Haints

MEGHAN PALMER

write!

For Mom and Dad, and the farm.

Thank you to my family, and to my husband, Mike Palmer, in particular.
You never doubted!

Part One

Chapter One

VOLA AND GRANNY WHITT STOOD together at the husk of the old woman's girlhood house. Vola's young hand in Granny's gnarled, stiff fingers, they regarded the familiar, weathered-gray boards and the sagging porch. Granite stones from the tall chimney that had been hauled up the Clinch River by traveling masons—stone gypsies, Granny called them—kept on their private migration from sky back to earth, tumbling down only when nobody was there to witness. Granny, who was really Vola's great-grand-mother, was stooped with age, and the rims of her once-piercing irises had faded to gray. What hair she still had was like the wispy clouds streaking the sunset over the ridge. It was the summer of 1996.

"Granny, why are there five doors that go into the house?" Vola asked. "And none between the inside rooms?" The old woman seemed not to hear at first. She gazed at the house, as wisps of hair drifted slightly in the breeze. When she finally spoke, Vola jumped a little, startled.

"The doors confused the haints," Granny said. "When I was a girl, there wasn't near as many people in the holler as they is now." The holler was really the whole neighborhood—all the houses tucked in the undulating pockets in the long valley, bordered by one big ridge to the northeast and smaller hills rolling away to the southwest. It was a nuanced word, "holler." It could mean everything they saw and then some, or it could mean one shady valley, a fold in the land. Their two hundred acres wasn't "the holler," though; it was "the farm."

"Now, you throw one of them black walnuts yonder, and you might just hit two or three people. When I was a girl, wasn't no*body* around for miles. If the spirits got their eye on you while you was doing chores of the evening or shutting up the chickens, why, you best get inside. Mom and Daddy used to tell me, 'Use a different door. Every time.'" Granny's story fell into the rhythm of her accent, part Appalachian and part just Granny. To the girl, listening to it was like feeling the soft nubs on her favorite crocheted afghan.

"But, wouldn't the spirits just follow you into whichever door you went in? If that was all it took, changing doors to confuse 'em, they must have been pretty stupid," Vola said. The old woman cackled, thinking that was the reason why old folks liked young ones so well; they said exactly what came to mind. They didn't have layers of years to temper their words. No reason to put up a face that was anything other than their own. Vola was more special than most children, even allowing for the Whitt family talents. She quietly accepted Granny, with her repeated stories, her traditions, and her superstitions. And that girl was always thinking, always squirreling away information and turning it over and over in the cheerful way somebody might examine a fresh peach from the orchard. Granny shook her head slightly. Her mind did wander sometimes.

She turned a hawkish eye on the young girl, considering.

"Honey, you ever lost something?" she asked, bringing Vola's hand up to hold in both of hers. It was young and soft in her gnarled fingers. "Maybe a teddy bear you left when you was out with Mom? Or one of them...hair scrunchies you like. It prob'ly like to drove you crazy, tryin' to figure where it was. It's like that, see. Haints come after me 'cause I was a treat to 'em. They come after me, and I went in a different door every time. They got confused, couldn't find me. They can't see the world just like we do. They can't see it that way unless they take our eyes from us." Vola shivered, though the evening was warm. Granny looked up at the black, glassless windows.

"They would wander from door to window to door," she murmured, lost in the memory of it. "Trying to find the way in…but there were too many ways, and haints ain't equipped with choice makers." She tapped Vola on the head. "Then they would stay on the porch a while. They would forget, see? Why they was there. Then they would remember again, but they had to give up. I was already upstairs, already safe. But they come back again."

They come back again. They came back, and they come back. Both were true. The Appalachian way—the Whitt family way—confused the past tense with the present. She didn't think much on it now, but someday, when she was older, it would strike her that the ways on which she grew up were different. Vola would reflect that it was probably not ignorance, the way Granny spoke. Or some deliberate way of avoiding "talking proper," as her classmates said with such disgust. Here, time was funny. People were close to the old ways, yet…the old ways were forgotten at the same time.

Granny pointed a knotted finger to the top of the crumbling chimney, to a hole the size of a deck of cards between two remaining stones. She'd shown that hole to Vola before. It had been there even when the chimney was new and strong.

"That's the witch's keyhole. If haints got inside the house, why, they didn't have long before they's sucked right back up the chimney, through the keyhole. Everybody had one of them."

Vola had a vague idea of how old her great-grandmother really was; she was older than most kids' great-grandparents. Older than most people alive. Her age was only part of what made Granny unusual. Vola loved listening to her stories, letting her mind flow in and out of the woman's hill drawl. It was hypnotizing in its way.

Young Vola and Granny turned away from the old shack and started the walk back around the bend to the white farmhouse where the family now lived. As if waiting for that signal, a shaggy border collie trotted over from where she'd lain in the shade of a blackberry bramble.

"Hi, Gitli," said Vola, brushing one black ear tangled in burs as the dog went by. "Good girl." Gitli liked to walk just in front of them, the tip of her curved tail flipping back and forth with each step.

When Granny was a younger woman, they had left behind the old gray house in favor of building a bigger house in the next fold of the valley. Granny'd told Vola it was because the old house was done bein' lived in. Vola guessed that was true; after all, the chimney was losing its great stones and the windows were all empty. That old husk of a house had none of the warmth, none of the people-live-here quality of the big house where the Whitts now lived.

As she walked, Vola hummed to herself, letting her eyes slide out of focus, letting each step make the world seem to slowly bounce up and down around her, and pretending she wasn't doing the moving at all. The house, glowing white in the fast-coming twilight, loomed bigger with each slow bounce. The kitchen light came on, followed by lights in all the downstairs windows in a series of bright, homey winks. They made fierce, square beacons in the darkening evening: a promise of comfort. Of safety. The blush that had silhouetted the ridge to the south and west of the house was quickly fading as the sun dove behind the ridge and sank the farm into gloom. Fireflies began a sleepy blink in the hayfield, with cicadas and frogs tuning up for their nightly dialogue.

Later in the summer, the evening cicadas would be almost deafening in their insistent, undulating whine. It was the seven-years' turn, Grandpa June said. There was a seven-year cicada and a fifteen-year cicada. They stayed burrowed down in the ground that long until it was time to come out and sing, and sing, and sing like queerly tuned, one-stringed fiddles. Vola supposed she'd sing her heart out, too, if she'd stayed silent that many long years in the dirt. The thought of cicadas burrowed underground for so long brought haints to mind.

"Granny," she said. "Why don't our house...I mean, how come there's so many doors on the inside, between all the rooms? Why ain't we so worried over haints, like when you was a girl?"

Granny didn't have time to answer; right then, Mama called through the kitchen screen door: "Vola! Go down the valley and find Uncle Lacey. It's supper time."

"Okay!" Vola left Granny at the stone walk to the front door. The girl had asked a good question. It was one that fit Granny's own line of thought lately. Thinking of doors, the old woman went up the walk. She pushed open the heavy front door—the one that served as a front door, anyway, because it was closest to the driveway, and it was the most ornate. But each side of the big house had its own entry. It was in a Whitt's nature to never be too many steps from the out-a-doors. Light spilled out onto the porch, by contrast, deepening the gloom that fell over the farm, now that the sun had sunk down under the ridge yonder.

Vola jogged along the gravel drive that went down past the big house to Uncle Lacey's trailer house, a quarter-mile or so away. Gitli, who'd trotted up onto the porch in anticipation of dinner outside the kitchen door, couldn't resist joining Vola's run. She bounded into the yard to intercept Vola just as she passed the barn, the feed pen in the back obscured in the gloom. This time of night was perfect for running; cool air drifted up from the earth in pockets after the sun went down, thrilling her each time she leapt into chill from the humid, summertime warmth. Fireflies jigged and glowed in a cloud around Vola as she stretched her tan, play-bruised and scabbed legs, with each step pulling the road behind her, sneakers crunching gravel. Her breath huffed in tune with chirping frogs in the creek. Gitli looked up, seeming to grin before hopping off into the tall hay to snap at grasshoppers and fireflies making their way from across the hayfield to join Vola.

"Ho, young 'un!" Uncle Lacey stood and watched from his chicken huts as his niece came on, a cloud of softly glowing bugs marking her general shape. She waved back to him, the motion lit by a glowing sweep of fireflies in the falling night. Lacey came to meet her through the low gate. Closing up the chicken yard, he snatched out a quick handful of fireflies from Vola's entourage. He held them close to his face and waggled his eyebrows at her—his face a Halloween mask, his one good eye shining in their glow, the bad eye like dull, misshapen clay. Gitli jumped and barked around them, in on the joke.

Giggling more from good-naturedness than at the old joke, Vola blew on the fireflies in his palms, setting them a-flight in the air once more. They drifted around his wild shock of hair, and for a moment, he looked both ancient and exotic: a one-eyed totem god with hair of cold flames. He sneezed and shook his head, breaking the spell.

"Supper time, Uncle Lacey," she said.

"Mmm. What's the spread tonight?"

"I think a mess of beans and cornbread," Vola answered, turning to walk with her uncle, cutting through the field toward the big house. He and Gitli jumped the creek ahead of her before turning to offer a helping hand. She couldn't see the water in the muddy trench, but she trusted her legs to navigate the familiar path in the dark. Besides, Uncle Lacey was here, a warm, tall, familiar presence at her side. All was right, here in the dark, fireflies trailing them in a bobbing, swirling cloud. The hills loomed around the broad valley, like silhouettes of giants sleeping on their sides around them. In Vola's sweetly optimistic eyes, the sleeping giants protected the Whitt family nestled in their circle: Granny, Vola's mama Clary, her Grandpa June, Uncle Lacey, and her. And Gitli, of course. And the cows. And fireflies.

Overhead, stars sparked in a velvet sky. Over the ridge to the north, a faint glow revealed the direction of town, only a couple of miles as the crow flies. But folks didn't fly as crows, and roads here in the county were twisted and steep, so it took a fair few more miles to get over yonder. To visitors from places like New York or Georgia or Florida, this place was remote and isolated. The nearest town of consequence was forty-five minutes over the Clinch mountain range to the southwest, or a little further if you drove north, over the border to Middlesboro in Kentucky. To city folk, this was as far out as the Himalayas. Or the moon. To the Whitts, it seemed as though the population was crowding in around the farm fast and thick, though—truthfully—there weren't as many people living here as there had been a decade or two ago. Or maybe it was simply that the nature of the place had changed. Atrophied. In Grandpa June's day, there'd been two used-car dealers in town, plus a bowling alley. Now there wasn't much more'n a Hardees, a dollar store, a drug store and a handful of folk addicted to pills or meth wandering around back of the court house, looking to score. Or looking for a sleazy way to get a little money to score. Hookers in Greasy Rock might have only been twenty, but they looked to be sixty.

Families, enchanted by the beauty of this land, came from out of state. And they went, young people with brains in their heads getting out as soon as they were able. Some people stayed on for good: folks who had it easy here (a small group) because of a family business or small-time political connection, or folks who had it so bad they were stuck (the bigger part of the population).

The Whitts? They'd been here forever. And they'd probably stay here just as long.

Chapter Two

WHITTS HAD LIVED IN THIS valley just as long as anybody could remember. Longer than Melungeons, who lived over on Newman's Ridge. Longer than the Indians, some said, though how that could be was hard to tell. It didn't make sense, unless you took into account that the Whitts were witches. Some still used the old word: shamans. But to a Bible-thumping Baptist preacher, it all amounted to the same.

Granny was the oldest living Whitt. She was over a hundred years old, though she didn't look hardly a day over eighty. June was her boy. June, short for Junior, though Granny never did say who her boy was the junior to. Then there was Clary, June's daughter, and Vola, the youngest of the family at eleven. Oh, and June's boy, Lacey; he wasn't quite right in the head, not since he was a boy, since the day his eye was knocked out. But he was a good 'un, as June said. He was a good 'un. Even if he did forget what he was doing right in the middle sometimes.

Clary had a job in town, and Vola went to school. She'd be in the sixth grade come September. But the other Whitts mostly stayed on the farm, with June and Lacey driving in to the co-op to pick up feed or fencing or some such when it was necessary.

The lives of the Whitt family were as quiet as could be from the outside. Their farm, bounded by seven points—small, worn mountains pretty as a watercolor from far away, yet still tough to climb when a body had to—held just about everything they needed. Tall hay that rippled hypnotically, like water, in the summer breeze. A few head of cattle. Vegetable garden out the back door, fruit trees set in a small, sloping orchard to the southeast of the house. It was idyllic.

To a foreigner, anyway. That's what the earthy people of Greasy Rock called anybody "not from around here." And they said "furr-iner," drawing out that first syllable, making it inhospitable in their mouths. It was a bit confusing that the only category of folks held in deeper contempt than foreigners in these worn, forgotten hills was a Whitt.

"Only thing I hate worse'n a Whitt is a black snake," Vola'd heard a man once say while leaving the town's one grocery store with her Grandpa June. She'd looked up at her grandfather, surprised and a little frightened at the vehemence behind the words. He glanced down at her, then only six years old, and looked as though he might just walk on and ignore the man currently spitting a brown stream of tobacco juice onto the sidewalk behind them. He might have, too, except the man kept on.

"Queers and Whitts," the man said, words muddied with the wad of chew in his lip. "Ain't nothing worse but a black snake."

"Well, now," said Grandpa June, turning around. "I'd say that makes you a damned fool, Jared Greer. Black snakes is useful. They eat vermin. Rats." He tipped his battered hat to the man before setting off down the sidewalk again, grocery sack in one hand and his granddaughter skipping to keep up. They'd already started the old farm truck and headed toward home before Jared could figure out whether he'd been threatened or chastised.

"Grandpa," asked Vola, unsure of what had just happened but exhilarated all the same, "What's a queer?"

"What?" the old man turned to her, a brief spark of sunlight through the windshield making his eyes glow like sapphires under the brim of his hat.

11

"Jared Greer. Said queers and Whitts is bad as a black snake."

Grandpa June gazed ahead in silence while trees glided past at the edge of the weathered blacktop. They passed over the Clinch River on the old bridge, its rusted metal cage throwing stuttered shadows over the truck. Straight ahead was a steep face of earth, thick with trees and boulders. Their farm wasn't far on the other side of it, but the ridge was too steep for a road to cut through, so they turned left and followed along it until they came to Sturgill's Hill, so called because the man named Sturgill had once careened right over the side, bypassing the road altogether and crashing down into the creek running below it. He'd said it was due to icy conditions, but rumor had it the man had taken too much of his jar of medicinal white lightning. Vola'd heard different versions of the story, and she'd confused the images in her head so that sometimes she thought old Sturgill had been driving an antique jalopy, and sometimes she thought he'd been in a horse-drawn wagon. She felt her weight settle against the back of the seat as Grandpa June shifted the truck down into low gear to climb the steep hill. She wondered idly if Sturgill'd been in a wagon, what had happened to the horse when they crashed? She decided he was in a jalopy instead.

"Anybody different than them, sugar," June said, finally. "Some folks can't tolerate different." Which didn't really answer Vola's question. They had a satellite television, so Vola eventually figured out what old Jared Greer meant by queer. For a while she thought Grandpa June just didn't want to discuss the idea of homosexuality with her—which annoyed her, him thinking she was too young or not smart enough to understand it. But it came to her one day that Grandpa June's words were more elegant and more true than she'd originally credited.

The thing was, folks like old Greer thought they was living right by the old ways, hating queers and foreigners. They thought they had the Bible on their side, and that made 'em right. Made 'em righteous. But there was ways older than the Bible, and the Whitts still kept them. The people who had lived here long, long ago—now they was called Cherokee, though that was a modern name; then they had called themselves People. Those People had accepted a body's nature, had respected a person's strangeness for what it was: just a part of them. The world had been sweeter in some ways, back then, and much, much harder in others, and People just didn't think it important to sit down and list out all the ways to hate.

As Vola had grown, she'd realized that lots of people in town held her family in a strange regard. Some were kindly enough, it was true, but meanness was always louder than the rest, so she often saw small acts of petty insult. Sometimes she was the butt end of jokes at school; sometimes the kids pretty well ignored her. Either way, her mama had made sure to give her stern warnings.

"Don't show anybody else that you got talents, you hear?" Clary'd knelt down, so she was at eye level with Vola. "You're a bright girl, Vola, bright as a star, and other folks prefer dim."

"Why?" Vola'd been scared when her mother had said that. She'd always had the freedom to do and be what she was at home. But Clary shook her head.

"Because it makes them more comfortable, I reckon," was all she would say on it. Vola saw, in time, how right her mother was. She was too intimidated when she started school for her talents to shine through, anyhow. And when she saw the smarter kids in class cut down for "talking proper" or acting like "city kids," she understood it would go much harder for her if they all knew what she could do. So she never called the honey bees to her on the playground or touched the small flowers in the grass to make them grow taller and brighter. She pretended to be invisible much of the time.

Until she was home, on the farm. Then all her talents could glow out of her in great bursts, and she could find peace.

Vola gazed up at the soft morning light on her ceiling. She loved mornings in the summertime. Loved that sense of anything-can-happen that tickled her with the early breeze. She rolled over to gaze out the window at the foggy valley from the very edge of her bed. She'd just about decided to ease on out from under the warm blanket and see about breakfast when a shotgun blast from outside, loud enough to rattle the window, made her jerk and fall to the floor with a sharp cry, as she flailed in the sheets tangled around her. Gitli was unfortunate enough to be sleeping where she fell, so the two of them had to wrestle their way out from each other and out of sheets that had turned into twisting snakes of cloth, with Gitli barking in dismay.

"You get him?" Granny called from somewhere in the house—sounded like the living room, just below Vola's bedroom. Clomping boots on the porch floorboards that could only be Grandpa June's accompanied words Vola couldn't quite make out. She guessed he hadn't got whatever varmint he was after. Probably a possum. Vola didn't hate much, and definitely had a stronger understanding of creatures than most, but she did not like a possum. They'd eat a chicken while it was still alive—sharp, evil teeth ripping into the poor thing's soft undersides with no regard for putting it out of its misery.

"Well, reckon I'm up for real, now," she muttered, and rolled off the pile of tangled sheets to stump downstairs to the kitchen. "Come on, Gitli."

Grandpa June stopped short when he saw her in the hall, shotgun still in his hand.

"Morning, Glory," he said. She gave him a wave on her way by.

"Mornin', Grandpa," she said, stifling a yawn. "Did Mama go to work already?"

He nodded. "We got new neighbors. Did your mama tell you?"

"We do? No, she didn't say anything about it." Vola reached into the pantry for cereal.

"She talked to 'em in the road, driving by on her way home, yesterday afternoon. They're just over the southeast fence, yonder." He gestured with two fingers, as though he could point to the new neighbors through fields and hills. "From Florida." Vola shrugged and nodded. New neighbors from out of town were a little bit unusual in a county where folks were mostly related to one another—or at least related to somebody that was related. But still, it happened, and it didn't have much effect on an eleven-year-old's daily life. Vola wasn't terribly interested.

"They got a kid. Girl, about your age."

"They do?" Vola was interested, now. "Where'd you say they come from?"

"Florida, your ma says." His mouth twitched under his moustache, grinning at the excitement on her face, breaking through like a sunrise. "Anyway, I wanted to remind you about that border ..."

"Yeah, I know, Grandpa, stay off the Byrne land."

"That's right. Don't even touch the fence." He shook his finger at her. "The new neighbors, they're right next to the Byrnes. So if you should go visiting, remember: don't even touch the Byrne fence." She nodded. When she was younger, it used to scare her when he got so serious. Grandpa June had eyes that would go so still when he was angry, and that stillness was more terrifying than anything. Her mama would yell when she got mad, and Granny would fuss around (like a pissy hen, Uncle Lacey said, and it made Vola laugh), but Grandpa June's face would start to settle, eyes alert like he was out in a field and came up on his anger out of nowhere. Like the anger just sort of leapt out in front of him, and he had to figure out how to see around it. Vola saw his eyes dancing now, with none of the stillness that came with anger. He was amused by her, and that made life normal. It made life all right.

She let Gitli out the kitchen door to get the dog food Grandpa'd set out before she scarfed down her cereal and bounded up the stairs. She was set on getting dressed and cutting through the woods on a cow path she knew well. She was headed to the southeast boundary to check out her new neighbors from Florida.

Rounding the corner of the house, Vola saw Granny ruefully inspecting the porch railing. It was pocked and gouged, freshly ripped wood showing through many layers of paint, looking mildly obscene, like someone's injured flesh.

"Grandpa do that?" Vola slowed down to look, too.

"Yup. Law, how a possum can pretend to be dead but move so fast when you aim a shotgun at it. Only thing June hit was the dad-blamed house." Granny waved the girl on, flapping her hands. Like a pissy hen, Vola thought, stifling a giggle. "Go on, now. Stay off the Byrne property."

"Yes, ma'am," called Vola, trotting away up the gravel drive, Gitli on her heels.

—⟫⟫⟫⟩ ⟨⟨⟨⟨—

Haints used to be bigger. Not bigger in the sense that a grizzly is bigger than a black bear. But they loomed up in life, like the threat of starvation or of freezing to death in the coldest, deepest nights of winter. All those things seemed like so many fairy tales these days, with every house strung up for electricity, every house with an indoor commode. Food was plentiful, food stamps even more so around here. Hell, even the tumble-down hunting shacks over in Snake Holler had satellite dishes perched on their roofs. People's lives seemed to have lost something. Some kind of...of immediacy.

It worried Granny, how the threat of haints had faded away like the once deep-auburn color of her hair. Folks in Greasy Rock found it right easy to remember how Whitts were outcasts—witches, they said —but they didn't rightly remember why.

Nature balanced, somehow or another. All the Whitts knew that. Actions and reactions, hot summers and cold winters, and dry and wet seasons. Yin and yang. Granny was born and raised in Appalachia, but she wasn't uneducated. She'd read her share of books. It didn't surprise her a bit how human thoughts went around and around the world and how even if one kind of person looked and sounded different, when you got right down to it, their stories all proved how similar human minds were to one another. Human hearts, too. Hell, in Japan, folks used to believe illnesses came in the form of demons jumping right into a body to make 'em sick.

Sounded an awful lot like haints to Granny.

16

She wondered if Japanese folks was forgetting their old stories, too. She wondered if there was houses up in the forests in Japan, far away from the cities, where the old ways were forgotten and satellite TV dishes sprouted on roofs. She wondered if younger generations was forgetting all about hunger and freezing...and haints. Was that happening all over the world? She reckoned that was probably the case. Where folks could afford to forget, that was. Folks living in what the newscasters called 'first-world countries.' Like worlds stacked up on one another, overlapping but not the same.

She sat on the porch, rocking. Thinking. She watched as the sun rose and painted more of the hay field in its golden rays. Chickens, still a little spooked from this morning's ruckus with the possum and June's shotgun, scratched out in the yard below Granny's feet. She reckoned she understood it, after all: why folks forgot all about haints. People had proved to be far more terrifying than misty forms in the night. It was people who dropped bombs and shot guns. Maybe that's what it meant, when a society made their way to first world. People got meaner than haints. Just look at her boy June; he'd seen more than his fair share of grisly things in the Great War. But she couldn't lay down her vigilance, even if other folks forgot about haints. Even if haints was *obsolete*. She was a Whitt, and Whitts had a reason. A purpose.

And all this forgetting people had done, deciding that central heat and air and indoor plumbing made all life's hardships into myths—including haints. That forgetting worried Granny. It seemed to her that forgetting was some kind of yin, and she wondered about the yang. She suspected mightily that yang was haints, biding their time. She'd have to be ready. But she was old.

⟫⟫⟩⟩✦⟨⟨⟪⟪

It was going to be a hot day. Vola could tell by the smell: wet clay seeping up from the ground, mixed with pungent weeds and the occasional gust of fresh, cool pine. It would be bearable up in the woods, but down in the full-sun hayfield, it would be cooking by this afternoon. Gitli was already panting, her long tongue hanging down from the side of her mouth.

Vola had once asked why the air felt so sticky in the heat of the summer.

"That's 'cause the plants is working so hard at growing," Granny had answered. "Makes 'em sweat." It was humid much of the time in the hottest part of summer, making her shirt stick to her back and her hair plaster all around her face. But, occasionally, there would be days that came so clear—not much cooler, really, but the wet stayed out of the air, so it felt like an ice-cold drink, a day like that. Those days made her feel funny, like a bear blinking stupidly in the sun after shuffling out of her dark cave. On days like that, she felt like napping, like her senses were simply exhausted from all that clear air.

Today wasn't one of those days. She was in the mood for adventure! Vola followed the cow path until it split, pausing for a moment to gaze around and get her bearings. She usually took the path that meandered down the hill, toward the pond Grandpa June'd had dug out to be bigger with a big, growling backhoe into the cleft between two hills yonder. The path she took now—the high path, the one that would bring her up on the southeastern ridge—it didn't rightly make her nervous, but...well, it wasn't familiar, was all. The shadows looked different. The moss and the boulders all peeking up from under clutching tree roots, they faced her with an almost-stranger's regard. Like she was a distant cousin who didn't come around too much. Gitli sat with a "whuff," waiting for Vola to make up her mind to go on, one way or the other.

If she could fly up like a bird, she'd see an irregular bowl of land with a couple of legs of hill jutting into it and a pond glimmering in the sun to the east of those. There'd be great big patches of gold, where the woods were cleared off the valleys and hay grew. There'd be two intersecting veins through the fields, where streams ran even during the hottest parts of summer. Seven points, those were the borders of the Whitt farm, though they wouldn't be so obvious from a bird's eye. These were the old Appalachians, not the young Rockies, and points around here were more like massive mounds worn from years and rain and wind. Vola couldn't fly up like that, but Uncle

Lacey claimed he could. Claimed he could leave his body right down on the ground and lift his sight up to see and see and see. Said he had one eye in the spirit world.

"That's why it ain't in my head no more," he said, winking the good eye as green as new grass. "It went on to the spirit world and done left this clay lump instead." Clary would smile a little and shake her head in sisterly disbelief whenever Lacey said that.

Since she was a little girl, Vola'd been warned to stay right clear of the southeast border. It was just over the fence from the Byrne place, and Byrnes and Whitts didn't hold much with one another. Sticking her hands in her shorts pockets, the way she did when she was a little nervous, Vola mused about the Whitt and Byrne feud as she went along up the cow path, Gitli following behind. It was Grandpa June's fault, really, but it was on account of love. He stole Vola's grandmother away from her family years and years ago. Long before Vola was born. Vola's grandmother was a Byrne, which made Vola part Byrne, and though the southeastern neighbors were technically kin, they and their land were off-limits.

With her hands down in her pockets, Vola's feet took her one step at a time, stork-like, up the cow path to the top of the ridge. She had to pull her hands out to scramble up a few rock outcroppings, gripping saplings that stubbornly grew out of cracks in the steadfast granite and crumbling slate. Her hair flashed brilliantly in the dappling sun as she passed between overlapping shadows on the forest floor. A wooly worm caught her eye, and Vola squatted down, hands tucked behind her knees and pressed in between the backs of her folded legs. She lurched sideways a bit to pull one out, reaching gently to rest her fingertips in the air just above the wooly worm's deep burgundy fuzz, grinning when each roll of its little body brushed soft spikes against her fingers. She hummed a nonsense tune, one like her and Uncle Lacey sometimes made up when they went exploring together. It wasn't long before more wooly worms humped and rolled their way to her, making curious brushy noises against the dry leaves on the forest floor. Gitli watched passively. When she was a puppy, she would dance and bark excitedly when Vola called insects to dance and play with her, but Gitli was past her puppy years. Now, she watched with something akin to boredom, though she did feel a comfort like having her ears scratched whenever Vola used her talents nearby. It just felt...nice.

Through the trees over the next rise in the land, just out of Vola's sight, the sagging barbed-wire fence that marked the border between Byrnes and Whitts twanged. It glowed as though the sun shone directly on the rusting wire, though the morning light lay soft and quiet in the foggy woods while the sun itself made its slow ascent, still below the treeline. Vola didn't know the power of her own talent. Oh, she knew that she could bring in the wooly worms with her song, and she could dance with fireflies, and send butterflies soaring and swirling to make her own heart pound with joy. All the Whitts had special talents, Vola knew that.

But just as Granny mused on yin and yang and the shadow cast by the light, her great-granddaughter danced through life without a care for how her actions might bring consequence. Vola's wooly worm song called up more than little brown-and-black critters. When she sang her ancient tune so close to that fence—the very fence Grandpa June'd sung over years and years before, to make the border strong and deep and impenetrable to more than just people—she called up something that would give her cause to regret her eagerness to meet the new neighbors from Florida.

⟫⟫⟫⟩ ⟨⟪⟪⟪

Down in the valley, Lacey gazed out the dirty window over his kitchen sink. The sky was awake, but the sun hadn't quite popped over the eastern hills where he could see. Over at the big house, they could see the sun already. The predawn light made a glow in the valley yonder, gold diffusing the fog rising up out of the creek. Down here, between the low ridges in the back-hundred acres of the Whitt family farm, morning came a little later. It's where furtive little creatures stayed, down here in the gloom. And Lacey, of course. He liked it here, too.

What was he doing? He shook his head as though to clear it and yawned. He blinked, his bad eye feeling gummier than usual this early morning. He couldn't see the waking world through it, that gray lump. Looked like creek-bed clay, that bad eye. It was ruined. He yawned again.

Breakfast. He looked down and saw the last half of his boiled egg in his hand and grinned. He liked boiled eggs. The yolk was especially bright in this golden, early before-light time. It was almost orange. He'd had store-bought eggs before; pale, tasteless things. But these were eggs from their farm, from his own chickens: his ladies, he called them. And these yolks were rich. His ladies feasted on grasshoppers and other bugs. Lacey was always fascinated, studying on that: it was the grasshoppers that made these eggs so good.

But he was forgetting again. He popped the rest of his egg into his mouth and chewed, whiskery cheeks bulging. Swallowed it down with orange juice from the IGA in town. Not rightly juice, his mother had always said; it was sugar water colored to look like juice. Good though. Orange—like the good yolk of his boiled egg.

Lacey went out to perform the morning rituals. Some folks might call 'em farm chores, but to Lacey they had the weight of importance. It was how he called the new day to their valley: letting chickens out of their huts after another dark night. His daddy had his own chickens up near the big house, but Lacey was always comforted by the strutting, softly croaking and cackling hens, so he had his own flock down here by the trailer house. After he opened the chicken huts and scattered a little grain for a treat, it was time to put out feed for the cattle over at the barn. He'd stop to raise his arms to the morning, welcoming another turn of the Earth. Face lifted to the sky, shadows of his Indian ancestors fell on him, making him seem both familiar and ancient, if anyone had been there to witness. Sometimes Gitli made her way over the field to greet him, of the morning, but she wasn't here today. Lacey figured that meant she was off somewhere with Vola.

Like all the Whitts who were born and raised—and buried here, too, Lacey had been to the family archives. When he turned twelve, just like the rest of them, back to the beginning of memory, Granny had taken him to the archives in the old house. Told him the important stories. He reckoned it would be Vola's turn, soon. He knew the family history, at least as well as he could. Each of the family had their own talents, their own abilities. He wasn't much on book learning; the words swam all around on the page when he tried to pin them down with his eyes—well, his one eye, since the other'd been knocked out years and years ago. But he didn't need the books to speak with the family spirits. Not haints; the family spirits were like...what was it Granny said? Like yin to yang. Lacey couldn't remember which ones the haints were and which ones the family spirits were, but he knew for certain they swirled all together. They balanced out, yin and yang.

He realized he'd been daydreaming again, going through all the motions of his morning ritual with his body, but his mind had been looking inside. He stood outside the chicken huts, watching them scratch and chase after grasshoppers and worms and what-all in the grass. He took up a stick and scratched a spiral in the dirt, around and around and around.

He had it, suddenly—what it was that made him so daydreamy this morning. Why his mind wanted to gather wool instead of pay attention to what was in front of him. The Byrne fence. That southeastern border, the one Daddy'd always warned him about. It was awake. It was awake, and Lacey could feel it pulling like a bright thread that stretched from the center of his belly, straight up through the trees to rusted barbed wire strung up at the edge of the forest. It was a wonder he hadn't seen it before! It was so bright, so...*immediate*. But he didn't rightly know what it meant. Lacey started down the road to the big house. He didn't go through the field this morning; it was sodden with dew, and he didn't like the feel of all that wet, green fescue grabbing his ankles. Granny and Dad would know what it meant, that thrumming barbed wire fence. And why it made him think about the coat tucked away in the chest at the end of his bed.

Vola giggled and the spell broke. Wooly worms milled around the toes of her sneakers. It was quiet now that she'd stopped singing. Not a bird chirped, not a creature disturbed the brown leaves on the forest floor. The rich, green canopy above stood witness with the solemnity of a cathedral ceiling. Only when a cow called from deep in the valley did Vola realize she'd been holding her breath, and she let it out with a whoosh. The wooly worms had all dispersed.

"Reckon I'll go on," she said aloud. Gitli stood up in agreement, the tip of her wagging tail sweeping leaves behind her.

Continuing up the ridge, this path felt more foreign than ever. Vola shoved her hands back into her pockets and was relieved when squirrels started their scolding, shooing off birds harassing a nest somewhere nearby. That silence had been eerie. But...under the silence, almost underneath hearing, there had been something, hadn't there? A humming. She'd felt it through her shoes, she'd thought. Unless, maybe, she'd just been imagining things. Or maybe her feet had started to fall asleep; she'd been squatting down there with the wooly worms for a while. It wouldn't be the first time.

Reassured, she went past the Byrne property with plenty of space between her and the old, rusted fence. Bob-wire, as she and Uncle Lacey always called it. She craned her head to try and see more of the backyard, but the fence line was weedy and, anyway, most of what she could see was just heaps of trash. She went on, walking toward the log cabin-style house to the east of the Byrne property. Granny had once told her that folks who didn't have pride in themselves didn't have pride in their homes, either. When Vola said that the Byrnes had trash all over the place—and they seemed awfully prideful, considering they wouldn't speak to Whitts at all, even after they became kin—Granny laughed.

"That ain't pride, child," she said.

"Then, what is it?"

"Plain old stupidity, that's what."

Vola thought she'd been clever and quiet and, well...sneaky, but she knew she'd been spotted by the new neighbors—one of them, anyway—when she caught sight of the woman on her back porch. It embarrassed her a little, to be caught out before she'd had a chance to study the house a while. The woman waved to her, and Vola waved back tentatively before climbing through a sagging place in the fence and picking her way through the trees. Gitli came too, not the least bit embarrassed.

"Good morning!" Vola called. She was at the edge of the woods now, uncertain of whether she should go up through the clearing to the house or wait to be invited. Around here, if somebody didn't call out "Come in!" you waited to enter their yard. But she was already here...Vola was suddenly, painfully, aware that she was a country girl, and that she had very little experience with meeting new folks outside of school. She thought frantically of all the television shows she'd seen where people met for the first time. On TV, teenagers were always calling each other up on the phone first, laying on their beds and making plans, and twirling the twisty phone cord and looking glamorous, even if they weren't especially dressed up. Or there was *I Dream of Jeannie*, and she just appeared with a magical POOF! Vola wondered how that would be, if she just jumped out from a cloud of smoke and yelled, "I'm your neighbor!"

The woman put her out of her misery.

"What's your name?" she called, beckoning.

"I'm Vola," she said, a little shy. She went up to the porch.

"How old are you? I think my little girl is your age."

"I'm eleven. I live down yonder," Vola turned to point in the general direction of the Whitt house. "We're neighbors, though I reckon you can't see the house from here."

"Oh! I think I met your mother," said the woman, "Well, it's nice to meet *you*. I'm Jayne Watson. Come on in; I'll see if Lily's around." Jayne Watson was a little strange, Vola decided. She was too bouncy, like she was trying very hard to make their conversation cheerful. Gitli lay down at the bottom of the porch steps while Vola followed her new neighbor inside and waited in the kitchen, half unpacked boxes still stacked haphazardly on the counters and floors. She looked around curiously. So this was what the house of someone *from Florida* looked like. She had a queer sense of double exposure; it looked like a regular Tennessee house. But she still felt like she might see the beach if she walked into the next room, sand and blue water washing up on it. Well, not that, exactly, but maybe something more sophisticated than just a couch and rug in the living room. A couch and rug from Florida. Her thoughts caught up and embarrassed her a little, which reminded her again of how country she really was. She was pink-faced when a girl with a blond ponytail trailed into the kitchen after Jayne Watson.

"Vola, this is Lily." Jayne still spoke with exaggerated cheeriness. Lily waved, unsmiling.

"Hi," said Vola, waving back.

"Do you two want to go play?" asked Jayne. Lily shrugged and Vola, somewhat awed by the girl's nonchalance—a sure sign of superior coolness—scratched her nose and shuffled her feet a little.

"We could...I could show you our pond," said Vola.

"Okay," said Lily.

"Here," said Jayne, snatching a ball cap and a sweater from the row of hooks near the back door. "Put these on, Lily. You don't want sunstroke. Or a chill. It's still a bit chilly out. Do you want to take a snack, or..." But Lily had already grabbed the sweater and pushed past her mother to bound down the back porch steps. Vola gaped after her and waved goodbye to Jayne before following.

"Be careful!" Jayne called after the girls. "Don't get lost! Don't..." But the girls didn't hear whatever Jayne's last warning was; they were running through the woods, Lily leading the way and Gitli bounding along delightedly in their wake.

"Don't worry, Mrs. Watson!" called Vola over her shoulder. "We won't get lost! I know right where we are!" She followed Lily until they were out of sight of the house, and then Lily collapsed to the ground. Vola was a bit alarmed at first, thinking Lily had tripped or gotten hurt somehow. But she soon realized Lily was playing for effect. Playacting, Granny would say.

"She just...she's so *suffocating*," said Lily, laying back with her arms spread wide.

"Oh," said Vola. "She seems nice," she added, completely at a loss. This new girl was kind of dramatic, and her mother... Vola wondered if all this had been a good idea after all, trying to make friends with the neighbor from Florida. She sat carefully nearby, resting her chin on her knees and wrapping her arms around her legs. Seeming to enjoy the game, Gitli rolled onto her back next to Lily. Her white, furry belly was too much for even Lily to ignore, and she rolled to her side to scratch the soft fur, grinning at Gitli's happy grunts. Vola felt vaguely betrayed by this.

Chapter Three

BY THE TIME LACEY STEPPED onto the farmhouse porch, Granny had gone back inside and upstairs. He studied the pockmarks in the railing. They were fresh. He reckoned his dad had tried to shoot a varmint this morning; now that he thought about it, Lacey'd heard a bang early on. He stood, pondering. Daddy shooting the porch didn't feel like a very good omen in Lacey's mind. He let his thoughts sort themselves; it was best to ride them like a leaf in the wind when he got to feeling like this.

He had a cocoon jacket in a wooden chest, and he liked to take it out every once in a while. He had taken it out for a while this morning before breakfast. It gave him comfort. He knew Granny didn't like it when he did; she didn't think he was responsible enough—too "airy-minded," to use her own words. She reckoned it should only be touched when strictly necessary. Which meant only at funerals. Probably—he had enough in his brain to know this—Granny would prefer to keep hold of the coat herself, to keep it safe. She was the story keeper, after all: the family archivist. Now there was a word he couldn't spell to save his life. But, no, the keeping of the jacket was Lacey's job. Everybody in the family knew that. Even the ancestors knew it. So Granny contented herself with clucking over the coat from time to time, shaking her finger toward her grandson and telling him he'd best leave it alone, leave it safe and *tucked-away-until-they-needed-it, good-lord-forbid*.

But he knew better, Lacey did. He'd taken it out this morning and checked it over. He knew it was made of living things, and all living things needed attention, as long as it was the right kind. He didn't wash it, no, no. That would ruin the coat and probably hurt the cocoons, besides. *See? Not so airy-minded*, he'd thought, gently patting one sleeve of the coat, spread out on his bed. He wouldn't wash it, but he would take it from the box and spread it out, checking each and every cocoon and making sure they stayed supple and thick. That's how you could tell it was still a healthy cocoon; if it got too crumbly and dry, that meant it wasn't no good: the lovely creature inside had gone away, and he would have to sing it back.

It was thick, the cocoon jacket, with every available inch laid in a furry, thumb-sized pill of a unique color. Some were ancient, their woolly threads fading…many were brilliant, glinting with captured splinters of light. Some were prickly, maroon and black like woolly worms that old-timers used to predict the harshness of the coming winter. Lacey had gently pet one of these with the tip of his finger.

"One, two, three, four stripes," he'd crooned. "Snow storms ahead." He couldn't remember which color stripe meant bad weather and which one meant mild. It didn't matter, no-how. These weren't the same woolly worms you could find on the gravel road that went from the farmhouse to his little trailer, humping along in an undulating, fuzzy wave that always fascinated him. Lacey chuckled. No, they weren't worms but cocoons, and these stripey cocoons, and all the rest, were very special indeed.

He'd put the jacket back in its wooden box, not grand enough to be called a chest. He'd made the box himself, special, with salvaged boards from the old house in which Granny grew up. The same old house that kept the family's stories hidden away in its dusty bones. He kept the box at the end of his bed, and though he took the cocoon jacket out to inspect it and talk to it every so often, Lacey only actually wore it to funerals.

Absently stroking the gouged porch railing, thinking he'd work on fixing it later, Lacey turned and wandered into the house, wondering if there were any scraps of breakfast yet: a round of cold sausage, maybe. Or some toast. Or a biscuit. Lacey scrounged around the kitchen, looking for bits of food and thinking about funerals.

The last one had been years ago, to bury Granny's brother.

⟫⟫⟫≺≺≺≺

The day they buried Granny's brother it was early summer. That had been a good year for calves, Lacey remembered. Calves and storms. But the morning of the funeral had dawned clear.

Lacey'd put the jacket on, that morning, after scrubbing up in the shower and combing his hair—which didn't do much good—and putting on his pants and the good-shirt-with-the-buttons. Then, he'd put on the jacket, and it made him look woolly and bulky in the mirror, his tanned face under a wild fuzz of dirty-blond hair seeming to float on top. The whole family had climbed up the northern ridge to the family plot, where some graves were marked by a wedge of slate so old that the names and dates scratched on them had worn to nothing. The whole family went up except Granny, but she was already there. She'd stayed up there all night to keep vigil. Lacey hadn't known his great-uncle so well; the old man hadn't lived at the farm. He'd been at the old folks' home over in town for as long as Lacey could remember.

That had been a little strange, hadn't it? Lacey's great-uncle living at the old folks' home. Because Whitts generally lived right here, on the farm. Lacey had asked Granny about it, and she'd looked sad, which had scared Lacey, because Granny was always stern or laughing or gruffly kind, but not sad. So he hadn't asked about it anymore. His daddy told him, later, that Granny's brother had been a good man in his own way, but he'd liked the hooch too much. As if that explained anything. But then the man had up and died, and the Whitts buried him with their own, because he was one of 'em.

29

The day of the funeral, the sun lit the mist through the trees on the north ridge. The morning reached them there at the grave before its glow could be felt at the farmhouse down in the shady valley. The mist glowed around them so that they bathed in liquid light as Granny spoke the traditional words. They each came to touch his hands, the man wrapped in his shroud, even young Vola. The hands were the only part of him exposed to the swirling, glowing mist.

Last was Uncle Lacey in his cocoon coat. It might have been made of rough wool at some point, but now it was knit together organically by those little, furry, parti-colored lumps. This morning a bright yellow butterfly arrived through the glowing fog, hovering as though observing the scene. Lacey wondered how it could fly in the cool morning, through the heavy drops of mist in the air. The fog should have been too thick for its delicate wings. The mist—as though hearing his thoughts—parted around the flitting butterfly and swirled thickly like drops of elderberry syrup falling into clear water. He watched, hypnotized, as it landed on his shoulder, delicate wings shivering before it flew again, this time to land farther down his sleeve. It seemed satisfied with the spot, for there it stayed and remained until Granny finished the chant of the elders, and Lacey's daddy helped Clary put the shrouded man into his grave. They all pushed the good, dark earth—not rich and red like the clay down in the valley—over his body until it was covered and all mounded up.

As the body settled and became part of the earth, the ground over it would sink. They would add more earth and tamp it down. It was respectful, according to Granny, and Lacey thought of it like making the bed each morning...maybe pointless 'cause you were just going to rumple it all up again come evening time, but neatening things up showed that people were here and that they cared. One more thing to keep out the haints.

They made their way back down the mountain, through woods on a path that was old and tangled, almost wild. They clambered over downed trees, ducked under thick vines, and wove around brambles. This was another way to keep the haints deep under, where they belonged; they could smell a well-traveled path. The dead were vulnerable. It was best to keep the way to them protected.

Young Vola walked fairly well alongside her uncle, ducking through archways and tunnels in the vines. She was part of this land, just like all the Whitts, completely comfortable navigating the roots and slope of this wooded hillside. She craned her head around, catching glimpses of yellow on her uncle's sleeve, though it seemed that less of the butterfly was visible each time she saw it. She took to staring at it and walking just behind and to the side of Lacey, so she could follow what it was up to. It was making its own cocoon, but it was all in reverse, since it was caterpillars that went in and butterflies that came out, usually. Toward the bottom of the hill, Vola was so distracted that she got tangled up in briars and Clary had to help her pull thorny branches off her sleeves and jeans, so those two were the last to emerge from the leafy edge of the woods into the dew-sodden hayfield, sparkling in the fully-risen sun.

She stepped quickly to Lacey's side to peer at his sleeve and clucked a sound of disappointment. She'd missed the final bit where the butterfly sealed itself inside. It was really something, the cocoon: a rich brown color shot through with lovely gold threads. Lacey caught her eye and winked. She smiled back and pointed at the cocoon, her fingertip almost close enough to touch it. He shook his head at her, and she snatched her hand back.

"Got to keep it safe," he said, one good eye twinkling. "Until the next time we need them." She was about to ask what he meant when Granny called her name.

"Honey," the old woman said, beckoning, "We got to go on to the house. Got to get dinner on, or it won't be ready when folks come midday."

"What folks, Granny? Are we having a party?" Everybody walked along the road, back to the big house. Everybody except Uncle Lacey; he stopped into his trailer to carefully fold away the cocoon jacket. Vola was sorry to miss that; she so rarely saw the inside of her uncle's special wooden box. But

Granny's mood warned her that this was not the time to ask if she could go with Lacey.

"When folks die, the living come eat." Granny smiled down at the girl, taking her hand and patting it.

"Mama, you know nobody's going to come down here. They ain't…" June stopped at the old woman's expression. "Not for that old man," he finished, looking down and shaking his head. Later, when June had gone out to check a fence row—something he did often when he was feeling pensive—Vola asked her mother why he'd said it.

They stood alone in the living room. Clary hesitated before taking Vola's face in her hands. The girl was getting taller all the time; the top of her head was almost to Clary's belly. She looked just like Clary: rich, brown hair and brown eyes. People used to say the Indian really showed in Clary's face. She could see it in her daughter, too.

"Honey, folks don't visit us. Not if they can help it. And most funerals around here, they happen at the funeral home in town or at church." Vola didn't ask which church; she knew there were almost more churches than people around here. Whichever church was nearest, she figured her mother meant. And she also knew other folks didn't approve of the Whitts' holding their own kind of church. "So your grandfather, he just meant your Granny shouldn't expect too many visitors, even in respect of her brother."

⟫⟫⟫ ⟪⟪⟪

Deep down, Granny knew better than to expect the town to act friendly. She knew better, but she followed her own mother's traditions—the *old* traditions, because the ancestors were always close. So Granny made food: pies and greens and roasted chicken. It wouldn't do to go against her mother's traditions. That was the trouble with folks dying…the heart grieved more than just the most recent death. And the older she got, the more people she had to grieve. Granny missed her own mama, dead for years and years. And she missed her daddy, too. They'd had some good times, when her brother had been right in the head, and they'd all lived on the farm together.

Granny's mother had been friendly with folks in town. In her day, folks would have added to the spread of food with their own dishes, honoring the dead by comforting the living with sustenance. But that was a different time, when folks hadn't turned their eyes away from the land in favor of a talking, glowing box and voices over the wire. Folks had come for help, back then, with birthing goats and, sometimes, babies. They had exchanged herbs and gossip and visited with smiles and respect. Even the Bible-thumpers had stayed in the shadows then, and church hadn't had the menacing sway it seemed to hold now.

Maybe I'm the reason all that changed, Granny thought. At least partly. She pulled a sweet potato pie from the oven. She'd been hostile to outsiders as a young woman and outwardly indifferent as she'd aged. Now anybody in the county who might remember who she was knew her as a sullen woman. Her brother remembered her that way most of all, by the time he'd died. She sighed, closing the oven door and passing one hand over her brow.

She'd been young in a time of distrust, with revenuers coming around looking for moonshine stills and the Depression tightening belts on home-spun pants. Then the government cut the community's legs out from under them with the Tennessee Valley Authority. Their land had been spared flooding by the TVA; the rich, riverside farmland in the neighboring county had been swallowed up with man-made lakes. But the welfare checks held folks down worse than the floodwaters, and now...now Greasy Rock was heavy with poverty and drugs both homemade and dispensed by so-called doctors.

No, nobody was coming for a proper wake, a respectful breaking of bread with the deceased's family. But still, the Whitt family would eat well in her brother's memory, and they would sprinkle some meat, and pie, and bread in the field and chant to the sky and to the earth. It was the kind of ritual that would bring haints sniffing under their feet, but it was also the kind of ritual that bound living, loving folks together, and that was part of the magic that kept the haints down underfoot.

⇒⟫⟫⟫ ⟪⟪⟪⇐

Later on that afternoon, Vola took Gitli and sat out under her cedar tree next to Uncle Lacey's place. Gitli was just a puppy, and she'd been left behind for the funeral. Leaning up against the shedding trunk, Vola absently played her fingers along a hump of root shrugging out of the duff. It was needly, under the cedar, but she was rarely poked. They all lay just so, flat under her, so the sharp ends were harmless. It was always that way. The dog chewed a stick happily.

Vola hummed, still softly stroking the little bend of cedar root. She sang a little nonsense song, and as the melody came out of her, her disappointment eased. She felt it more for Granny than herself; nobody had come to eat after the funeral.

The cedar stretched overhead, the shade velvety under the thick, green-needled branches. The air was sweeter under this evergreen canopy. Dust motes sparkled in thin, golden rays of sunshine. Vola started to feel better. She'd come here to sing under this tree every time she felt sad, for as long as she could remember. It had been so tiny, at first, and now look at it. Her own mama had remarked on how this tree looked like it was decades old, not merely as old as Vola herself. She'd said Vola's singing was special. It made the trunk taller and the branches stretch out over the roof of Lacey's little trailer house. Not that he should worry about one falling on his house, no! Vola had heard Grandpa talking about that one day, how one of those thick, reaching branches could just up and fall and crush Uncle Lacey's roof, maybe with Uncle Lacey underneath it. So she came right out and sang it to the tree: how it should be strong in those branches and never fall on Lacey's house.

The roots grew, too, thick and deep. She couldn't see those, but she could feel them under her, burrowing through the wet clay and shale. A few of the deepest had even come to black, dark air—they'd pushed through the earth

34

and rock, finding cracks and twisting aside when they met impenetrable granite, down, down, until they emerged into one of the caves deep below. Sometimes Vola followed the roots with her thoughts, her deep-down brain, as Grandpa June called it. She closed her eyes and traced them down to their deep places, down to the unexplored caves where blind creatures lived their lives in the trickles of water. She had trepidation about this; Grandpa had told her tales of what sometimes dwelled down there in the dark, secret places below.

He didn't know she already knew all about these places, that the living, growing roots could take her there if she concentrated hard and followed them down. She'd never told him. She was afraid he'd make her stop. She didn't want to stop. It felt so good, touching the roots like that. It made her tingle and soothed her all at once, just like when her mama sang and braided her hair on the back porch in the fading summer light.

Now, she followed the roots down and down, pushing with them as they broke through, more thick fingers of root curling around rock, through clay and gripping the earth in a twisted fist...she couldn't stop, didn't want to stop, would keep singing deep down into the earth forever because it *wanted* her to! And suddenly, she did stop—one quavering note on a jagged breath—frightened by the intensity of what she felt. Her hair stood out from her head as though she'd rubbed it with a balloon. There was a smudge of earth under her right eye. She shifted and yelped as one of the cedar needles turned up and poked her.

"Goose walking over my grave," said Granny in the kitchen across the field. Clary nodded her agreement; she'd felt the shiver, too. The women turned to gaze through the dining room, out the big picture window. Away over at Lacey's place, they thought that maybe that big cedar had grown a little bit more. Vola must have been singing.

⇢⟫⟫⟩ ⟨⟪⟪⟵

In the regular order of things, cedar trees do not feel excitement like a little girl does. Cedars, with their richly gnarled branches close to the trunk and fractal-patterned fronds at the very tips, reaching out into the sunshine and the air, releasing sweet evergreen breath...cedars don't feel anything at all in the realm of emotion—much less the drive and wonder of exploration, the desire to see what the air is like a few inches closer to the sky, or how the damp, cool clay feels farther down below its last roots.

But Vola felt those things. And Vola was a very special girl, so when she sang her sweet, sad songs to the cedar tree, some of her wonder, and curiosity, and the richness of life through her eyes imbued itself into the tree and encouraged it to move and achieve a little bit of greatness in the only way a tree really can: by growing, and growing.

One little filament of root, a tiny push of sweet song and whimsy from up above, broke through a barrier of shale the size of a fingernail. It was dark down below, blacker than night (which was lit up, after all, by brilliant stars and moonshine, and the dull-orange glow of sodium arc lights from the little town over the ridge on cloudy nights). The little root quested for wet soil and rich minerals and nutrients to travel through its questing finger, up into its rich, thick trunk to make the tree even stronger.

The usual root, wending its way to a void in the bedrock full of blackness, would not attract any kind of attention at all. It would creep along, gripping the underside of the rock, soaking up the moisture that dripped over it in its slow travels to the water table down below. But the usual root did not break through with a whisper of a giggle.

Haints came to the root, drawn like fish to a sparkling, floating mote. They bumped and chafed in the confines of their dark prison, trying in vain to suck up the sweet, human energy that had come to them like a whisper of perfume on a breeze. But they could not because a root, even a root as unusual as this one, affected by one special girl of immense vitality—a root was not the origin of any kind of thought or feeling. A root was not human.

The haints were riled. They were mad. But they could do no more than roil in their formless way, crashing into the rock ceiling like noxious smoke, bursting apart and reforming, the substance of malice.

What if we followed.

Follow the giggle.

Followed the root-the-girl-the-giggle-the-song.

There is a crack.

The root made a crack.

But they could not follow because the Whitts had made a boundary, had laid it thick and strong like a tight quilt under the earth, and even though a small thing like a root could push through, haints could not. When the Whitts made a boundary, it stuck.

Vola went away, and Gitli went with her, and even though they came back to sing the cedar every now and then, the haints never could get through that way.

⇒⟫⟫⟩ ⟨⟪⟪⟸

This summer morning, years after his great-uncle's funeral, Lacey leaned against a porch column, having found a cold biscuit to munch, contemplating boundaries in his methodical way. The cracks in boundaries, to be precise, the...the places where two borders might join together. Like in a house, where two walls came together. It made a crack. Yes, a body could plaster up the crack and join it tight together with nails on the inside, so nothing could push through, not even the thinnest edge of paper.

"Hello, son," said June, softly. He'd come up on his boy and knew from years of experience two things: Lacey was deep, deep in his own mind and June would best serve him by not startling him. His son was an odd one, "queer," the old-timers might say, in a way that rhymed with "choir." It was a word that meant many things, but in this sense, it meant out of the norm. Lacey himself claimed his clay eye could show him the spirit world. June had been on the Earth long enough that he wouldn't totally discount his boy's claim…but, whether or not the boy had the spirit sight, he did have a way of wisdom.

Lacey turned at the sound of June's voice and shook his head slightly, coming out of a dream of thought.

"Hey, there, Dad," he said. "Cold can still get through." June blinked at him.

"It can?"

"Yes. Cold and blusters. Shaking storms. Even if you put the cracks tight up together in a house, like." Lacey pressed the palms of his hands together so that the skin on their sides went white, the blood momentarily pressed away. Then he reached out and pressed both hands to either side of the porch column and raised his eyebrows as if to say, *See?*

"You feeling the cold over in your trailer house, son?" June crossed his arms, trying to follow Lacey's logic. Some people thought he wasn't quite right in the head, not since the accident that took his eye. But June remembered that his boy's mind worked in its own rhythm, and if he could be patient, he could mine precious information from it. Even so, how Lacey's thoughts bubbled to the surface could be distracting.

Lacey was already shaking his head, his one good eye shining with intensity.

"No, Dad, no, I mean things get through cracks. Where walls come together, like. Even if you put 'em tight together, things get through. So we got this lid on the haints, right?" Lacey pushed down on the air with both hands. "And we got a wall 'gainst those damned old Byrnes, too." He mimed rubbing his hands against a wall. "The wall comes right up against that lid. Don't it?"

"And you think it makes a weak spot. A place haints can come through." June took his sweat-stained hat from his head and rubbed at his thinning hair. "Yeah. I reckon that could be."

"Well, anyhow," said Lacey, taking a deep breath, relieved his dad got the picture, after all. "Anyhow, there's a line pulling on my belly button, here," he pointed at his belly. "It pulls on up to the bob-wire, right up to that Byrne border." June nodded thoughtfully. He knew what Lacey was driving at. Something was off. Something was...was coming. And for a Whitt, that was often something worrisome.

Chapter Four

UP IN THE WOODS, VOLA was extremely uncomfortable. She'd just wanted a new friend. Well, she'd wanted *a* friend. Most folks around avoided a Whitt like the devil, and Vola, well...she knew she was considered by her classmates to be a dork, even without being a Whitt. She'd thought that maybe a girl from out of state would be easier to befriend. But this one was...well, it was like trying to pull pants on like a shirt, talking with Lily. It almost worked, but it felt out of sorts. First, Lily was so dramatic about her mom and how she always was on her *case*, and how Lily hadn't wanted to move away from all her friends, *anyway.* It was so off-putting that Vola grew quieter and withdrawn, until she had stopped even attempting to answer Lily with "hmm" and "uh-huh" and started absently brushing at the tiny flowers and delicate shoots of grass questing their way toward the thin forest light. Lily stopped, midsentence.

"What are you doing?" she asked.

"Hmm?" Vola looked up at the girl, then down at the flowers at her feet, tiny forest violets that had all sprung open under the arc of her sweeping hand. "Oh, just...nothing, really."

"What's that you're singing?" Lily looked wonderingly at the patch of flowers and back at Vola's earnest face. "It sounds...it sounds like an Indian song. You know, that throat noise." Lily tried a poor imitation of Vola's warble. Gitli gave her a look that was so incredulous it was almost human, and it changed everything. Vola burst into laughter so genuine and sunny that Lily could not resist joining her. With that, it was like the sun coming out after a bitter storm, and the two girls started over.

"Seriously, though," said Lily, propping herself up on both hands, legs crossed in front of her. "You just made those flowers bloom."

"No, I didn't," said Vola, the corners of her mouth still twitching. The denial made Lily suspicious. Most kids would boast at something so cool as magic or even making an illusion (which was what magic really was, after all). What was Vola covering up?

"You did. Show me how!" Lily insisted. Vola hesitated, then swept her hands over the tiny plants at Lily's feet.

"Pass your hands over, like this," Vola said, and when Lily did it, Vola sang her warbling song and passed her own hands, too. Tiny purple flowers opened like fairies stretching their wings. Lily crowed with delight. Drama with her mother completely forgotten, she lost herself in the woods with Vola. And the girls began the real business of getting to be friends.

Not fifty paces up the old forest road, barbed wire at the Byrne property line glowed and thrummed.

⤙⤙⤙⤛⤛⤛

It was almost dark when Grandpa June stumped his way into the house. He'd been out checking fence lines most of the last half of the day—after he and Lacey had mended the porch railing. They had cut out a length of it and replaced the worst of the shotgun-blasted wood, then filled in the rest of the holes with wood putty. Granny would put up with farm life—there was a wholesomeness to the dirt, and the work that wasn't never done. But she would not put up with a redneck house. Truth be told, June was a perfectionist himself and kept the homeplace neat as a pin. After fixing the railing, he went out on the ridge to check the fences he hadn't laid eyes on in a few months.

41

He checked fence lines and the deeper boundaries, the ones down in the earth. What Lacey'd said troubled him. He saw the truth to it, but he wouldn't be foolhardy enough to charge up to the Byrne-Whitt line and challenge it, just to see if it was still strong. If it was weak, testing it might break the whole damned thing open. He'd have to go up on the southeast ridge tomorrow, though. No way around it. He couldn't push too hard, but maybe a little investigation would help him see more clearly.

"And she likes the same TV shows as me, too!" Vola was washing up in the kitchen with Clary, bubbling over with excitement for her new friend. June was glad to see his granddaughter happy like that, preoccupied though he was.

"You went on up to meet the new neighbors, I take it?" he asked, ruffling her hair before sitting down to supper.

"I sure did! The girl's name is Lily, and she's nice."

"That's good, darlin'. You didn't touch that fence, did you? The Byrne line?"

"No, definitely not. Definitely." She flipped her ponytail back from her shoulder in a way June had never seen before—though he would have recognized it if he'd spent five minutes with Lily.

"I didn't think you had." June smiled at her and took a bite of supper that he barely tasted, slipping into his own thoughts while Vola chattered away, Granny and Clary and Lacey—who was still up here at the big house, later than usual—letting her go on. It was an unusual day, after all; the youngest Whitt had made an outside friend.

After supper, after Granny had retired to bed and Lacey headed off across the field to his own little house, Vola happily flopped onto the couch to watch television, with Gitli on the floor at her feet. Clary leaned down to kiss her daughter's head before she went out one of the many screen doors to the porch. For some reason, the creak of the door spring reminded her of Granny's decrepit childhood home…an old building that was now more monument than structure. They'd done some things different when they built this newer house. You could get anywhere inside the house you needed to without having to leave and come back in, for example. But there were still plenty of doors leading outside. And there was still a witch's keyhole in the chimney, even if it was hidden from view in the attic. The Whitts moved with the times, you could say, but some things they never would let go of. Witch's keyhole, five ways in...and haints. But you couldn't let go of haints, could you? Even if you wanted to. It was like riding the wildcat. Once you hopped on, you stayed on. Or you'd get eaten up. Clary spotted the silhouette of her father out on the porch, having his evening beer.

"Hi, Daddy," Clary said, settling into the rocking chair next to June in the dark.

"Howdy," he replied, taking a sip from his bottle. There was a time he'd had to drive all the way to the county line for his beer, but politicians had decided this was a partially dry county now. You could get beer at the package store. But not anywhere within a hundred yards of a church—damned near impossible to avoid being within a hundred yards of a church, around here—and not on Sunday. That was all fine; it suited June to live in a partially dry county. A damp county. He chuckled to himself at the thought. Anyway, liquor wasn't the problem in these parts. Pills and dope. That was the problem. When June was young, dope meant Coca-Cola. It was a nickname holdover from the days a Coke had the real thing inside: a lick of cocaine. Of course, they'd taken all the dope out of a Coke these days. But dope was rotting the people in the town from the inside-out. Crystal meth, oxycodone. Drugs either made in the bathtub or directly dispensed by those crackpots down at the health clinic. June fetched a deep sigh, then took another drink of beer. Hell, haints wouldn't hardly have much to get after, if they was after souls to eat here. The dope did their job for 'em.

"Deep thinking?" Clary said, after a few moments.

"Yeah," June grinned at her in the dark. He'd let his mind wander, sniffing around from one ornery thing to another. Mary had always teased him about that, had accused him of going on the hunt for something to get his hackles up. Clary didn't tease like her mother had, but she could tell when he was in that mood. Like now. She couldn't see him, but she heard the smile in his voice.

"Yeah," he continued, smile fading out. "Lacey said something to me about that Byrne border today. About how it's a weak spot, on account of how it meets up with the bigger boundary." He gestured toward the hay field and the hills beyond, his arm a vague shape in the deepening gloom.

"Is that a problem?" Clary asked.

"Maybe."

Something new occurred to her. "Should Vola be allowed on the back ridge, then? Visiting her new friend?" The feud between her mother's kin and their family had always made Clary uneasy, anyhow, and this thing that was causing anxiety in Clary's daddy was one more little bug of worry.

"Well..." June rocked in his chair, considering. "I don't know yet. I thought I'd have her come with me while I check fences tomorrow. See if her being up there makes any kind of difference."

"Okay." She rocked one or two more times. Talk of haints and the boundary...her feeling of unsettlement grew stronger. Years and years ago, when Granny had taken her into the archives, into the old stories and memories all stored up in that old house...maybe she should have felt a revelation, when she was twelve. Maybe she was supposed to settle into her place in life as a Whitt, but all she'd felt was a vague wish to run away, a feeling that only grew sharper as Clary had gotten older, until she'd left. And then come right on back home with Vola in her belly. Vola...her baby girl would turn twelve next birthday. And it would be her turn to hear the ancestor-stories. Clary got up to go back inside.

"That's it?" June gazed after her, a vague shape standing in the flickering glow from the television on the other side of the living room window. "End of discussion, huh? This is your family, too, Clary. I know you're not here as much as the rest of us. I know you got a life in town..." *There you go,* he could almost hear his dead wife's voice in his ear. *Sniffing around, looking for something to growl over.* The voice might be right, but he couldn't help himself. He was irritated, starting to get scared deep down, and the feeling lashed out like a flash fire.

"That life in town pays for things for this family!" Clary's temper flared. "For satellite TV! Dad, I know you're not thrilled I got a job at the clinic—"

"Oh, the clinic. Where they hand out pain pills like candy. Doing good work." His words were heavy with derision.

"Yes! Yes, dammit! We do good work, too!" Clary rubbed her eyes with both hands, taking deep breaths to calm herself. They'd had this discussion before. Too many times.

"...I'm sorry," said June, looking out into the night. The fight dropped out of him abruptly. "I believe you do, honey. I do." Clary let her hands down.

"But you've closed off to our life here," he said. "You stopped...paying attention."

"To what? To haints?"

"Yes, to them. And to our duty. To our—our connection with this piece of ground we live on. And your connection with the rest of us, too." June's voice grew softer.

"Dad, I...I can't believe in ghost stories anymore. They ruined my life. I never had friends, never had anything normal." Clary sighed. "And, you know, Vola finally has a friend. And I don't want ghost stories to ruin her life, too."

"So, what? What are you saying, Clary? You want to leave again? Take her away?"

"No, I don't want to leave. I just...wish things were different." *But that's a lie, ain't it? I do want to leave.* Clary shook her head and turned away.

"We all wish that sometimes," said June, speaking into the night. Clary had already gone back inside, the screen door softly banging behind her. She mourned what she lost—her mother, dead the year Vola was born. Her snarled-up childhood, filled with memories of mean children and their small-minded parents, of being an outcast when she longed for a life on the inside of society. It was never so bad for the rest of them, Lacey for example, even with his ruined eye. He never seemed to care as much for the regard of others. Clary yearned for acceptance more than any of them ever had. That made it all the more raw for her: this life on the farm, at the edge of a town full of folks that would just as soon spit on her as look at her.

Chapter Five

EVEN WHEN THEY WERE CHILDREN, Lacey was more likely to accept things as they were—Clary's brother was never a worrier, even before he lost his eye and his mind became...simpler. But Clary was. She worried over the weather. She worried over what the girls at school might say to her, might say about her, or might do to prank her in the bathroom, on the playground, or in the lunchroom. There were so many things to worry over and so many stages for bad things to play out.

And most of all, Clary worried over what had already happened.

"Let go, child," her mother would say. Mary Whitt was never serene, never like a mother from a storybook, who would just gently press Clary's hair behind her ear and lead her into a sunlit field of calm. She was boisterous with her love, tickling Clary when she didn't want it. Roughing her out of being broody. Sometimes even scolding her raw when she'd had enough of her daughter's moods. Though, Clary admitted to herself, her mama sure could make her laugh...and it did seem to break her morose moods. Mary was frank with her love.

"You're going to worry yourself right out of a life," she'd say, when Clary was just a girl. "Fretting about the past all the time or terrifying yourself with what hasn't even happened yet—that ain't the way to be, Clary. And as far as all the things that might-could go wrong? Burn that bridge when you get to it."

"Don't you mean, 'Cross the bridge'?"

"Huh?"

"You said, 'Burn that bridge when you get to it.'" Clary grinned, thinking she'd caught her mama out. "But it's supposed to be, 'Cross the bridge.' "

"Is that right?" Mary winked at her daughter, turning back to the clothesline, her hair suddenly fiery with the late afternoon sun behind it. "These clothes will be dry in the wink of an eye, hot as it is today!" Clary helped her mother hang the laundry, still uncertain that Mary'd understood about the bridge...and yet, wondering if she knew something Clary didn't. Clary's mama often had that effect. She put people wrong-footed, and yet they seemed to enjoy it every time. At least, other folks enjoyed it. Clary, in the long tradition of daughters the world over, just got irritated at her mother.

Clary and Lacey knew they had family over the southeastern boundary. They grew up with the knowledge like other kids grew up with red hair or knowing they had family all the way in Michigan. It was normal in their lives that they didn't have Sunday suppers with the Byrnes, or play with their cousins, or even see them at all except for the occasional encounter at Greene's Grocery in town. Once, they saw their Uncle Matthew in the Wal-Mart over the mountain, in Morristown. He'd nodded to them, then immediately seemed appalled at his action and hurried off to the hunting aisle.

"What was that about, Mama?" Lacey had asked.

"That's my brother," Mary'd said, curtly. The kids hadn't asked any more about it. Clary and Lacey grew up. Then Vola was born, and it was only months later that Clary lost her mother.

It was after Mary had died—the cancer stealing her away from everything she loved just as surely as June had stolen her away from the life she'd hated—that Clary had started to wonder why the Byrnes hated them more than most folks did.

"Granny," she said, as they walked in the woods in search of ginseng. "Why don't Mama's kin ever come to visit?"

"They cain't," said Granny, stooping to sweep away dead leaves from a tender, green shoot. "Lookit that." It was a yearling plant with only three leaves. Not ready for harvest. "We'll have to remember this spot, eh, my girl?"

"Because of the boundary?"

"What?"

"The Byrnes can't come over because of the boundary, right?"

Granny stopped a moment and leaned on her walking stick. She took a handkerchief out of the pocket of her faded, patched overalls and mopped her forehead. "Yes, honey. Your daddy stole Mary from her kin and put up a boundary to keep her safe from them." Clary stood still, shocked. She'd known the story; she and Lacey had grown up with it: June had romantically swept Mary away to marry him, and they lived happily ever after at the Whitt farm. Until the cancer got her. But she'd always thought it was...embellished. Romanticized. She stood confounded with a raw secret that had been common knowledge all these years—hidden in plain sight by the casual attitudes of adults who explained a thing to children as though that's just how it is. The sky is blue and the sun rises. The Byrnes don't come onto the Whitt property because your daddy stole your mama from them.

"So you're saying...they physically can't come here?"

"Nope."

"Because...they got mad at Daddy, so he banished them? Like the haints?" Clary started to feel indignant. She was unsure why, just...she wanted to feel like she had some kind of handle on her weird family. Somehow, if Clary could only reduce their actions to the decisions made by crazy hill people, well, then, she'd be superior. And aloof. And she could shake her head at them, siding with the saner crowd.

"He protected us. And your mama." Granny pierced Clary with keen eyes. Eyes that said they knew just what her granddaughter was thinking about her family. "And them." The way she spoke the words gave a chill to Clary.

"Because he would have killed them."

"He would have had to. Clary, did your mama ever tell you about her daddy? About the kind of way she was raised?"

"Yes," she answered defensively. Her own mother would have told her the important things.

"He hit her, child. And he did worse than that. He taught your mother that she was unimportant, all the best parts of her: her heart, her mind. Her fierce spirit. He taught her..." Granny laughed, suddenly, with real joy that startled Clary. "He *tried*, I should say! Hee hee...lawksy, he *tried* to teach her that meekness was the way of grace." She spat the words with sarcasm. "But your mama never was one for meekness." Clary smiled to herself. It was hard not to agree with Granny's fiery views on the rightful place of a woman— namely, that it was wherever she happened to be. And you'd best give her an extra few inches of space all the way around, according to Granny, for good measure. A woman has to be strong, she always told Clary. She has to seize what's hers 'cause no man's gonna give it to her.

"Walk behind her man. Give it all up to God. Never question thy father— thy mother be damned. Eve is the root of sin, a woman is sin incarnate..." Granny stuffed her handkerchief back into her pocket and set her walking stick in the earth, hard. "That's the bullshit your mother ran away from. And your father took her in his arms, and so did we all." Granny's smile was sad, and its tenderness brought tears to Clary's eyes.

"I miss her so much," Clary said, sitting on the ground.

"I know, baby." Granny lowered herself to a jutting rock.

"Granny..." Clary rubbed the tears from her face. "If they were so bad, why did Daddy make Mama live here? Right next door, where they were always just over the ridge. Why didn't he take her away?"

"You think he should have taken her over to Morristown? Or…Ohio? Maybe all the way out West? Somewhere she'd never see her family at the Wal-Mart and never be reminded of all their hurty ways?"

"Well, yeah. Yes."

Granny thought a while. White tendrils floated away from her once-thick braid, now diminished by age. The birdsong of the woods seemed to mark the flow of the old woman's thoughts. Clary was comforted by this; she'd been set adrift since the death of her mother—the woman who'd planted her firmly in love and had never laughed at Clary's worries, though she'd tried to teach Clary how to laugh at them herself. She'd tried to show her that they were too unimportant to steer the wagon. *At least I still have family*, Clary thought, taking in a shaking breath. Her mother was gone, but Clary hadn't been banished from the rest of them, like her mother had been. She felt like she was being shown a painting she'd walked past her whole life but had never stopped to really see.

"Hurts and memories and…a scarred spirit, they never can be left behind," said Granny, startling Clary again. Even the birdsong quieted, the forest itself listening. "You can go to Siberia. You can go to yon sun." She pointed a gnarled finger at the leafy canopy above. "You'll take them with you, and worse…if you don't face them, they will grow like mushrooms in the dark." An unbidden image of haints, drifting like malignant smoke below their feet, came to Clary's mind.

"*Wherever you go, there you are,*" Clary murmured, pushing her hair back from her face. "I read that somewhere."

"Exactly. And if you get your mind right, you can be anywhere at peace. It's all in here." Granny tapped the side of her head, grinning crookedly. "Now then. I think I know where we marked a 'sang plant that should be just about ready. Let's go, Clare-Bear." It was the nickname they had called Clary as a little girl, and it almost surprised her into tears again. She swallowed them down and stood to help Granny to her feet.

Later, when Clary sat cuddling her own little girl, watching the sunset spark the hay field to glowing, she mused over what she hadn't spoken of to Granny: her own longing to leave the Whitt farm and her suspicions that her mother might have felt the same. For years, she'd entertained the thought that her mother was a prisoner, stuck here because June would never leave, because Whitts didn't leave—or if they did, they always, always came back. She rocked Vola, breathing in the girl's smell of sunshine and sweetness, and discovered something else: Granny had already answered that concern. Wherever you go, there you are. Mary wasn't a prisoner here; she was content, and Clary supposed she'd always known that. And Clary, rocking her daughter, wanted so badly to reach that same place of contentment in herself. But she worried that she never would. Mary would have laughed if she could hear Clary's thoughts. *You're worrying about worrying,* she'd have said. The idea made Clary smile a little bit.

June came around the corner of the house. Clary looked up and pulled him to her with the string she held inside herself, that part of Whitt talent she had. He felt it and surprise flitted across his face; she'd been distant since her mama had drawn her last breath. June knew his daughter blamed him and couldn't quite convince himself that she was wrong to do so. He came to her and put his hand on her shoulder. Clary laid her cheek on it and sighed. They watched the last of the light fade from the sky together, lost in their separate thoughts of the Mary they loved.

⟶⟫⟫⟩ ⟨⟨⟨⟵

June remembered the first time he saw the future mother of his children. Mary Byrne. She wasn't, strictly speaking, the prettiest thing he'd ever seen. There was a way about her—the tilt of her head as she read her book. The way her hair fell over her forehead. The unabashed way she smiled up at him, without a lick of self-consciousness. It was all teeth, that smile, and not a bit coy.

The new glass factory was going up in Church Hill, and June was part of the crew building it. He had masonry training, and the work paid good.

He rode the two hours every day with Billy Venable in his old Chevy. Before dawn. Billy was a good man—didn't give a rat's hindquarters about whether June was a Whitt or the Pope. Billy's people weren't from here. They didn't have roots here, and they didn't stay long, not by the town of Greasy Rock standards, where your people had to have lived here for four generations for you to be rightly "from here." And some, like the Melungeons up on Newman's Ridge, well—they could certainly claim residence hundreds of years back, but they lived side-by-side with the white folks in an uneasy truce. Not so different from the Whitt family, really. Matter of fact, some of those Mullins and Collins probably were related to the Whitts, if they looked far enough back in the gnarled, convoluted family tree.

The war came, some years after June fell in love with Mary. The war came, and he and Billy went overseas. June came back. Billy didn't. His people left soon after they got the telegram. They got his dog tags back home, but not Billy, and it was a damned shame was what it was.

Might have been hot the day June saw his future wife. Might have rained. It didn't matter; that day was perfect. Mary'd loved hot summer days. She'd kick off her shoes and sip iced tea in the shade, just like a Southern belle, but without the fancy dress. She never did need a fancy dress, his Mary. Her smile would light up the room, no exaggeration to it. Fine, white teeth and curly hair—even if it did come out of a bottle, she looked good with curly hair. She just...just looked good. God, he missed her.

There was a short fella who laid brick up at the new glass factory with June. He was strong for his size, but what he was really good at was moving his ass up the scaffolding. He'd heave on the pulley ropes, bringing up loads of brick and buckets of mortar. The boys' lunches, too. He was a good fella. What was his name? What was that little guy's name? Anyhow, he was married to a great, big woman. June remembered that much.

And Church Hill was a dry town. Not a lick of alcohol to be found outside the bootlegger's trunk, and the constable was keener than most on keeping shine where he figured it belonged—anywhere not in his city limits. But it wasn't too far to Gate City, where a man could buy himself a beer or two. Every payday the masons would pile in together and buy themselves a cele-bratory drink up in Gate City.

This particular day, one of the boys had some news: his wife was expect-ing a baby. He was young, and it was their first young 'un, and he was right proud. They all bought him a beer, then bought themselves another round for good measure.

"May that kid be purtier than you, Gill!" Billy'd called out. June smiled at the memory.

"Naw, naw, but he better get your wife's smarts instead of your big ears!" someone else yelled. Gill had blushed at that, but he was still pleased. They all gave him blessings and goodwill anointed with warm beer.

But, Lord, then Jeremy's wife—*yes, that was it, the little 'un's name was Jeremy!*—she'd burst right through the door, face almost purple with rage.

"Gawd-damn it, you little son-of-a-bitching-whore-lover! I'm about sick and tired of you drinking away all our rent money!" And June was shocked to see her—truly, a huge woman—march over to where Jeremy perched on his stool, and she scooped him up under her arm and marched him right back out. June couldn't see the little man's face from where he sat, but he could see his legs kicking, making him look every bit the scolded boy snatched up by his mother. They were gone quick as she'd come in. The whole scene seemed unreal. All the men sat in shocked silence for a minute before Billy commenced to giggling.

"D'you...did you *see* the size of that woman?" Before long, all of them were guffawing into their beers, unable to control their laughter.

"And...and...if Jeremy's a whore lover, what's that make his woman!?" June lost it, then, about falling off his bar stool in fits. He didn't even mind picking up Jeremy's part of the bar tab, truthfully. It was too good a night.

But the morning, oh Lord. He'd passed out in the back of Billy's car—thank the Lord for bench seats. The morning brought a hangover the likes of which June'd never had before or since. The light pierced right through to his brain and set his head to aching something fierce. The only thing he could keep down was small sips of water, and only after he'd thrown up everything he'd eaten in the past week, it felt like. He wasn't going to work that day, no sir.

Billy made excuses for June to the foreman, who had his own suspicions of what went on the night before—the masons were a rowdy bunch on this job, and they always looked pretty bad the day after payday. Smelled pretty bad, too. June hitched a ride in the bed of a pick-up going back over Clinch Mountain, hoping to sleep it off. Luckily the next day was Sunday, a day for working the farm and a rest before going back to laying block Monday morning.

But he never did get to sleep it off. Something else was in store for him that day.

The truck driver reached his arm out and banged his door with a fist when he pulled into Greasy Rock, and June hopped off the bed, stumbling a little and willing his gorge to settle back down. He rubbed his eyes and scrubbed one hand through his hair before he set his cap on his head and started the long two miles that would take him over the Clinch River. On the other side, he'd have to climb up the steepest part of Deer Ridge, where there wasn't no road, down into the valley of the Whitt family farm.

He looked up, though. Something caught his eye, and his body wasn't under his control anymore. His feet stopped sharp, right in the middle of the blacktop, and June's eyes met hers. She sat on the other side of the plate glass window, at the counter at Aunt Bea's Soda Shop and Drugstore, reading a book—from one of the pile she'd got from the library, he'd find out later. Sipping a soda. She'd looked up right when he had, and their eyes had them both pinned like raccoons in the beam of a flashlight. Then she smiled, and he might have happily died—almost did, actually; he stood in the middle of the street like a damned fool, and the sound of screeching tires and the laying on of a horn broke him out of his daze enough to fall back on his ass as the car went on by, couple of teenaged boys—vaguely familiar—laughing at him as they burned rubber out of town.

June looked up to see she'd gotten halfway down from her stool, concern shining in her eyes but hiding a smile behind one hand. And that was it. He was hers. Forevermore, he was hers.

Later, when Billy told him she was Mary Byrne, and her daddy was a Baptist preacher—the hellfire and brimstone kind—and that there was no way he'd let her be courted by a roughneck like June, let alone a Whitt, June only shrugged. It wasn't that he didn't believe Billy; he'd heard about Old Man Byrne and knew he was a man who shuffled just shy of madness. Hell, they were neighbors, Whitts and Byrnes. But he was too in love to think a little obstacle like an unconsenting father, even a crazy one, would stop what he felt. It was elemental. It was deep. And if Mary was willing, June would lay down everything that he was for her.

But he hadn't. It was Mary who'd laid it all down for him.

⊰⊰⊱⊱⊱⟫⟫⟪⟪⊰⊰⊰⊰

After supper on the day his belly button seemed to have woken up with a direct line to the southeastern border of the Whitt family farm, Lacey had wandered back down to his trailer house. He was in a strange mood. The whole dad-blamed family was in a strange mood. Made him think about how cats got all cagey when there was about to be an earthquake. He'd seen that on TV, sometime or other. It made him smile, thinking about them all like moody cats, stalking around the farm with tails raised up high.

Vola was happy, though, and that was good.

This kind of feeling, it seemed to dredge up all the sad things and the worrisome things. Like sadness and worry never really left when you forgot 'em but were kept in a basket deep inside. And his brain pulled the basket up on a rope and pulley when Lacey felt low enough and brought out everything inside it for inspection. He stopped just past the barn and looked up at the starry sky. He felt a furry body press against his knee, and he knew Gitli had

56

slipped out of the house and decided to spend the night with him. She did that, every now and then. That made him glad—the border collie had enough good nature to help him through tonight. He figured it would be a bad one.

Lacey missed his mama, too. It had rained and rained, then rained some more when she'd really gotten sick, almost as if the sky itself was sad Mary Whitt was dyin'. He took his sister's hand one day, about a week after they buried Mama up on the ridge with the rest of the Whitt family—those dead ones, anyway. Mama wasn't born a Whitt, but she married one and mothered two of them, so that counted, according to Granny. And if Granny's word hadn't sealed it, the cocoon had: after they put her in the ground, a delicate violet butterfly had winged its way over to Lacey's shoulder and woven herself right into the jacket. Tonight, Lacey went into his trailer house, opened his special box, and looked at the small, silvery-gray cocoon.

"Hi, Mama," he murmured, before shutting the lid. It was a beer kind of night. He took one from the fridge and settled on the couch before letting the memories flood in again. Gitli put her chin on his knee and fetched a sigh that might have been melancholy and might have been satisfaction. Lacey thought about how Clary had been so sad, like losing Mama had been her own fault.

Lacey took his sister's hand and said to come with him.

"Let's go see about the pond," he said. "Now the waters have gone down a bit. Might be there's something to see." Clary'd left Vola with Granny and gone with him, like she usually did. She was a fretter, was Clary, but she was a good 'un, and she was Lacey's sister. And he hated to see her so sad, her eyes always puffy from crying, her nose red. She had a baby now, after all, and needed to buck up to take care of that young 'un. Babies needed a whole lot more'n just food and diapers changed. They needed the joy of love from somebody, preferably their own mama. So Lacey figured he might-could help Clary find that again, that joy of love.

They made their way through the woods, using the secret deer paths instead of the broader road beat down by the farm truck. The ground had finally dried up enough to be firm, but the weeds and flowers and ivy and what-all was going crazy with all the water they'd been given. It was hard going a time or two, getting held back by ankle-grabbing tufts of grass or strainer-like branches hidden in the burst of undergrowth. But they made it down to the pond, down to where Lacey had his homemade boat hid on the bank.

It had mostly been covered up in mud and water from the flooded pond, but Lacey's frog-boat (that's what he called it) was too heavy to be carried away by anything less than a flood of Biblical proportions. (Not that they wanted any such thing around here, nossir.) He'd made the boat out of heavy sheets of plywood, wetted and warped and painted and nailed to a frame. It was ugly, for sure, and it was heavy as a bastard, but it floated. It was good for cruising around in the pond, spooking frogs so they'd make their twangy rubber-band croak before plopping heavily into the water, out of the thick weeds. It always made him chuckle, that twang-plop combo. Frogs were ridiculous, really.

"Help me, sis," he panted, trying to pry the frog-boat out of the mud. She came over and started tugging along with him.

"Damn, Lacey, what'd you make this thing out of? Rocks and steel plate?" She slipped and cried out in surprise as she landed on her butt in the muck, splashing slime and mud and a dash of pond water all over herself and Lacey and the boat, but it didn't really matter; the boat was covered in the stuff anyway.

Lacey couldn't help himself; he started off in a giggling fit that got worse when he saw how furious his sister's face was—bright red and starting to puff like, like...well, like a frog. She started splashing water and mud at him, but it only made him laugh harder, and finally, Clary started to see that it was all ridiculous and messy and funny after all.

"Oh no!" she cried, when she could get enough air. "Look how muddy we are. We're gonna get the inside of your frog-boat all dirty!"

"No, no, we can't have that. We'll lay down some towels. Or rags." Lacey used the back of his hand to wipe tears of laughter from his cheeks but succeeded in only smearing mud around, making him look like a crazed Indian warrior, with his tufted hair and bad eye.

"Ain't got no towels. Nor rags." Clary shook her head in mock sadness. She scrambled out of the mud and helped Lacey with a final heave, pulling the mongrel boat over to rest right-side up in the shallow end of the pond. Lacey put his hands on his hips in an uncanny imitation of Granny, then went to pull some broad leaves from a gnarled shrub jutting over the pond. He fussily placed them over the wooden plank that served as their seat in the boat, and Clary pretended to arrange invisible skirts as she settled in. Lacey jumped in after her and produced a paddle, and pushed them off toward the deep end of the pond.

"Looky there," he said. "The water left behind curtains." The rain had brought more than just moisture; it had caused a craze of life, a bloom of anything that lived in their part of the world. Sheets of drying green algae hung from low branches, weeds, and shrubs at the water's edge, marking about an eighteen-inch swath of bank that had just recently been underwater. They paddled over to inspect it.

"Dried flood slime," said Clary. "What do you bet that's something we ought to collect for Granny?" The late afternoon sun peeked through just then, making the dried algae glow like tiny green panes of stained glass.

"Yup." They floated over to the bank and started pulling algae. It was crispy for the most part, but there were slimy runners that wanted to slip out of their fingers. It's a universal rule of human behavior that handling slimy things makes for giggles, and so they were at it once again. Plopping frogs calling out like they'd all swallowed jaw harps only set them off worse.

It was only after they'd stowed the heavy boat once again and fought their way through the woods to the main track that Clary grew serious again. She studied the plastic Zip-Loc bag they'd stowed the algae in—they always roamed with one, in case they saw something Granny would want—and said, "I miss Mama." It was such a simple thing to say, and plaintive. Lacey stopped and held his arms out to hug her.

59

"I miss her too, Clary." And they cried together, standing under a lovely blue sky that was somehow worse than rain, because their mother would never see it again.

But, Lacey reflected later, those tears were the good kind. Back at the house, when Clary washed up and took baby Vola into her arms, Lacey saw her really look into her girl's eyes, and the life started to come back. They would heal without Mary, and that was terrible in its own way, but it's how life was. Lawd, Lacey knew that; life didn't care a bit when you lost an eye or a mama. It just went on along until you chose to join it once more.

He put his thoughts of grieving his mama out of his head, took a final pull on his beer and laid over on the couch to sleep. Gitli climbed up over his legs and settled her furry self in the nook behind his knees.

Chapter Six

JUNE HAD FULLY INTENDED TO go up to the back ridge just as soon as he was out of bed the next morning, but what with one thing and the other...it hadn't worked out. The Whitts were pretty good at walking the path that was laid before them. Sometimes life put too many obstacles pushed right up in their way, so they turned aside and walked another way a while. Each thing had its own season, and it was hard to know when that was sometimes. But being a Whitt was an exercise in patience. Some of the family was better at it than others.

One of the cows had her calf. It was out of season, and June thought he had a few more weeks until she dropped. But Gitli came to him, whining and acting mighty anxious to head over to the edge of the pasture, where the mother—it was the auburn-colored cow he called Red—was having a rough time with birthing. While he was there helping her along, he noticed the fence had a hole busted in it by a falling branch, and he was going to have to round up some cattle from the woods where they'd taken the opportunity to wander away. That was easy enough; he just needed to bring some sweet feed over and call 'em in for a treat. But then, he'd need to fix the fence. Seemed his whole life was fencing sometimes: haint fences down below and regular old bob-wire fencing up here, to keep in the cows.

"Good girl, Gitli," June said, rubbing the collie's black ears. Her warm, brown eyes spared him a quick glance, but she kept watch at the woods beyond. It wasn't unheard of for a coyote to attack a newborn calf, especially when the mother was having a hard time. Gitli was canny.

Red's calf came along, and June put them both in the barn to keep a closer eye. They'd be all right, he reckoned. Red was a good mother. She'd had a healthy calf yearly, pretty much like clockwork—for how long, now? Maybe six, seven years? She was getting on in years, he reckoned, but she wasn't all that old. She should still have a few calving years left. This early birth was troubling. Might be a sign that things were getting up to a simmer here on the Whitt farm.

So it was that a couple of days passed before June was able to head back toward the Byrne-Whitt line. The unease built deep inside him.

⟫⟫⟫⟫–⟪⟪⟪⟪

Before she left for work in the morning, Clary stopped to squeeze her father's shoulder. He sat at the table with his morning coffee, gazing out over the foggy fields. His hat was laid on the table next to him, like a decision yet to be made.

"You finally taking Vola up on the southeast ridge today?" Clary asked. The girl was still in bed.

"Yes. I was planning on it." June looked up at his daughter and smiled as he put his hand over hers.

"Okay," she said, nodding. "Be careful." He gave a single nod in return before letting her hand go. It was a hollow thing to say: "Be careful." Careful didn't really fit the Whitts. Vigilance, yes. That fit. Kindness, philosophy, history, and responsibility. Even magic, of one kind or another. Those things were all part of the Whitts' lives. But careful? Whitt kids stayed innocent of the outside world for too long sometimes, but they were warriors, after all. Fierce shamans. Even Clary fit the mold.

62

"I'm off to work," she said, walking through the kitchen. She kissed Granny's cheek, opened the door, and left for the day. Clary had stopped in to see her daughter's sleeping face before coming down the stairs, as she always did before going to the clinic each morning. She crept into the room and touched Vola's soft, sleep-warm hair. She was growing up, her face losing its baby roundness. Clary kissed her daughter's temple, feeling the swell of love and the ache that comes with being a parent: knowing that each moment is equal parts holding tight and letting go. She wondered if her own mother had felt that way about her.

June and Granny watched her beat-up little Honda disappear around the bend of the driveway, before Granny went upstairs for her morning constitutional, as she called it.

June was anxious today, more'n he wanted to let on. It was his way to cover up his worry or sadness or anxiousness with gruff words. He suspected Clary knew that about him. Problem was, June Whitt was a man of demons, different from those malicious spirits he kept pinned down with a long-sung boundary in the earth. When he got to fretting, sometimes it opened up a gate to all the things he kept in the back corner of his mind.

Today…he had awoken with the feeling that the gate blew wide open, and it was all he could do to keep it together. Missing Mary, worry over that back property line at the Byrnes' place, worry over Clary. And the war. Those memories were a lifelong sickness.

Mary could always calm him down when she was alive. She handled him like a frightened horse, speaking softly and laying her hands on him with a gentleness only she could give. But she was gone, and it was probably all his fault. He'd killed her, just as he'd killed his platoon mates over in Italy. Brothers, they'd been, and they were gone. Dead, every one. Like Billy.

"Grandpa?" Vola's sleepy voice shattered his rumination, and June looked up at her. He realized he'd been clutching his fists hard enough to ache. He took a deep breath and opened his hands.

"Mornin', Glory," he said, but he could only muster a half-smile, and Vola knew. She had so much of Mary in her, their granddaughter did. She could see into him like Mary always could. He opened his arms up, and she ran into them, hugging tight.

"We got to check on some fence today, sugar bug," said June. She nodded against his chest. He gave her one last squeeze before sending her into the kitchen for breakfast. Usually, he could ride the waves of his bad days until the swells faded down to ripples, but today was different. Today, he thought he might drown if he couldn't grab hold of something. And he couldn't afford that now, not when the uneasiness below their feet was getting stronger. The sweet, bright spark of his granddaughter would help him get through what he needed to do. Maybe.

Down below, haints cruised in the black ever-night underground, in the chambers of earth—worn through by water and years like haphazard honeycomb. Like vultures riding thermals, they glided under the tide of June Whitt's despair. It smelled delicious. If only they could have a taste! They called to it: the spirit-rotting sadness that weighed him down, that told him he deserved death; he shouldn't enjoy his life when men who'd depended on him and when his own dear wife could never again enjoy anything. They couldn't get to June, but they could smell his weakness, and they could whip it up into a storm that would blow him away! And how, how could they do this, when they'd been trapped down below rock and rich clay? Because he let them, pure and simple.

Somewhere inside, June knew it. But he let it happen.

Because he deserved it, as far as he was concerned.

⇛⇛⇛—⇚⇚⇚

Later on, Vola and Grandpa June followed the cow trail up the hill and into the forest. Gitli was nowhere to be found, but that wasn't terribly unusual. Probably she was off at Lacey's.

"After we check the fence row, can I run over to see Lily?" Vola asked. June grunted his assent, picking his way up the path, preoccupied with his own thoughts. As they walked, Vola played a game with a little cloud of white butterflies, jumping up to catch one before releasing it to the swirl. It was a rigged game, of course; Vola could call them to her whenever she wanted. But it soothed her and helped push down her growing anxiety about Grandpa June.

Sometimes he got like this, broody and gruff, and apt to growl shortly when Vola asked him things. She thought his mood had something to do with the Byrne property, which maybe made him think about Vola's dead grandmother—the one he stole from her own daddy, who was a Byrne on the other side of the fence. And sometimes, all that thinking put Grandpa June down a spiral that turned all the way down to the pit inside, where he kept his war thoughts.

Absently, Vola pushed aside a thin tree branch, gazing at the ground without really seeing it and automatically climbing after her grandfather over downed trees and boulders pushing their way out of the scree. She listened— to the woods, to her grandfather breathing. To his mood. Her sneakers kicked up a rich, growing smell in the dark forest soil. Spears of golden light drifted down between leaves, sparking brighter when she walked through them. Tiny white butterflies followed along like a comet's tail.

Pushing through a dense stand of stunted cedars, Vola stopped short at the sight of her grandfather, just standing, shoulders hunched.

"Hey, girl," he said, sitting heavily at the base of a poplar. "You want to go on now." She took a hesitant step toward him.

"Grandpa?"

"I thought...well, anyway," he said, pushing the brim of his hat up, mopping his sweaty forehead with one sleeve even though the morning was still cool. "The tide is rising inside me." She understood, from the apology on his face, that he'd thought they would be all right in each other's company. She could see that all the darkness that dwelled down deep was coming up.

Now. She'd never witnessed this before. She knew it happened, had seen him looking pale and all drawn out after one of his episodes. But he'd always been on his own, when the tide in him rose up. Until today.

Vola stood frozen in place by what she saw. She couldn't even rightly understand it. June—her grandpa, a man of stoic nature and deep calm—he strained against a mantel made of grasping hands, clutching him at the shoulders, arms, and neck, reaching to clutch his hair under his hat. Taking a deep breath, Vola stepped to the side and cautiously circled around him, trying to see. Butterflies followed, swirling behind her. The hands belonged to arms, stretching back to angry men, howling—silently, to her, but from the strain on her grandfather's face, he could hear every word—and clutching at June and each other, with eyes like black sockets, mouths like gaping holes. They made no noise for her, but their rage kicked up an overwhelming tempest, bringing tears to her eyes and making her instinctively look around for shelter, even though the trees around them remained still.

"Hey, now," she said. "Hey." The men stretched out as though caught up in a gale, blowing out behind and boiling up the poplar tree behind Grandpa June. He tipped up his sweat-stained hat and wiped his brow with a trembling hand, causing an outraged ripple in the ghostly legion scrabbling at him. When he looked into Vola's eyes she stepped back, her own entourage of fluttering white butterflies disturbing out and around her before settling back into orbit. Without knowing it, she'd called more of them to her—dozens, hundreds, and enough to match Grandpa June's dark, weighty cloak, their white wings flashing in the sun. Vola's trailing cloud of butterflies was the mirror of Grandpa's mantel of suffering; together, they were life and death, dark and light. Yin and yang, and if Granny were there, she'd understand the dance they made best of all.

His eyes were wild, full of rage and death but mostly—pain. He was in pain. Vola saw it clearly, just like the stray dog she'd once found on the gravel road after it had been hit by a car. June's breath came fast, sweat pouring down his face.

"I can't take it," he said. And Vola saw that was the truth. "Make it stop. Put me out of my misery." He put his hand into his canvas vest and pulled it out with a gun gripped inside. He always carried that gun on his rounds of the farm, just in case. Still sweating and trembling, he tossed it toward her feet. Vola barely glanced at it before turning back to her grandfather. In a flash, she remembered that run-over dog and how Grandpa June had taken it out behind the barn and shot it. Put it out of its misery. It was a kindness.

"Haints is bad," June said, so low that Vola had to lean in to hear. "But people. People...men like me, men do terrible things." He reached out one trembling hand to touch his granddaughter's cheek, the stream of ghosts behind him rippling and writhing.

"Please," he whispered. Shining butterflies whirled faster and faster around Vola. She reached out for the gun. The demon-men gripping Grandpa June writhed and howled silently and more terrible because of their silence. Full of rage. Their tempest pulled at her, sucking at her shirt and trying to consume her, too. Vola lifted the gun, its grip still warm from being in Grandpa June's vest.

Below the ground, unseen, haints writhed.

<hr>

Back at the house, Granny fell down into a well of thought. She'd learned to do this gracefully, with years of practice; her thoughts were intense enough to grip her and run away, and she'd be dragged if she didn't grab the mane and jump on for the ride. She reckoned it was part of being a Whitt, or part of being old. And she'd been old long as she could remember, seemed like. She came back downstairs and sat at the dining room table and gazed out the big picture window, not seeing the sweet summer morning on the other side.

Appalachia—the place, the concept—was a test of mettle for some people. That's what Granny thought. There were those who drove the flashing neon of the strip at Pigeon Forge or Gatlinburg and believed in the cartoon hillbillies they saw: barefooted and clutching a crock with "XXX" emblazoned for moonshine. Other folks listened sympathetically to National Public Radio segments on "Life in Appalachia," expounding, mostly, on "life" in Appalachia as they were most comfortable seeing it: a thing passed by and forgotten by the modern world. Since the days of the Great Depression, and the Great Flood perpetrated by the Great Tennessee Valley Authority, and the Almighty Welfare Check handed down magnanimously to poor, benighted hill folk, well. Ever since those days, folks from outside somehow didn't see the part of Appalachian culture where a lot of people got along fine. They didn't see folks living in middle-class, brick ranch-style houses, driving down to the mall to buy clothes that look more or less like the clothes most Americans buy, including—against all clichés—shoes.

Then there were those who passed by the mini-golf courses and mega pancake houses, the incongruous mountainous plaster alligator next to the equally improbable plaster lumberjack, silently hollering "Souvenirs! Beach wear, 50% off!" even though the nearest beach was more than half a day's drive. Some tourists drove by the flashy stuff, and they saw forests and mountains looming beyond the advertised Appalachia, and they went on. They sought the quiet, the refuge, and the peaceful green and cradling comfort of the hills, both familiar and unsettlingly foreign. These people, these pilgrims, refugees from the increasingly crowded world of middle-class America, saw locals in these parts as down-to-earth. "Earth-ey," in fact. Maybe even slightly mythological. Characters in a story set in place to welcome them to a new, enlightened life. Like in a made-for-TV movie, folks thought if they came to the "real" Appalachia, they'd be transformed by an unlikely encounter with an overall-wearing, cigarette-smoking wise elf in this semi-derelict, forgotten corner of the country.

Granny shook her head, thinking of it. Maybe that's why folks in small-town Appalachia didn't take kindly to strangers; travelers from out of town seemed to not see hill people as, well, real people.

She wondered about those new neighbors from Florida, living up past the southeastern border. Wondered where they fit in. Folks came here to start over, to shock their wearisome lives into something more wholesome, more meaningful. Granny remembered talking with Clary those years ago, about finding peace where you were. She knew there was truth in her words, but she also suspected she, herself, could never find peace in the crowded towns and cities, where farms got sliced up into tiny plots, just big enough for a slapped-up house and a few blades of grass out front.

There was *something* about the hills.

The startling views that opened up between tall trees on the ridgebacks. Not ancient trees, no. Granny had an almost-memory of those towering behemoth trees that once marched along farther than a body could go in a lifetime. An almost-memory…probably a family memory, stored in her bones. Most of the forests here today were regrowth from turn-of-the-century logging, aggressive enough to raze the land as absolutely as wildfire.

But the land was still here, and the forests came back because in places like this, well, rebirth was still possible. Sometimes an acorn could regrow a forest.

Granny's thoughts jumped.

Sometimes it took a young girl with dirty knees and crumbs of granola bar in her pocket to help an old man start over.

Granny passed a trembling, old hand over her brow, steadying her thoughts. People said things come in threes, didn't they? Bad things. The first was on its way; Granny felt it right alongside her ghost-memory of the ancient forests, in her very marrow. June was about to go to the very brink, and Vola with him—but that girl could dance along the edge and never stumble, and Granny wasn't sure her son could. She wasn't sure at all.

But, before this summer was over and done, the Whitts would have a Three. And the first was a-coming. Maybe it was here.

Grandpa June was in the war. Vola knew that; she'd heard her mother and Granny talking about it, though her grandfather didn't like to, much. Somehow those stories, tempered by their soft, feminine voices, seemed far removed from the warm man she knew. He took her out into the woods, after all, showed her where ginseng could be found, and how to tell the birds apart by their call. She helped him haul firewood. She'd learned how to be a steward of their land by watching Grandpa June and listening to how much he loved it. He was gentle; he was steady.

Sometimes Grandpa June was troubled, Vola knew that. But she'd never known this part of him, this raging pain, these dead men who clutched at his mind and heart from the reach of time and distance and life itself.

"Who are these men, Grandpa June?" Vola asked quietly, gun still gripped in her hand. Leaning back against the storm, she stood from her crouch and stepped closer, her butterflies swarming, causing the mantle of demons to writhe and silently howl still harder. She could make them out in more detail now: the black blood caked on them, moustaches on some of their pale faces. Their hair rippled in an invisible current, mud and blood crusted in it. Vola shivered. She crossed her arms and hugged herself, tucking the gun under one armpit. Frenzied butterflies, some of them flying so furiously around her they crashed into each other, fell to the ground.

"I killed them," said Grandpa June. "I killed them all." He buried his face in trembling hands, his ghosts railing at him and at each other. Vola thought she recognized two of the men from an old photo album. They'd been part of his platoon, his brothers-in-arms. Those two, sensing her focus, quieted down a little, silent screams becoming groans, and watched her, as they clutched at each other and at June, kicking at other apparitions trying to get at the old man.

"No, not all," she said. "You didn't kill those two." She knew that, knew it from the stories. Grandpa had helped those men, not killed them. She pointed at his old friends, and they stopped writhing, quieted their silent groaning, and stopped clutching and kicking. They gazed at her and let go completely, drifting off into the morning sunlight until they weren't there at all. Grandpa June trembled more violently, tears spilling down his weathered face.

"The others," he said. "Please. Make them stop." Vola closed the last inches of space between her and her grandfather, gun in her hand, pointed at him. He stared into the blank eye of the gun barrel, sobbing aloud. She reached out with the gun, still pointing it toward him, and he realized she was handing it back.

He shuddered and took it from her. She dropped to the ground next to him and wrapped her skinny arms around him, putting her strong, young, living flesh right through the rotten ghosts that still did not want to let go. Her eyes were inches from theirs, her life light piercing the black sockets just over her grandfather's shoulder. They stuttered in their howling, losing their grip on June, and turned their ire on each other. White butterflies swarmed, covering Vola and June, and the poplar tree pushed the ghosts of the men June had fought beside and men he had killed in war into the spears of sunshine, burning them up. Even in this realm, this beyond-death, the apparitions held tight to their anguish, beating against the white moths with muck and blood-blackened hands.

"Burn them up," Vola whispered to the butterflies. "Burn 'em." June wrapped his arms around his granddaughter and sobbed into her thin shoulder, one hand still holding the barrel of the gun.

⟫⟫⟩ ⟨⟨⟪⟪

"You're better," said Vola handing Grandpa June half the granola bar she'd stuffed into her jeans pocket that morning. It always paid to have a snack or two on you.

"Yes," he said, but he looked pale. His eyes were clear, though, like a beach washed clean after the storm. They sat together and ate quietly. White butter-flies lay on the forest floor all around. Vola risked a peek at the tree behind her grandfather and the sky beyond. Empty. No ghosts, no demons. Just the woods and a drifting wisp of cloud above.

71

"Reckon I ought to go on back to the house. Lie down a while." He smiled at his granddaughter, too tired from his shock, too...clean and new and alive to yet marvel at what this young girl had done. He would have time to think on that later. She was a Whitt, and all Whitts had something special, but what she'd done...well, that was altogether different.

But. Just because Vola was sweet and just because she helped June sever his demons from his heart didn't mean it was any less painful. Letting loose all that sorrow felt just as bad as mourning his Mary had been. Maybe worse, because he'd been using his old war memories and holding tight to the night-mares as a kind of penance. Taking forgiveness from his granddaughter— from Mary's granddaughter—tore a hole in him. He felt raw and sad.

"What about checking that Byrne fence?" She looked anxious—was still hoping she'd get to visit her friend, he reckoned.

"I'll have to get up there another time. I'm plum wore out."

"Can I go on up there by myself?" Vola could see the answer in her grandfather's tired face. He was nervous about her passing by the fence, at least today.

"Well...could Uncle Lacey drive me over to Lily's, do you think?" She looked a little embarrassed at showing her eagerness. He chuckled softly, which only made her blush harder. She could face down a legion of ghosts, but wanting to play with a friend made Vola shy, June thought. Lord, they were country folk, weren't they?

"I reckon. Prob'ly should call her on the phone and ask her mama, first."

"Okay," Vola said, cheerful once more. She folded up the empty granola wrapper and tucked it into her pocket.

"Grandpa," she said, "Do you have PTSD?" She'd heard about PTSD on television. He looked into her eyes with a serenity she'd never before seen on his face.

"I did," he said. "And I reckon I'll still have the occasional bad dream. But, I think...I think you just had me cleansed. Saved and baptized in the fires of forgiveness." She grinned, catching his poke at preacher talk.

"Those weren't haints, were they, Grandpa." It wasn't a question.

"No," he replied. "They weren't. Those were good old-fashioned personal demons." He lay back on the ground, letting warm sunlight dapple over him.

"They wanted to be let go," Vola said quietly.

Down, down in the black earth, haints smelled something new. They'd been in a frenzy, snapping at each other with ineffectual teeth, smoke biting at smoke. With June's death near, his despair at the breaking point...something else had happened then, and the little girl had changed everything.

She changed everything.

Chapter Seven

LACEY WAS LUCKIER THAN MOST; he knew that. He chuckled at the thought, tossing out grain for his chickens to run after in the yard. He only had one good eye, and he was a strange 'un by any measure—he wasn't too strange to know it. But he was here in the valley, and the things that lived all the way around him—they were his world, and he was part of theirs. Most folks never realized that part; they were a part of the world around 'em. Folks somehow thought they were separate.

The old ones—the ancestors who first laid down the blood on this land to make it theirs and their children's and their children's children's land— believed that when a man lost an eye, he gained something else. He had half a vision in the world on top and half a vision in the world underneath. Sometimes Lacey saw things he knew his daddy or Granny or Clary couldn't see. Vola, now, she was a whole 'nother story. Vola could do and see things none of them even guessed. Lacey knew just enough to know that about his niece.

Sometimes, late at night, Lacey would get a feeling about the cocoon jacket stashed away in the chest at the end of his bed. He would get up and pull the woolly thing out, and his eye—the one like old creek-bed clay— would show him there was a cocoon that needed tending. A knitter might get to darning, or a crafty person might go on down to the Wal-Mart and pick up some liquid thread to fix an old jacket. He knew all about liquid thread; Granny'd used it to fix up some seams on the curtains hanging in the living room up in the big house. She'd been pleased as punch about not having to sew a stitch.

But this jacket wasn't anything like a normal jacket, not even an old antique jacket. It was made of thousands of little cocoons that had knit themselves together in the fabric of the thing, and Lacey could see when one of them was sick.

The cocoons didn't get sick like any normal critter would. They would start to fade, unravel, and become, well...less focused to his eye. To his bad eye, which was really what he thought of as his underneath eye. And when he saw that, he would strip down to his underpants and go out to the creek and dance to the ancestors. The dance he chose depended on which ancestor needed his focus. The ancestors waited many long years tethered to their cocoons, and sometimes, the magic and mystery of the universe called them away. So he had to bring them back and help them realize their living family still had need. He didn't know when it would happen, when the Whitt family would have to call the ancestors out of their tiny beds. He didn't know the future. His underneath eye didn't have anything to do with the future. But he knew the haints were still there, still down below the earth, and as long as that was true, they'd need the cocoon jacket.

Last night he'd danced for his great-uncle. He was a recent enough ancestor that Lacey recognized him clearly, and he'd sung a little bit of *The Glow Worm* as he danced in the moonlight. His great-uncle had loved the Mills Brothers version of the song.

Curious, Lacey thought, tossing out the last of his handful of grain. It was a funny thing that he hadn't known Granny's brother at all in life. The old man hadn't spent his days on the Whitt farm, as most of the living (and dead) family did. Granny had once told him it was because her brother had gone a little queer in the head (she'd said it like the old-timers: quoir) and when Lacey had asked if the haints had done it, she looked at *him* queerly and wouldn't answer. Lacey couldn't plumb the depths of her mind to find out; the underneath eye couldn't do that either.

But he'd sung his great-uncle back to the cocoon last night and felt him curl up, content, and the rest of the jacket sort of settled back into itself. Lacey was their keeper, those souls in suspended transition. They weren't in purgatory—he'd looked that word up, once, and been appalled by the bleakness of the concept. Folks came up with some truly horrible ideas in their religions, Lacey thought. His cocoons were just...in storage. It was different. No torture, no wandering in sadness or confusion.

Clary, on the other hand...sometimes Lacey wondered if she was in purgatory. If she was, it was a state of her own making. How can a body show how to see—either underneath or on top? The world they lived in, the world they were a part of themselves, was a fine place. To be in it was a fine thing. Lacey shook his head. He did a little shuffling dance among his chickens and sang a bit of a tune for his sister. Some Aerosmith, which had been one of her favorite bands, when she was a teenager. Maybe his love for her would help her come home within herself. He didn't know if his talent would work on the living Whitts or not.

"Uncle Lacey!" He looked up to see his niece running to him on the gravel road, with Gitli bounding along behind. "Uncle Lacey! Will you drive me up to Lily's? I called, and her mom said 'yes.'"

He grinned at her, stowing the feed bucket on a shelf in the old shed. "'Course I will, young 'un," he said.

⟫⟫⟫⟫⟩ ⟨⟨⟨⟨⟨

Even though it would have been a short trek through the woods, Lacey drove Vola to Lily's house more times than he could count over the following weeks. Lily's mother drove her down too; she didn't think it was strange, all that driving back and forth, when the girls could easily cut down through the woods to visit each other. Apparently folks did a lot more frivolous driving down in Florida.

But it suited the Whitts fine, keeping Vola and her little friend away from the southeastern fence line.

Sometimes they hadn't been parted but twenty minutes when one girl would call the other on the phone, remembering something she just *had* to tell her friend, something that couldn't wait until the next time they were together. It made Clary smile, tears pricking her eyes. June shook his head, not at all understanding why they had to tie up the phone line all the time; what if someone had something important to call about? Never mind that Clary explained about call waiting and how a person could still get through even if Vola was using the phone. Not that anybody ever called them anyhow, unless it was a wrong number. But June grumbled good-naturedly because that's what he did. Granny watched, keeping her opinions in reserve. She wondered about the rest of the "three" she'd sensed was starting. Some kind of change was still peeking at them, she could feel it. She supposed she liked the girl, Lily, well enough. And she was glad Vola had her a little friend. And Lacey was Lacey, pleased when things went along.

He still felt that tug on his belly button, though. It still worried him. Made him check on the cocoon jacket to soothe a fret he couldn't quite name. June walked up to the fence between the Byrnes and Whitts. There wasn't anything wrong, not that he could put a finger on it. So he watched and waited.

Chapter Eight

"**S**O...IF YOU'RE ALL WITCHES, ARE these your familiars?" Lily held up one of the kittens recently born in the hay loft. Light filtered through cracks in the barn walls. Hay dust floated in it like specs of gold. The morning had dawned cloudy, and the wet grass testified to rain the night before. But the day was shaping up to be sunny. The kitten mewed, a sound like the tiniest rusty hinge.

"It's not really...I mean, we're not witches," said Vola, rolling her eyes in imitation of her friend. She held her own kitten in her lap. "Besides, cats don't work well for what I do."

"You mean getting all the animals to do what you want? Snow White-style?" Lily lay back on a pile of loose hay, its sweet smell in the heat of the day making her sleepy. She didn't know if this place would ever feel like home to her; the heat here was softer, like a thick quilt. In Florida, the heat of the summer was sharp, like the rasp of sandpaper on the skin when she'd walk outside from the air-conditioned house. But it had been home. And she missed it. She liked it in Greasy Rock much better now that she had Vola, though. With her, it felt like she was on a constant adventure.

"Yeah," said Vola. Her talent with insects and flowers and the way she could communicate with animals in the woods was something she normally didn't talk about. She kept to herself at school, and nobody in her family thought it was an unusual thing. And she only ever spent time with folks in her family in the summertime. So drawing attention to the thing that made her different in the wider world made her feel funny, like her deepest parts were on display. And she wasn't sure whether that was good or bad yet. It probably depended on how Lily reacted. "Cats just always do what they want."

"Really?" Lily sounded impressed. She'd been teasing and hadn't expected her comment to lead anywhere so interesting.

"Yeah. Granny says cats got lumped in with witches back in the old days because of that. Cats and independent women: they didn't need nobody tellin' 'em what to do!" Vola's impression of Granny was close enough to set both girls giggling. Lily's kitten, splayed on her tummy, bounced with the girl's laughter, setting her to laughing even harder. Gitli gave a sharp bark from down below; it made her anxious, when the girls climbed the ladder to the loft.

"Oh," said Vola, with a sigh. "It's getting hot. Let's get out of here and go someplace cooler!"

"Okay," said Lily, reluctantly putting the kitten down in the hay, where its mother watched placidly.

⊰⟫⟫⟩—⟨⟨⟨⊱

The cold push of air coming from the mouth of the cave made Lily shiver. It hadn't looked like much from the dirt road above, just a dent in the ground with a trickle of water pouring over the top. The girls had picked their way down the slope and passed a rusted car on its side, old and strange enough to seem like it could have been set down by aliens instead of rolling down here from a long-ago mudslide. Inspecting the kudzu slowly wrapping its rusty frame, Lily felt like they might have been in an *Indiana Jones* movie. A thrill sent goose bumps down her arms, and she giggled happily.

Gitli between the two girls, they stood at the mouth of the cave proper, old sneakers soaking wet from the creek running down into the dark. Lily

79

could see how big the thing really was, now that she was up close. You could fit a little house in there. Or maybe a big shed. She said as much to Vola.

"Yeah," said Vola. "Uncle Lacey talked about parking an old VW bus down in there to live in. Granny said she wouldn't consent." Lily grinned at the thought.

"Lily?" Vola sat on a rock in the creek and turned over little pebbles, setting mud swirling in tendrils in the clear water.

"Huh?" Lily sat next to her, watching.

"What's Florida like?" Vola grabbed at something in the water and held up her hand, grinning triumphantly. "A crawdaddy!" The dog came over to sniff at her hand, then, unimpressed, went to lay in the water downstream.

"Oh, cool!" Lily looked around for her own crawdaddy, lifting rocks in the water like she'd seen Vola do. "Um...Florida's nice."

"Does everybody go to the beach all the time?"

Lily shrugged. "Sometimes. We swim in the pool a lot. And we play out in the cow pasture, too. My brother and I..." She stopped abruptly, resting her chin on one knee folded up, the other leg stretched into the cool creek. Vola looked up at the pause.

"You have a brother?" she asked.

"Had," said Lily. "I had one." She cleared her throat. It was heavy, being reminded of her brother out of the blue like this. She felt plunged into the deep end of the pool, suddenly, where the weight of the water made her heart strain in her chest. She cleared her throat again and there was Vola, putting her arms around her friend and hugging tight. It was a completely different sort of hug from the soft embrace from her mother, or the gruff squeeze of her father's one-armed pat. Vola's arms were bony, and she smelled like hay and sunshine. Since Conner had died, Lily hadn't had a single hug from a friend; they'd all avoided her on the playground, unsure of what to do or say to a kid whose brother was dead. Would she explode with emotion, like the kids on television? It was too risky, too weird. They studied her from a safe distance, whispering behind their hands. Lily closed her eyes and squeezed Vola back.

She hadn't realized how much she needed to tell somebody all about it—how Conner died. Her parents talked about it, usually in tense voices, when they thought she couldn't hear. She was pushed out of their grief. They'd done all the hollow things: asked her how she felt in stiff conversation and sent her to a grief counselor, who told her all kinds of things that sounded like they came out of a pamphlet in the waiting room. Adults, they tried to...to *sterilize* grief. But she needed to tell somebody about it, like a story, like an event that had happened without judgment or carefully composed expressions of sympathy. Conner was a boy of dirt and laughter and skinned-up knees. He'd once gotten his hair caught in the barbed-wire fence in the cow pasture next door to their house, and he'd howled until Lily had run over to him with scissors and cut him loose. Their mother had been furious!

Lily told Vola about this and other stories. And she told what it had been like, finding him in the ditch at the entrance to their neighborhood. She cried some in the telling, but...not as much as she'd thought she might. Vola held her hand, and they kicked their feet in the creek, and she just listened. She asked questions at the right parts—*What did your mama say when you cut his hair!?*—and stayed quiet at the right parts, too.

When the girls came back to the big farmhouse late that afternoon, Clary thought they looked different. Like they'd gone down under somewhere and come back out again. Even Gitli looked thoughtful.

"Did ya'll go down into the cave?" she asked. They shook their heads.

"Just down to the creek," said Vola.

"Well, did you girls have fun?" Clary prompted, relishing how the words felt in her mouth. It was the kind of thing a *normal* mother would say. They nodded, grinning, though still more subdued than usual. Maybe they were just tired.

"Ma?" Vola asked. "Can Lily sleep over? We'll camp in the yard if you let us."

Clary considered them both, thinking maybe they'd spent enough time together for today. But, after all, what was summer for, if not squeezing everything you could out of one day?

"Sure," she said. "I'll drive you up, and you can ask your mother. And pack a change of clothes if you want."

⇒⇒⇒⇒⇐⇐⇐⇐

Jayne Watson was a woman on the brink of divorce.

She and Dan had decided to move up here to the woods because it was too much. Too much to drive into their neighborhood every day, past the place their son had died. It was painful to see the places where he and Lily had played together. Even the bathroom was haunted with Conner's memory. Potty training, bath time. Him bursting in while Lily was in there, cackling wildly when she shrieked for him to *Get out! Get out, you slimy little freak-azoid!* They had left Florida because it was too much, but Jayne suspected that even though they'd given lip service to starting fresh, to working on their relationship together, to getting back to Mother Nature...well, they'd known it was just about over.

Two people might fall in love with just each other, but when they had kids, well, that changed everything, didn't it? You had to stretch your love out in those sleepless nights when your babies cried and cried. You re-stitched your soul to fit those little tiny people inside, until you were different and your marriage was a different thing, too. And when one of those people was hit by a car and left to bleed out his life in the ditch...you might as well have issued a death certificate for her marriage right along with Conner's.

She sat on the back porch, rocking and gazing out at nothing in particular. Dan had taken a job that required travel, far more travel than he'd done in Florida.

"It's just for now," he'd said. "We're lucky this position came up. The pay is good, and it means we can move up to the mountains, just like we'd always talked about."

82

Had they talked about it? Probably, on one of their family vacations. Despite Dan's reluctant words, Jayne was pretty sure he seized the job with relief. A chance to escape the pall of sadness? An opportunity to avoid being in the same house with his wife, whom he could no longer bring himself to love, and his daughter, a constant reminder of the other child he lost? Sign him up! Sign her up, too, for that matter. Jayne could use an escape.

She was grateful for the little neighbor girl, Vola. She was a funny thing: pretty, in a way Jayne couldn't put her finger on. She looked like she had some Indian blood in her somewhere. The way she'd appeared in their lives, like a wood sprite. Jayne didn't know if she'd ever seen her daughter take to another little girl like this. They were fast friends. And what could be more wholesome than her daughter exploring these lush woods around them? *There* was the saving grace of this whole mess, Jayne thought. Her daughter would be all right after all.

The crunch of gravel under car tires got Jayne out of her chair. That would be Clary, Vola's mom, bringing Lily back home. The sight of her daughter, cheeks flushed and hair a mess, made Jayne almost cry with gratitude. There was something to live for, wasn't there?

"Mom! Mama, can I spend tonight at Vola's?" Lily crashed into Jayne's middle, hugging ferociously. "Grandpa June says he has an old tent, and we can go camping, and we'll look at the stars and catch fireflies!"

Jayne laughed. "Sure, sweet pea." She looked up at Clary, eyebrows raised. *Was it all right?* Clary smiled and nodded.

"It'll give me a chance to unpack more boxes," Jayne said. But she knew she probably wouldn't. Somehow, it was hard to find the energy.

⟫⟫⟫⟫⟩ ⟨⟪⟪⟪⟪

It wasn't on the first sleepover that Lily and Vola argued their way into their first big fight. Nor was it the second. Those nights were ideal: filled with sparkling starry skies and fireflies and mist settling over the valley while the girls and Gitli slept out in the yard, so they woke up in a foreign place, where

83

vague, looming shapes could be mountains, or they could be ships at sea. The fog did things to sound, too. Dogs over in the next holler would bay, chasing some unlucky rabbit on the trail, and each bark echoed around them until the sound itself was part of the fog, shapeless and everywhere at once. Gitli would give little, muffled *whoofs* as though she'd like to join in the chase, but she stayed with Lily and Vola.

It was nothing short of magic for Lily, who had spent much of her social life watching Disney movies and taking ballet class with the other well-kept girls. She and Conner, and the occasional neighborhood kid, would sometimes run around in the cow pasture next door to the subdivision; it was true. But it was different. Back home, the outside was kept outside. These people, the Whitts, blurred all the boundaries between in and out. Sometimes it was like they were more creatures of the woods than people. Other times, it was like...like they were more human than anyone she'd met in her life.

It was Lily's third sleepover at the Whitt farm, and they ate a hearty supper. It was normal for the Whitts to put on a big spread, but it was the kind of meal Lily's mom only cooked on special occasions. Only after Uncle Lacey heaped a third helping of mashed potatoes on her plate did the Whitts seem convinced she'd gotten enough food. The whole event had a holiday air, and it was deeply comforting. Granny's faded apron, Clary's fussing around after Granny in the kitchen, June sneaking bits of chicken to Gitli under the table, and Lacey groaning with pleasure, both good eye and bad half-lidded while he chewed...it was almost overwhelming after months of nearly silent, quiet meals, mostly with just Lily and her mother at the table.

If their mealtime was comforting, their language was foreign. It was English, mostly—sometimes Lily thought they were speaking Indian words, especially to the dog—but the way they used the words was altogether different. Even Vola's hill accent was thicker with her family all around.

"Y'uns want more mashed taters?" Lacey had asked, giving the spoon a shake over her plate, so a glob of golden, creamy potatoes plopped onto it.

"You young 'uns orter check on the doodles after supper," June said, a broad grin making his otherwise stern face instantly likeable. "They're mighty cute."

"What's...what's a doodle?" Lily asked, flushing pink with embarrassment. She wasn't sure if *they* were wrong—they certainly didn't pronounce anything the way her own teachers had emphasized in school—or if she was the foreigner in her own country. When they were packing up to move here, her dad had joked that East Tennessee might as well be a separate country. *People there march to a totally different drum*, he'd said. She hadn't understood what he meant then, but now she was starting to. She suspected she understood better than he did, in fact.

"It's a chick, honey," said Clary, pushing another hot biscuit onto Lily's plate.

"Oh." To cover her confusion, she brandished the biscuit, taking a big bite. "These are sooo good! They taste different from my mom's!"

"Well, they're the Whitt family recipe," said Granny, clearly pleased. She didn't often get to feed folks outside the family. "We add extra goodness. Herbs and things."

"And REAL butter!" crowed Vola, anxious to show off her family to her new friend. "Granny makes it herself! Not like that ole margarine from the IGA."

"Mmm!" Lily took another big bite, sparing herself the need to find something else to say.

After supper, Vola took her friend by the hand and led her down the long hallway, toward the front door.

"Let's go see the chicks," she said.

"The doodles, you mean?" Lily asked, shyly. Vola grinned back at her. As the summer passed, Lily had settled more into herself. Vola thought she was...more like a real person and not like somebody trying to act out a role on TV. She still had her moments and her mannerisms and tendencies that were almost unfathomable to Vola, but she found herself getting used to all that. They passed by a cabinet that caught Lily's eye.

"Wait," she said, tugging Vola's hand, "Is that a guitar? What are these other instruments?"

"Yeah, that one is," Vola said, pointing to the guitar her Granny's father had made years and years ago. The wood glowed faintly in the dim hall light.

"That's a mountain dulcimer and Grandpa June's mandolin, there, and Mama's banjo. Lacey plays the juice harp. Also called a jaw harp." She pointed out each thing in turn.

"Wow! What do you play?"

"Well, I reckon I play just a little bit of everything. And I sing." Vola smiled shyly.

"Can I hear?"

"Maybe," said Vola. "I'll ask Grandpa June, after he gets through with milking. Come on, let's go." The doodles were every bit as cute as June had promised, though they weren't quite what Lily was expecting: some were fluffy-yellow, just like she'd always thought they should be, but some were black and some were kind of yellow with black marks. The girls only tried half-heartedly to catch them.

"We don't want to spook 'em," said Vola. Gitli watched anxiously as the chicks ran from the girls, cheeping.

"Your dog is, like, a chick babysitter, huh? A doodle-sitter." Lily plopped down under the shade of a sprawling oak, just down the hill from the chicken coop.

"Yeah. Gitli takes care of the chickens. Keeps the coyotes away, that kind of thing." Vola sat next to her friend.

"Well, what about Gitli?" Lily contemplated the dog. "Is she one?"

"Is she one what?"

"You know, a...a familiar. You said cats don't work, so...?"

Vola laughed, crouching down. The shaggy border collie wiggled all over, licking Vola's face with gusto.

"No, she's just a good farm dog. She looks after the new calves until Grandpa June can find 'em up in the woods sometimes. But she can be a complete coward! She runs and hides if we set off fireworks. Once ran a clear mile down the road! We had to go get her in the truck." Vola continued scratching Gitli's ears.

"My grandma had a dog once. A poodle. Dad says he was—" Lily's voice deepened in a poor imitation of her father "— a little jerk! He'd sit on Grandma's couch with this dog, and every time Grandma was gone, it would act like it liked Dad. And then, when she walked back in the room, it would turn around and BAM! Bite him!" The girls giggled.

"This goofball isn't always perfect," said Vola. "Granny like to tan her hide when she was a puppy 'cause she kept pulling laundry off the line. And there was this one time..." she pointed off toward the edge of the mowed yard, to where the hay grew thick and tall. "I was up in my room when I heard this crazy...like a bleating sound. So I came runnin' downstairs, and there was Uncle Lacey a-goin' like his hair was on fire, yelling."

"What was it? Making the sound? Was it Gitli?" Lily sunk her fingers deep into the thick black and white fur.

"No." Vola's face was solemn as she shook her head. "Gitli was chasing a brand-new baby deer, still with the Bambi marks on its back, and Gitli was totally, totally quiet."

"Wow."

"Yeah. And Uncle Lacey caught sight of me, and he yelled out for me to stop Gitli, so I ran out and tried to grab her. But she wasn't bothered about me, nossir; she only had eyes for that deer. And then, when I finally stopped her, I had to grab her tight," Vola hugged Gitli's furry neck to show how she'd done it, "and she still wouldn't stop, so I had to lay down on top of her!" Vola lay on the dog, whose tongue lolled in pleasure. "I had to stay there until Uncle Lacey got to us, and he shooed that baby deer along to go hide. And then, when I looked into Gitli's eyes…" Vola sat up, her own eyes wide and earnest. "There wasn't no brown there. No brown at all. Only black. Her pupils swelled up so big, they was just big, black holes where her brown eyes should have been." The girls contemplated the dog's eyes, half-closed in contentment with their attention but still clearly a mild, coffee-brown.

"The wolf came out," breathed Lily. "She smelled that baby deer, and she just…"

"She went feral," Vola finished, nodding. "Yep."

"So, why didn't Uncle Lacey let her just have the deer? I mean, this is nature and all that."

"Lily! It was a *baby* deer!" Vola looked affronted.

"I know! I know! But, you guys, you eat grown-up deer!" Lily threw her hands up.

Vola tried to look offended, but she gave up and shrugged instead. "Yeah, I know. I asked Uncle Lacey the same thing."

"Hah!" Lily poked her.

"He said it was a bad idea to let Gitli chase down baby things. He said, 'Next thing, she'll be taking down the calves.'" The girls nodded at this wisdom.

"But, you know what I think?" Vola gazed down at the dog.

"What?"

"I think Uncle Lacey couldn't bear to see our little Gitli killing something like that. Something so…well, it was Bambi!"

"Yeah." Lily gave the dog a quick, tight hug, glad she hadn't killed Bambi after all.

"Hey, Lily?"

"Yup?"

"What ever happened to that poodle? The one that bit your dad when your Grandma came around?"

"Oh, it died. It was really old. But Mom says it got sick from biting Dad. Says he gave it some kind of infection."

"No!"

Lily started to giggle. "Well, she said it was like a 'gross guy' infection." They laughed together, not because it was so funny. But because it was summer and they were friends, and it was too, too sweet to have any excuse to laugh aloud. Even Gitli seemed to enjoy the joke.

⟫⟫⟫⟩ ⟨⟪⟪⟪

As it turned out, it was Uncle Lacey who convinced Grandpa June to play an impromptu pickin' session on the porch that evening. After Grandpa June consented, taking his mandolin into his lap and picking out a sweet progression of notes, the rest of the Whitts took up their instruments and played along. Lily was spellbound, a child of the radio, of the *Weekend Top Forty!* and pop songs that fit the sun-bleached world of her childhood. If she'd thought the hills of Tennessee would be like Florida, but with less palm trees and steeper land, well...sitting enthralled on the porch of the Whitt house, listening to them pick out songs that seemed both ancient and bright, watching fireflies swirl in the twilight, with the last of the rosy sunset fading into fog...there was no doubt, now, that Lily was somewhere other than anything she'd ever known before.

She didn't know it, but Lily would spend her life comparing its events to this night. Her first kiss, falling in love, sitting on a balcony while on vacation in a tropical paradise...deep down, in her heart, she would think, "Does it feel like that night? Does it compare?" She wouldn't even consciously know what it meant, but Lily would search her lifetime for this feeling: thrill and comfort and exotic tucked into a sense of complete rightness.

Whitt bluegrass wasn't anything like most kinds of bluegrass, as Lily would later discover. There was too much wild in it, too much of a driving beat that made her think of Indian drums. Even the twang of their voices echoed with more of an Indian ululation than East Tennessee accent. It was

89

amazing. Before she even realized it, Lily was in the yard with Vola, dancing and twirling to the music, humming along, hands flung out in eddies of fireflies by the score, with Gitli barking and seeming to dance along with them.

All too soon, it was time for bed, but even this wasn't so bitter: they rolled their sleeping bags out under the night sky, and Lily barely had time to wish on the scattering of bright, shooting stars before she slept profoundly.

⊰⊱⊱⊱⊷ ⊶⊰⊰⊰⊰⊷

Lily woke with the dawn, her sleeping bag covered in finely beaded dew. She gazed at the muted land beyond the porch, where the girls lay. It wasn't like Lily was completely lacking in experience with the outdoors. It was just that the outdoors here were…different. Ancient. The land here seemed layered in years like a gypsy in shawls. She was half-convinced that some time-lost mountain men would wander out of the foggy valley and ask for directions to the nearest buffalo herd. She was so lost in this fantasy on the morning after her third sleepover on the Whitt farm that she shrieked a little when Grandpa June came around the corner of the house, his worn work hat and shotgun distinct shapes even through the fog.

"Good morning, girls," he said, chuckling a little, and he was gone again, slipping into the fog.

"Where's he going?" Lily asked her sleepy friend, who was still rubbing her eyes and yawning.

"To check on the boundaries, I expect," answered Vola, rolling over in her sleeping bag. "Haints've been active lately." She mumbled something else, but the words were lost in Vola's pillow. Lily lay back down herself, but she was too thoughtful to go back to sleep.

Later, when the sun was high and they ate snacks in the shade of the woods, she asked Vola about what she'd said.

"What's a haint?" she asked. "Is it like…like a ghost? Haint, like 'haunt'?"

Vola looked intensely uncomfortable. "Sure."

"Then why...what was your Grandpa doing with a shotgun before the sun was even up? Everyone knows you can't shoot ghosts with a gun." Lily crossed her arms, sensing that she was on the outside of something. Nobody likes feeling as though your friend has secrets from you, but Lily had felt on the outside of her family ever since Conner died, and she'd just started to settle into the world she and Vola made together, out of sun-baked afternoons and shared hair scrunchies. Chasing crawdads. Climbing hills through tangles of vines and towering woods. All that stuff seemed...well, it seemed inviolate, and if Vola had secrets she wouldn't share, it cast a grimy shadow over all of it!

"Look, Lily, there's things I...Whitts, we...I mean, I can't tell you some things." Vola looked miserable, but Lily was nettled.

"Fine. That's fine. Don't tell me. I'm only your best friend in the world, and I've only told you everything about me. Even about Conner." Some part of Lily knew she was being petty about this, but she couldn't help herself.

"You *are* my only friend. You're my best friend and my only friend." Vola spoke quietly, looking at her hands in her lap.

"Well you're not MY only friend! Maybe I should just...just find someone else to hang out with. Maybe the neighbors next door have a kid my age." Lily knew she'd struck a chord; Vola's eyes got huge, and she gripped her friend's hands in hers.

"No, don't say that!" Vola was so earnest that Lily almost—almost—forgot to be angry. "Stay away from the Byrnes. They ain't nice people." Gitli whined, ill at ease with the high emotion in the air.

"I bet they are. I bet they're just fine, but you don't want me to have other friends."

There it was again, Lily's dramatic streak. For Vola, it was cruel; she was used to dealing with things with frank openness. She wasn't armed against manipulation. She studied Lily's exaggerated toss of hair, her crossed arms and pouting face. Vola took a deep breath.

"Well," she said, "If that's how you feel...I'm sorry for it. Maybe you should go on home, Lily."

Lily was shocked her gambit hadn't worked, but she couldn't back down. She was too far in the game.

"Fine. See you later." She got to her feet and hurried away, tears stinging her eyes. She was mad at Vola and mad at herself and...well, more than a little bit ashamed, though it would be hard for her to admit that aloud. She knew her friend well enough to treat her better than she had. But Lily had her pride, and she wouldn't show her real tears to anyone, not while they were hot. She hesitated only a moment at the edge of the woods. She knew the way well enough now; right would take her down the long gravel drive that gradually became the county road. That way would get her home. Left would take her up the track that was much shorter, but that took her past the Byrnes' ramshackle property. Lily could almost feel Vola's gaze between her shoulder blades. What else could she do?

She took the left.

PART TWO

Chapter Nine

IF LILY THOUGHT OF THE Whitt lifestyle as full of life, as deeply connected to the natural world, more human than most...she'd have been struck with horror at the squalor of her other neighbors. Vola's grandmother Mary would have been horrified as well, but she probably would have acknowledged her kin's disintegration as something of the inevitable. Her daddy had pounded his version of the Bible with a disdain for others, disdain for themselves, and a heavy scorn for most things, including his own family. How else could folks live with that much venom? They couldn't, really.

Boyd Byrne sat and twitched in the yard behind the house, staring without seeing past drifts of trash, into the woods beyond the rusted fence. He tried to use his peripheral vision, bloodshot eyes scanning back and forth, so sure he would see the creatures again. He rubbed his eyes with dirty fists. It felt like sandpaper under the lids. He'd been up for two days now, and would probably crash soon. A meth crash was always the worst. At least when he finally did sleep, he'd be blissfully unaware. Dead to the world.

There...in the shadow of the big tree, just on this side of the property line. Was it just a plastic milk jug? Did it move? All the trash made it hard to see where the *things* were. The *haints*. His mama would call them haints. He lingered at a turned-over rusted barrel...yes, there was one. He was still jumpy, still a twitchy effer, as his brother would say, but somehow he felt better knowing where the thing was. He'd never seen one, not for real. His mama had told him plenty about haints, along with heaping helpings of Jesus, since he was a boy. He had a morbid curiosity—a whisper from the devil, his mama would say. Where was she now? Probably inside, eating instant oatmeal and smoking her way through the day's three packs of cigarettes. Now there was a habit that would kill you.

Would a haint really eat his soul? Suddenly, Boyd was interested. He was very interested indeed. He shambled and twitched toward the turned-over barrel, a too-skinny kid in pee-stained sweats. He was drawn to it. It must be the devil's work, to tempt him so. Shit-fire, he was so high on meth his eyeballs were singing.

The haint made a hollow, creaking sound from deep in the barrel. Boyd reached out his hands.

"Boyd!" his mama's voice lit into him from inside the kitchen window. The boy turned back to the house. He would crash soon; he could feel the exhaustion seeping through the electric tension in his muscles. His mama's next words were lost in a coughing fit.

"What, Mama?" Boyd was irritated. He had been on to something, just about to grasp what the creature in the barrel was trying to say.

"I said," Boyd's mother began, still coughing, "Don't you go over the fence. Stay off the Whitts." Boyd stood in place, swaying and twitching. He knew the rule; Byrnes stayed on their land, Whitts stayed on Whitts'. It was an old rule, one reinforced by his grandfather's threats—back when the old man was alive—to give any Whitt lead poisoning with his old shotgun, should they be fool enough to stray over the line. He turned his back on the rusted-out barrel, thoughts drifting. He spun around again, thinking he shouldn't do that, shouldn't forget about it, shouldn't turn his back...on what, though? He'd lost the thread. His mind wasn't right. Not anymore. He stumbled over a rusted bike frame and fell.

Through the fence, from his vantage in the dirt, Boyd caught a glimpse of a thin, tanned leg and a pony tail higher up. A kid, then. Just some little girl. Probably the new neighbor; Boyd and his brothers had noticed a moving van at the house next door, just visible through the trees to the east. They'd had a passing fancy to see about what they could steal—what might be worth a little cash in those moving boxes. But then they'd gotten high and forgotten all about the new neighbors. Boyd gazed at the woods beyond the back fence, thinking about money. Neighbors, and what they might have for the taking.

The younger generation of Byrne boys didn't care so much about the old feud, especially since they started cooking meth in the bathtub. They had started doing it to earn a little money, at first. Boyd's older brother, Albert, had started them in the business. He heard down at the V.A. how some people were taking cold medicine and cooking it down with some other stuff and *whoo-ee*, it smelled like cat piss cooking, but it sure did make a man feel good.

"Makes you feel alive!" Albert had said. "Better'n that, you can kill a bear with your hands. And boys, it'll make us a little money." Albert had rubbed his thumbs over the pads of his other fingers, waggling his eyebrows. Making bathtub meth was cheap, and you could sell it easy. Boyd's daddy had been all for it. The family was drawing the check, as folks around here said. Didn't exactly make for easy living, being on the dole. But then, when you started taking meth, started off snorting a little and then smoking more...well, you didn't care much about money after that. Unless it was money to get meth, anyway. It was the ultimate painkiller. *Wonder if haints like to get high,* Boyd thought disjointedly, and he chuckled up into the sky from where he lay in the dirt. His mama, watching him from the window through a haze of cigarette smoke, shook her head and shuffled back to the battered kitchen table.

Boyd's daddy had developed too much of a liking for the stuff. He didn't eat much lately and had aged about thirty years in two. Now he stayed gone, mostly, and he stayed high.

Two Byrne boys were left in the house. Boyd was the youngest, and Albert was the oldest. The middle one, Hunter, had been gone for six months now. Boyd thought maybe he was in jail somewhere, maybe up in Kentucky. Hunter'd told Boyd about having him a lady friend up in Middlesboro, right before he disappeared. Albert said he thought Hunter was lying in a ditch, dead. Boyd tried to think about when he'd last seen either brother anyway... he couldn't remember.

Boyd's mama, Pauline, never touched the meth. She smoked three packs of cigarettes a day and dully put up with her husband and three boys' more recent enterprise—even if it did throw up smoke that burned her eyes and seeped through the house in an evil fog. Her sense of smell was gone anyway, smoking as much as she did. She coughed up phlegm every morning and sometimes a little blood, too. *Let 'em kill themselves*, she thought, shaking another cigarette out of the foil pack. It would give her less to worry over. Commend their souls into God's hands. The Good Lord knew she couldn't do a lick of good with her own.

She mostly spent her days shuffling around the kitchen and sitting at the battered table, staring out the window into the backyard and the woods beyond. She didn't care much about the old Byrne-Whitt feud herself; but she had always felt a kind of discomfort about those trees, the dark woods beyond the sagging wire strung up on their rotting wooden posts. Not two days ago she'd thought she saw the old, rusted wire glowing, as though lit with demon fire. She'd dismissed it as a trick of the eye at the time and told herself it was only the wire glinting in the morning sun, but her mind kept worrying at it, like a hole in her sweater sleeve. It was that uneasy feeling that made her keep her husband's family law about staying to this side of the line. That stuff her boys were putting into their bodies, she understood those demons. It was a shitty world and a shitty life, and she didn't much care what those boys decided to do about it. The Lord would judge His own believers, after all.

But those woods...they held demons she didn't understand.

It was one thing to give up on this life. Jesus himself said what lay beyond the veil was infinitely better. Infinitely better. Pauline sighed and tapped the ash from her cigarette.

It was one thing to give up on this life, but quite another to give your soul over to whatever lived in those woods. She held a fresh cigarette to her lips, lighting it with the coal of her spent one. Smoke trailed in front of her eyes, and she got up to gaze out the dirty window again. Drawn toward the fence and the woods beyond, she saw a kind of shadow moving around the rusted barrel at the edge of the property and shuddered before taking another deep drag and coughing out a cloud of smoke, hiding the yard and the woods from her view.

"Lord, though I walk through the shadow," she muttered, her voice rusty, and she took another drag.

⫸⫷

Lily knew Vola was right about the Byrnes; she had known it ever since she'd seen the trash-heaped backyard through a screen of brush between their two houses. But she hadn't been freaked out about them, not really. Plus, that much trash in one's own backyard? It was fascinating in the way that junkyards are fascinating to all kids. It drew her eyes, even as she went nervously past, moving almost at a run to get to her own woods and the safety of her porch beyond.

A sudden scuffling and thud, punctuated with a groan and volley of hollered conversation from whoever was now on the ground and somebody through the back window startled Lily so that she had to stifle a screech. Then she did run in earnest, heart thumping too hard in her ears to hear anything that Boyd and his mama yelled to each other. *Vola's right-Vola's right-Vola's right*...the words pumped like a prayer through Lily's mind, and her anger was completely forgotten under the thrill of her recent brush with the Byrnes. Maybe she'd call Vola tomorrow and tell her all about it, and their friendship would be mended.

⫸⫷

Boyd woke with a stiff body and a fierce headache. How long had he been asleep? He thought maybe for a full day. That wasn't so unusual; he tended to do that after being high for days. It was dark, now, and Boyd rolled to his knees and stood up slowly. *Oh, my dad-blamed head*, he thought. He had to pee.

He staggered over to the edge of the yard and stood with his legs apart, head back, while a steady stream of pungent urine battered the plastic milk jug.

"Maybe I should cut this shit out," he muttered to himself. Head still pounding, Boyd gazed up at the stars with blurred vision. No moonglow to outshine them this night. They had once had a yard light; most folks in these hills did. TVA run around and put 'em up all over, according to Boyd's daddy. "Makes the gawddamned electric bill higher, that's all it does," the old man said. "That, and makes it easier for a thief to see what they're doin'." Not that the Byrnes had anything at all to steal. Years ago, with an air rifle, the Byrne boys had shot out the bulb mounted on a tall pole. Their daddy had not bothered to replace it.

Oh, his head hurt. He needed a Mountain Dew or maybe a Gatorade, that's what Albert always said. Where the hell was that no-good sumbitch, anyway? And what the hell was that noise? He fumbled his dirty sweatpants back up, feeling a little less vulnerable with his ding-dong back in his pants.

The gurgling came again, from the shadows, driving Boyd's muddled thoughts away and dredging up a memory, a jangling warning about...haints. He was thinking about haints and about his mama—where was she, anyway? Where was any-damn-body? He peered around, eyes lingering on the rusted barrel, its hulking mass like a cresting water creature in a sea of trash. He shuffled over toward it, trying not to step on anything sharp in the dark. There— *there*! If he looked away and tried unfocusing, looking with his peripheral vision...yes, there it was, like a heat shimmer. No, more like the opposite of one. It was a cold and dark shimmer, darting around, but still sticking right to that barrel. It reminded Boyd of a TV show he'd watched about ocean critters that slithered and darted around a hole in an underwater cave. Luring in prey, attacking from the shadows. Desiring, desiring for Boyd to come closer, gurgling sounds that became more like words with each reluctant step Boyd took.

⇶⇶⤛⤛

Through the patch of woods that separated the Byrnes from the Watsons, Lily lay sleeping in her room. She dreamed about her brother. She dreamed about him often, sometimes with such unrestrained joy at seeing him again that she wept quietly when she awoke, bitter with disappointment. But tonight, the dream took on another feeling, anguish seeping into her heart. Her brother was still there, still playing with her in the sun-baked cow pasture like they used to. She ran and ran after him, always just behind, until he turned to her and he held out his small arms, and he asked her *Why?* Why had she let him die? She'd been his protector, his big sister. His hero.

"I'm sorry," she whispered. Tears seeped from beneath her eyelids, and she let out a shuddering sigh in her sleep.

Down in the valley, each of the Whitts had their own bad dreams. Through the woods, across ridges and hollows, sleeping minds plunged into despair, remembering loves lost and disappointments both petty and crushing.

And at the center of it all, the eye of the creeping fog of sadness: Boyd Byrne.

But not all by himself; Boyd would never be alone in himself, not ever again. Boyd had a new roommate inside his meth-soaked brain.

"What?" he whispered now, eyes starey, the whites gleaming in the dark. He'd heard something, something...words, but the sounds making the words were horrible, like leeches squelching them out of blood. It was a good thing he'd already taken a piss because he was scared enough to wet his stained paints. He couldn't seem to leave, though, badly as he wanted to; he couldn't turn tail and run to his mama the way he wanted to with all his quailing heart.

"Whaaaaat…s your naaaame…tell us your name…" he could pick out the words: moaning, distant sounds within the gurgling, that choking, phlegmatic sound, and he wished it would *stop*, oh lord, he did.

"Who are you?" He tried to make his voice louder, to scare the thing like you would a mean dog, but his whisper reduced to a hiss.

"What's your NAME!" The voice swelled to a scream inside Boyd's head, driving him to his knees amid the trash. The woods were dead silent, no cicadas or tree frogs singing. Over the ridge, down in the valley, Granny Whitt moaned in her sleep.

June, in his bedroom down the hall from her, turned over. He hadn't woken from nightmares since Vola'd swarmed his demons with her own butterflies. He didn't miss the horror of killing, waking up sweating, and stuffing his fist in his mouth to stem the screams that leaked from his mouth in soft moans. But giving up the blood and horror opened his mind to Mary. Tonight, he was lost in the melancholy sweetness of her. Sometimes dreaming of the ones you've loved and lost is a comfort, and sometimes it feels like sinking a finger down in a bleeding hole in your heart. You wonder how you can survive it.

<hr/>

"You all right?" Mary's hand lay in a wedge of sunlight on the counter of Aunt Bea's Soda Shop. He was remembering in his dream, remembering the woman who would be his wife, back when she was just a girl.

"Yes. Fine." June was acutely aware of how rough he must look—unwashed, scraped up from falling in the road. He probably smelled bad, too. He looked down at his own hands, both intensely regretting coming inside the soda shop and completely unable to leave. Say what you wanted about country boys; they were inexperienced in the world, sure, but they would go straight for what they wanted.

"I'm…sorry," he said, wanting to win her over with something charming but feeling too embarrassed about the state of himself. She was silent, and he stared at his hands a few seconds longer before he dared to look up at her.

Her eyes danced. "I ain't never had a boy fall down in the street at the sight of me," she said, voice bright with barely contained laughter. He grinned at her and knew in his heart he was unworthy, and even knowing he was unworthy of her, he knew he'd never be able to help himself from trying to get her.

"I'd fall for you anywhere," he said, and even though her eyes still danced, her smile was prim, and the set of her head told him she knew he was full of it. But she approved, at that.

"My name is June," he said, and he stuck out his hand. She shook it and answered, "I know just who you are. We're neighbors."

"What?"

"I'm Mary Byrne, you dummy."

"Mar—Mary? But you're just a kid!" He knew where her people lived, just over the southeastern boundary of his family's farm. But she'd always been a knock-kneed, freckled thing, out climbing trees and tending chickens when he'd seen her. Her daddy wasn't friendly with his family; he kept the old prejudices about Whitts being witches. June's shock set her to laughing again.

"Reckon I used to be," she said, "but I ain't no kid anymore."

"No, I can see that." She blushed, even though he hadn't meant to sound so forward. But, on reflection…he was glad he'd said it; her blush was pretty.

"Can I buy you a sody-pop?" June drawled, feeling more confident.

"I have one," she said, gesturing to her glass.

"Oh, well…can I buy you one another time?" But she was already shaking her head.

"Daddy ain't never gonna let that happen," she said. And now it was her turn to look embarrassed. "I'm sorry. I never should have let you think…" She stood up to go, gathering her small stack of books from the counter.

"Wait! Don't go, Mary," June was desperate. He couldn't lose her before he even got her. He'd never wanted anything so quickly and so badly in his life. He reached out to take her books from her arms. "At least let me walk with you." She glanced around, already looking as though she was in trouble, caught out by her daddy. Then she stood up straight, and her smile held a steely resolve that June would love about her for the rest of his days. *The hell with it*, that smile said.

" …All right." She relinquished her books and led him out onto the sidewalk. "I come into town every couple of weeks or so for library books," she said. "Daddy usually drives me, but today my brother did."

"Do you think you can get your brother to bring you from now on? Every weekend?"

She thought about it for a moment, then shook her head. June thought his heart would stop.

"Not every weekend. But every other, maybe. On Saturday." She pointed out her brother's truck, parked at the grocery store.

"Okay, I'll be here," said June, tipping his cap to her and handing her books over.

"I might not make it every two weeks!" In her distress, her country accent grew more pronounced. "Every" became "ever."

June was already nodding. "I'll be here. I'll wait." Her eyes widened, and she looked ready to protest, but there was that impudent grin on her lips, and he knew she wouldn't. By the time Mary's brother Matthew came out of the Kash 'n Karry, June had slipped around the side of the building, heading home, crossing the Clinch River bridge, and picking his way up the path over the backside of the northwest ridge of the farm.

It was curious, really, that neither of them thought to simply meet up in the woods, seeing as they were neighbors. It would have been an easy thing to slip out into the night for a stroll. But Mary's daddy was a daunting figure and meeting in town felt safer. In town, they were like two different people, somehow.

The next morning, Lacey awoke thinking about his cocoon jacket. It was on his mind a lot lately. In fact, he was already cracking open the top of its wooden box when he stopped, surprised at himself; he hadn't even realized he had intended to do that.

He'd had a hell of a night. Nightmares of losing everybody he loved, memories of his mama sick and wasted, dying of the cancer. Dreams of the day he lost his eye. His bed sheets were a silent testament to the rough night: twisted and damp with heartsick sweat.

That damned day he'd lost his eye. Lacey rarely thought about it. He wasn't one to dwell on the past. He was like his mama that way; you remember the sweet times, hold on to the folks you love, but you don't dwell. That way would only rot a man from the inside. He shuffled out of his bedroom and sat heavily on the couch, softly pressing against both eyelids—good and bad—with his fingertips.

Lacey was a kid when his eye was knocked out. He had attended the same school Vola now did. Played on the same playground. Avoided other kids, just like his niece did. But it hadn't bothered him, not badly, not like it had bothered Clary—the way other kids would taunt. Kids are like mean dogs. They can smell it, when someone is afraid of them. So Clary would draw fire. They would tease her, pull her hair. Push her down at recess. One day, some of the kids had her cornered behind the cafeteria, where the teachers could better pretend not to see.

"Heard you was all devil worshippers!" called out one girl.

"My pa-paw says devil worshippers dance naked in the moonlight!" another girl crowed. Lacey thought her name was Erica. "I bet that's what you do!"

"Eeeew!" the chorus of shrieks and giggles drew barely a glance from the teachers, who turned their backs in favor of watching the little 'uns on the swing sets. Ever, it had been this way: the teachers turned their backs. Adults of the town of Greasy Rock pretending it was the natural way of things for the witch-kids to be tortured. Different wasn't tolerated, not here.

"I bet you don't even wear drawers!" Erica hissed, darting forward to tug on Clary's skirt. That was the breaking point.

"Stop! Just stop it!" Clary cried, and the circle of kids stepped back involuntarily from her push, a hard shove they'd all felt, even though she hadn't touched 'em. Lacey felt it from where he was, still ten feet away, hurrying to defend his sister. She'd used her Whitt talent, the thing she always tried to hide. It was like poking a paper-wasp nest with a stick.

"Witch!" cried one of the boys, Jack. The girls were looking uneasy, looking around for an excuse to leave the scene. Lacey finally got to his sister.

"Leave her alone, you...you jackasses." It was a deliberate jab at the boy Jack, who'd cried witch. It was a stupid insult, one that would only ever rile a kid, but they were all kids. And sometimes, some kids don't need much of an excuse to start a war. Before Jack and his small, grubby gang could do more than take a menacing step forward, the bell rang, and the teachers began rounding up children.

That might have been the end of it, until the next day of teasing. Lacey and Clary might have finished the school year, might have weathered their days of being the butt-end of jokes, being social outcasts, and that might have been the worst. Still bad, but...endurable. Except that Lacey had had enough. Amiable, good-natured Lacey was done watching his sister, who never could ignore the meanness, being tortured by kids who thought they had a right.

"After school," he said. And Jack stopped cold. "We're fightin'." Jack turned and nodded, his Skoal-stained grin predatory.

That afternoon, Lacey stood nervously by the school bus. Clary sat in her usual seat, watching out the dusty window. But Jack and his cronies didn't come, and when the driver called out, Lacey turned and stepped into the bus.

He made his way down the aisle toward Clary, almost to her seat when there was a ruckus at the front.

"Hey, old man!" Jack called out to the driver. What was his name? Leroy, wasn't it? It was disrespectful, but there was something about the boy's voice that stopped Leroy from reprimanding. A feral edge. Two other boys chuffed and laughed quietly, nudging each other behind Jack.

"This ain't your bus, son," said the driver.

"Aw, I know it. But Lacey Whitt invited us to come for supper." Leroy looked back at Lacey and Clary, who both turned their faces toward the window. Without a word, he pulled the lever that shut the bus doors, and the three boys made their way to the back of the bus, barely sparing a glance for the Whitt kids on their way by.

Each stop on the route was agonizing. Each time Leroy opened the doors and let another kid off to go on home made the pit in Lacey's stomach ache. Clary quietly took his hand, powerless to help. Finally, Leroy stopped at the end of the county road, where the Whitt driveway began. Jack and his buddies waited at the back of the bus while Lacey and Clary walked to the front, down the steps to the gravel. Leroy kept his eyes forward when the three hooligan boys followed. He knew. He knew what he was condemning those Whitt kids to. After, he told himself that he'd thought it would just be a regular old schoolyard feud, a scuffle that would end in someone's bloody lip and hurt pride. *Let boys be boys.* That's what they said, right? But Leroy knew, in his heart, he did those Whitt kids wrong. He quit driving the bus after that. He couldn't see kids with innocent eyes, not anymore. Leroy knew well that the cruelty of some young 'uns was like a baby snake bite. They didn't know when to stop, so they kept pumping venom until they were all out.

Jack waited until Leroy drove out of sight, a plume of dust settling in the bus's wake.

"Now," he said. "I heard you don't wear no drawers. Why don't you show us?" He leered at Clary, who stepped back, trembling. It was a well-calculated opening foray; Lacey would never ignore a threat to his sister. He let out a screeching yell that was full of pent-up fear, a whole school year's worth of aggravation and plain old anger, and he flew at Jack. It was almost an even fight, at first, two boys scuffling in the gravel...but boys like Jack never fought fair, and his two buddies weren't there to spectate. One of them grabbed Lacey's shirt, ripping it a little, before he could get hold of Lacey's arms to pin them behind his back. The other one punched Lacey in the stomach once, twice, and Lacey puked at his feet.

"Aaaaw, that's plain nasty!" he crowed, and Jack forced out a mirthless laugh.

"My turn again," Jack panted. "You boys let up." Lacey fell to the ground, groaning, trying to get his breath, but before he could, Jack's weight was on his back. Clary turned and ran for the house. Lacey bucked. His vision dimmed. He needed air, couldn't breathe, and Jack grabbed a fistful of dirty blond hair at the back of Lacey's head. He slammed Lacey's face into the driveway once, twice, and the whole world burst into blood red.

"What the hell was that?" one of the other boys said. Pulsing—could have been the heart beating in their own ears, could have been the pounding of Indian war drums—filled the valley.

"Screw this, I'm outta here!" cried the other of Jack's buddies, and they ran off the way the school bus had gone.

"Pussies!" Jack screamed after them. He pushed himself off Lacey, breathing hard, one bead of blood trickling from a busted lip. Clary and her daddy came over the hill, the old man holding a shotgun.

"What are you gonna do with that?" sneered Jack. He was a boy that always had more bluster than sense. It was that lack of sense that got him crippled up in a car wreck a few short years later. June didn't answer the boy. He leveled the gun at Jack's chest and pulled the trigger, the bang echoing through the valley like doomsday thunder. Jack fell to the ground, writhing, blood seeping all over his chest, and his shirt in tatters.

"Get off my land," said June, mildly. His eyes had the still look of rage too deep to control. Jack couldn't see those eyes, but Clary could, and she was terrified. Nothing about this day was all right. Even her father saving them, even the man she trusted and leaned on and knew to be good down deep, even that part felt all wrong, when his eyes looked like that!

Jack crawled until he could get his feet under him, and he limped away down the road, chest full of rock salt. June handed the gun to Clary and knelt down.

"Lacey," he said, his voice careful. Gentle. He turned his boy over, and for a moment he was back in the war again, turning over yet another dead man in his arms. Trembling, June blinked. Lacey wasn't dead. He was breathing and bleeding but not dead.

"I can't see, Daddy," Lacey said. Where he'd once had two good, clear eyes, one was a ruined mess. Slammed into the jagged point of a rock in the road. June gathered his boy into his arms and walked with him down the driveway, back to the house, where Granny and Mary waited, Clary following along with the shotgun. Granny tended the boy and, shaking, June went into the woods until he was fit to be with people once more.

Lacey never did go back to school, not even after the fever burned out of him. Clary did, eventually, but kids pretty well left her alone after that day. Thought she was touched with the kind of bad luck that was catching. Their mama healed them, really healed them. If it hadn't been for her, Lacey might have lost that sweetness in him that made him who he really was. Clary had once begged him to forgive her, but he'd taken her face in his hands and said that he would not.

"Never was your fault, sis," he said. "Jack's like a rabid dog. He ain't nothing special, really, just ought to be put down. And he'll take care of that hisself."

"How do you know that?" Clary put her own hands over Lacey's.

"I told you! I got me a spirit eye, now. I can see things." And Lacey had waggled his eyebrows in that way that made his sister smile, and he knew she believed him—about the guilt. About how the guilt didn't belong to her, didn't belong to anyone, 'cept maybe Jack. Lacey couldn't see the future with his eye, not even about Jack. But he had a kind of simplistic view of the way of things. He trusted his intuition deeply.

Back in his own, snug trailer house, Lacey took a deep, shaking breath. Time to come back to the present.

"I'm going to speak with Granny about this," he said aloud. Then he nodded for emphasis. Her reassuring, gruff way would make him feel better. She'd put all this to rights, this uneasiness that had been building in his tummy ever since the day he'd felt the line pulling from his belly button, right up to the old Byrne boundary.

Lacey pulled on his old jeans, right over top of his faded, thin pajama pants. They bunched up under, making his legs and waist look lumpy, but Lacey hardly noticed. He pulled his flannel shirt on, then headed out the aluminum door of his trailer house with the grace and consideration of a freight train. He charged past the chicken coop, not sparing a thought for the indignant ladies inside this morning.

"Granny!" Lacey called, just as soon as he pushed open the screen door to the kitchen at the big farmhouse. It was early, so Clary was still home. Dad was, too, sitting over at the dining room table and drinking his coffee. Looking plum wore-out, with bags under his eyes.

"What's the rush, son? Something happen?" June put his cup down and rose from his chair.

"I need to speak with Granny," said Lacey, his one good eye wild, hair standing in tufts. "Something's the matter, and I need her to tell me about it."

"Well, that seems a little backwards, son," June started, but Clary put her hand up.

"I'll see if she's decent," she said. "Granny hasn't come downstairs yet." And Clary went on up, leaving her father and brother standing anxiously in the kitchen.

"What's this about, Lacey?" June said, putting his hand on his boy's arm.

"I don't rightly know. That's the problem, isn't it? There was the fence and that line," Lacey pointed at his navel, "And now the cocoon jacket is calling me."

"The jacket's calling you?" The alarm in June's eyes did nothing to calm Lacey. Before he could say anything else, Clary called out from upstairs.

"Dad? Daddy! GET UP HERE!"

Chapter Ten

BOTH MEN CLATTERED DOWN THE hall and up the stairs, rushing to where Clary crouched on the floor, Granny laid out on her side, still in her nightie.

"Granny!" Lacey rushed to her, already bundling the old woman into his arms, even as Clary told him to.

"What's the matter?" June asked, for the second time that morning. "Did she fall?"

"I don't know for sure," Clary said, her tone becoming businesslike. *This is how she talks to folks up at the clinic*, June thought. His mind was grasping details that made sense to him, putting things in order to find something useful—something he could do or change or fix.

"I think she may have had a stroke." Clary pointed Lacey toward Granny's bed, still unmade.

"She feels like a bird," said Lacey, looking down at his grandmother's face. He'd never held her like this. Even though she'd been smaller and frailer than him for almost all his life, Lacey thought of his Granny as completely formidable. He didn't know what to do with this thin, fragile body in his arms. He was worried her knobby spine might break against his forearm, or that he was hurting her knees where they lay together, crooked over his elbow. He gently put her in the bed, backing away quickly while Clary efficiently tucked the sheets up over her chest.

"Maybe we should get her to the clinic," Clary started, but June was already shaking his head.

"You know, well as I, that ain't gonna work," said June, quietly. She looked as though she might argue, but the fight went out of her fast.

"Yeah," she said. She held Granny's hand and pressed her fingers to the woman's wrist, feeling a thin, desperate pulse. Clary, like any Whitt, had talents. Much as she loathed to admit that her daddy was right about anything, he was right when he said she'd tried to turn her back on this particular family inheritance. But it was part of who she was, part of her makeup just like the color of her hair or the timbre of her voice. And it took her years to figure out that all the resistance she'd put up—running toward modern medicine, running away from this folk-remedy, shamanistic, backwards family—it was all a joke. It brought her back full circle because her special talent, that thing that came to life in her very blood, was a push-and-pull. The tide, like life, like seasons, and the energy that everything has. She could touch it, could use her touch to call a person to her, to find the sickness inside. And she could use the push to send somebody on when they needed it.

Clary sat next to Granny on the bed, and she held the old, frail hand in her own strong hands, and she felt for the woman inside her pulse, inside the shallow breath that still made Granny's chest rise and fall ever so slightly. For a moment, Clary felt lightheaded; the scene was too much like the way her mama had died. Her vision doubled, and she saw both her mother and grandmother lying in bed. She blinked hard and told herself to focus.

"Granny," she whispered. "Come back to us. Granny."

The old woman's eyelids fluttered and she pursed her lips, looking like the world's oldest child, pouting. Clary smiled, despite herself.

"Granny," she murmured. "We need you. Lacey needs to ask about..." She looked up at her brother. He and June looked utterly lost, standing together.

"We need to anchor her," Clary said. "Give her a focus. Ask her your question."

"I...I need..." Lacey looked ready to burst into tears, his hair wilder than ever. June put his arm around him. Lacey took a deep, shuddering breath and began again.

"I almost put on the cocoon jacket, Granny, and I don't know why. It called me over, and I...well, I don't know why," he finished, lamely.

Across the hall, Vola was dragging herself from a deep and troubling sleep. She'd had nightmares that her friend was stuck on the other side of the Byrne fence, that she kept getting trapped by piles of trash there, and that one of the Byrne boys was going to eat her. She'd dreamed that her Granny needed help, that she was, was...

Vola thrashed herself out of sweat-soaked sheets, sitting bolt-upright in bed and trying to orient herself. It was her room, just her room, and everything was normal. So, why did it still feel wrong? Gitli stood at attention, pointed toward the bedroom door. Her whole furry body expressed worry. Clary heard voices from across the hall, men murmuring, and her mother answering. Why was Mom still here? She usually went to work by now. Was it Saturday? Why were they all in Granny's room?

Sliding out of bed, Vola padded around the dog, over to her door, and opened it. The feeling of wrong washed over her like a tidal wave, strong enough to make her step back from the scene glimpsed through Granny's open bedroom doorway. Everyone was in there, the whole family, and Granny lay in bed. Vola wanted to shoo them all out! Didn't they know Granny needed her privacy? For goodness' sake, let the woman sleep in peace! She charged across the hall, ready to say all of this.

"What's wrong?" she asked instead, her voice very young. At that moment, Clary felt Granny with her pull, and the old woman's eyes cracked open, looking for Vola.

"Vola," she croaked. "Lily doesn't know. She doesn't know." And Granny's eyes closed again. They all stood, uncertain, until Lacey cried out in anguish.

114

"But what about the cocoon jacket!?"

Clary almost tried pulling Granny once more, but she took a deep breath and laid her hand gently on the covers.

"We'll have to figure that out, Lacey," said Clary, quietly, still using her "nurse voice," as June now thought of it. "But right now, Granny is very tired, and Vola needs breakfast." The last thing Vola wanted was breakfast, but Clary's push-and-pull wasn't limited to just sick people; everybody marched out of the room on her quiet orders.

"Reckon I better go up and check on that southeastern boundary," Grandpa June said, scrubbing his hands over his face. Vola sat at the table, picking at her breakfast. Clary gazed moodily out the window, and Lacey fretted, getting up to walk into the kitchen only to turn around and come back again. Gitli lay on the kitchen floor, watching them all, her friendly eyes concerned.

"Grandpa, you can't go up there," said Vola, letting her fork clatter to the table. "Granny's sick, and she needs us in the house." She crossed her arms as though her logic were irrefutable.

"Honey..." Clary began, coming over to lay her hand on Vola's brown hair. The girl looked as though she'd push her mother away, but she thought better of it, turning to wrap her arms around Clary's waist instead.

"Vola, your Granny don't need me in the house. She needs to rest, I reckon. And the farm needs me to make sure that line stays strong up on the ridge, honey. Especially now that Granny...especially now," June finished, awkwardly.

"Why? Why?" Vola's voice was plaintive, laden with every question she wanted to ask.

Grandpa June stopped, battered hat in his hands, and looked searchingly at his granddaughter.

"Because, honey," he said, haltingly, "Granny ain't sick for no reason. Do you see? The cocoon jacket, the...the line from Lacey's belly button." He looked vaguely silly pointing emphatically at his own belly. But nobody laughed.

"But, but...that's why we need Granny whole. Healthy and here." Vola stood up, arms crossed.

"I know, honey, I know, but..." Clary looked at her father helplessly, unsure of how to explain things, unsure of what was actually happening. "Granny's...well, she's doing something." She put her arms around her daughter, faintly surprised, as always, at how tall the girl had gotten.

Lacey jumped up again and paced down the hall before coming back.

"I'll go up with you," he said, and June nodded, settling his hat on his head. The two men left, June carrying his shotgun cradled in the crook of his arm.

"Why did he take the shotgun?" Vola asked.

"Just in case, darlin'. Just in case." Clary watched her brother and father until they disappeared into the woods before sitting heavily at the table. Shit, as they said, was hitting the fan. The Whitts were prepared for things in a way completely different from other families. They knew loss, and they expected a battle on the horizon, always. They were warriors, after all. Shamans, imbued with the sense of doom just around the bend. Sometimes there was joy in their lives. Joy in their love of one another, in their quiet existence on this farm. Today, there was only bewilderment and grief. What was Clary supposed to do now? She was blind, feeling in the dark for her next steps. She needed some time. A few minutes to herself, a few minutes to study on the shape of the thing—the sickness, the tidal wave of impending loss that had stolen into their house—even if the true shape of it was unknowable, only touchable in mysterious parts. Like the fable of the blind men with the elephant.

"Vola, you go on up and see Granny a while," she said. And when the girl hesitated, she gave a smile full of love and weariness. "Go on."

Vola went slowly down the hall. She took each step, one at a time. Not skipping any, like she usually did. Gitli sensed her heaviness, and she followed along meekly, not trying to bound up the steps ahead of the girl as she sometimes did.

Walking into Granny's room, knowing she was sick (*dying. Please don't be dying*), Vola felt a kind of vertigo. She knew folks in her family were dead, had even been to her great-uncle's funeral some years back, but death wasn't a real thing for her. At least, it hadn't been. But she could feel it now: a presence, like a shroud over everything. She crept up to the edge of Granny's bed and took the frail, blue-veined hand that lay on the covers. Searching her great-grandmother's face for any kind of emotion, any kind of reaction to her being there, she saw only sleep. Vola climbed onto the bed and curled up next to the old woman, her head on Granny's shoulder.

Sleep came like an animal lying in wait, and it pulled her under like a sudden fall, and there she was: Granny, looking at her, laughing. But it wasn't the old Granny now lying in the upstairs bed; it was Granny as she'd been more than eighty years ago, Granny as a young, lithe woman, running in the ankle-high hay field, barefoot and laughing.

"Come with me, Vola!" Granny laughed and took her hand, and Vola couldn't have resisted her even if she'd wanted to. They both ran and ran and launched their bodies into the sky, each leap a short flight higher, higher than they'd ever jumped in the waking world.

"Granny!" Vola shrieked, laughing and out of breath, "you're all right!" Granny was young again, and that meant she wasn't dying. That scene in the bedroom was false after all!

"Oh, of course I'm all right, young 'un," said young Granny. "Having a sick body don't mean nothing, not to me." Vola's smile faltered.

⇒⟫⟩⟩⟩─⟨⟨⟨⟨⟨⟸

Clary washed up the breakfast dishes, scraping the family's largely uneaten food into the trash. She fought tears, and it was like trying to push down a flock of birds in her throat, her grief rising to choke her. Harsh, muted sobs escaped, and she sank to the kitchen floor, burying her head in her arms and shuddering. Granny had been tough on Clary most of her life, making her pick row upon row of green beans when she'd rather play in the woods as a girl. Callously shaking her head when Clary'd wept as a teenager because she was an outcast to all the kids in town. But Granny had welcomed her with open arms when Clary'd come up pregnant and hadn't wanted to admit who the father was. Granny had embraced her, had dried her tears, and had told her it was an old story, but it was hardly unique; lots of babies didn't know their daddies.

"But this baby," Granny had said, holding her granddaughter's tear-soaked chin in her hand, "will know its family. And it will be loved. Just as you are loved." Clary leaned back against the kitchen cabinets, her storm of grief quieted. Her dad and brother were checking the boundary, keeping up family duties. Clary had to do her own part in that, even if she had always struggled to find her place—struggled against her family and struggled against this backwater town, full of addicts and superstition and just plain meanness. But Clary had always tried hard to find the good, and there was usually at least a little bit to find. There were good folks in town, along with the bad, and there was such painful sweetness to be found alongside the loneliness of living in this hollow, on the Whitt family farm. She'd continue to do what she knew how, put one foot in front of the other. Or so she told herself, finding a shred of comfort in this vaguest of plans of action. Pushing herself up off the kitchen floor, Clary wiped her face on a dish towel and made her way upstairs to join her grandmother and her daughter.

They lay together—Granny and Vola—on the bed, knees and forehead touching, hands interlaced, both breathing deeply. The dog had climbed up on the foot of the bed, curling up at their legs. She couldn't go where Granny and Vola had gone, so she waited here, patiently. Clary caught the smell of young hay and sunshine, of early summer—even though, outside, it was late August, almost time for school to start back again. She let out a breath she hadn't realized she was holding and stepped into the room. The air was thick over the bed, and Clary thought she knew what was happening. Granny was having a talk with Vola, sharing a dream and telling her things that would be so much harder to tell from inside the confines of Granny's old body. Realizing this, Clary felt suddenly chilled: if it was time, truly, for Vola to know the whole truth about the family, then a bad wind was on the way. It was early. Vola was only eleven. This was a family of tradition, and they always waited until the Whitt children turned twelve to show them the stories.

When she was a girl, when it had been her time, Clary'd been told all about the family, and the threat they kept at bay, but she'd spent her whole life deciding it was a hoax. Or, if not a hoax, then an ancient problem, like poor sanitation or saber-toothed tigers—a thing that used to matter a lot but was no longer such a big deal. Was history, really. She had no idea how closely her thoughts mirrored Granny's own frustrations.

But, now...the oldest and youngest living Whitts lay together like a glimpse into time itself, Granny's silver hair mingled with Vola's glossy brown hair, both wearing the faint smiles of a sweet dream. Clary sat in a chair in the corner of the room, the walls of her steadfast defiance falling down around her.

<hr />

Lacey was anxious. He followed after his dad, lost in his thoughts, not even pausing to study the markings of a box turtle's shell or note the crop of mushrooms growing on a deadfall. Usually observant in a feral way—taking the pulse of the land through the details of its life—Lacey's brain had room for only a klaxon of alarm. *Granny's sick, and who will tell me what to do?*

Moving steadily along the path, June ruminated, too, in his methodical way. He stopped a moment to look around, adjusting the carry of his shotgun.

"It will be all right, son," he said, worried at the panic kept barely under control in Lacey's face. His son's good eye swelled with tears and he abruptly sat on a fallen tree trunk.

"Dad," said Lacey, "I don't think it will." But he looked calmer, with his biggest fear said aloud. June sat next to his son.

"Well, maybe not right now, it won't be okay," said June. "And maybe not for a little while. Son, I think you're right about that boundary. What you said about the crack it makes where two of 'em meet."

Lacey nodded and said, "Is that why the cocoon jacket is awake? It's like an itch I can't get to, that thing, the way it's always in my mind."

"Yes, I believe so."

"But why is it happening now, Dad?"

June sighed. "I don't know for sure. Maybe Vola did it somehow."

"Vola? She wouldn't."

"No, not on purpose, of course she wouldn't go and bring up haints. But she don't really know the whole story about them—about how they're connected to us and to her...and she's mighty powerful." June thought about how she'd freed him from his own ghosts, and the fierce joy that had been in her eyes, so close to his. Vola was the most full-of-life creature he'd ever seen—excepting his own sweet Mary. And they were going to need her before this was all over.

"Granny's the only one of us living that seen a haint," he said, quietly. "Only one of us to kill one. And she always said it's hard to plan for it, hard to know how to beat it if one gets loose."

"Not 'if,'" Lacey murmured.

"What?"

"Granny didn't say, 'If one got loose.' *When*. She says, '*When* one gets loose.'" From anyone else, June would have taken this as an argument over semantics—splitting hairs. But Lacey was dead serious, and June thought it over.

"Yes," he said, finally. "You're right, son. Granny always did say 'when.'" She'd spent her life trying to prepare her family for an inevitable fight; it didn't matter how good their boundary was. Every fence had a weakness;

every wall could be breached. Even if it took time. *Especially* if it took time, the bad dreams below wearing down the Whitts' vigilance, wearing holes and cracks and thin spots in the fabric of their haint ceiling, that net of energy that kept their malevolence deep in the earth below the Whitt farm. Mistakes—they was something else that happened over time. June had thought making another boundary between their place and the Byrnes would be okay, had thought it was necessary at the time. He hadn't wanted to wake up with a bullet in his belly from his father-in-law's gun.

Chapter Eleven

JUNE WENT BACK IN HIS thoughts, to the day he told Billy about
falling for Mary on their next ride to the glass factory in Church Hill.

"I really did—I fell right out in the street for that gal." June laughed aloud
at the memory, feeling less embarrassed about it, now that he knew she'd see
him again. If making a fool of himself was enough to win him Mary Byrne,
well, that was all right. Billy drove with one hand on the wheel, left elbow
resting out the open window.

"She's something else, Billy." June was usually tight-lipped about ladies—
mostly because there weren't any in his life, as far as Billy could tell. He was
too surprised by June's sudden infatuation to even tease him about it.

"Aw, June," he said, scratching his head in consternation, the wind from
the open window ruffling his hair. "It just ain't a good idea. Old Man Byrne
ain't gonna let you go with his daughter. Everybody knows he hates you."

"Well, he don't know me, does he?"

"He don't need to. Not according to him," Billy said, quietly. "You're a
Whitt, boy." The two men sat silently for a moment, June's heart in his stomach and Billy shaking his head.

"What's got into you anyway?" Billy grabbed up his hat and slapped June in the arm with it. "You get drunk as a skunk on Friday, hop in my car come Monday and you're in love." June answered with a grin that was more like the man Billy knew.

"Well, how you gonna handle Old Man Byrne anyway?" Billy shook his head again.

"He don't need to know." June caught the look on Billy's face and put up both hands. "Not yet anyway," he said, laughing. "I can see a lady in town without her daddy's consent, can't I? It ain't like I'm a-going to steal her."

But that's exactly what he did. He climbed up and over the northwestern ridge of the farm and crossed the bridge into town every other Saturday. He put in his notice at the glass factory; it was just about built, anyway, and June felt more and more that Whitt keenness for staying close to home. The masons were moving on for other work. June wasn't going to move on with them. He had the farm, after all, and he had plans for running more cattle, maybe growing tobacco on it. And Mary. There was Mary, like a treasure hid right under his nose, most of his life. And now, he'd found her.

June came early to town every other Saturday, strolling up and down the few streets and trying to look nonchalant. It was bound to happen; the handful of shop owners up and down main street, the men working at the feed co-op, and the lawyers going in and out of the courthouse, they all noticed June Whitt. And if they didn't know him at first sight, the rumors flew fast and furious, they knew him pretty quick. The Whitts were celebrities in town, almost as well-known as moonshiners and small-time politicians. And pretty soon, they figured out he was beating the sidewalk waitin' on Mary Byrne, every other Saturday, like clockwork.

And pretty soon, Old Man Byrne knew it, too.

"Daddy knows," Mary said, just as soon as June stepped through the door and sat on the stool next to her. June's smile faded, and he signaled to Aunt Bea to pull two sodas for them.

123

"All right," June said, looking down at his rough hands. "And he ain't gonna let you see me, that right?"

"He says, well..." Mary's face flushed bright pink. She took a long sip of soda, trying to cover her embarrassment and something else—real sadness at the thought of having to give up June. She cleared her throat and started again. "He says I'm a Jezebel, and that you're no good, and that I needed to get right with God and go on and get married like a good Christian woman, since I'm old enough to start lookin' at men." She looked away. June noticed a slight tremble in her hands. He loved her a little more. He fairly ached with it.

"Then...marry me."

Mary stared at him in disbelief. "Marry you?"

"Honey, I'll ask him for your hand. I'll...I'll make him understand, and we'll be together." The desperation in June's eyes was sharp.

"Well, dadburn it, June Whitt, you ain't never even told me you love me yet, and here you are trying to get me hitched." The anger in Mary's voice drew Aunt Bea's eyes, and though there weren't other customers in the place right then, June knew their conversation would be all over town by late afternoon. Well, hell with it. He meant what he said. He wasn't embarrassed.

"I'm telling you now, Mary," he said, taking her hand. "I ain't got a ring. But I'll get one. I swear it." She hesitated, then nodded, cheeks flushing bright red. They finished their sodas, sitting in the bigness of their words. The promise they'd just made to one another. June held out his hand to her, like on the other Saturdays, and they walked out, nodding to Aunt Bea, who was trying (and failing) to act like nothing-at-all-juicy had just transpired in her own soda shop of a Saturday afternoon.

"You know, June, Daddy don't know I'm here. I told him I was a-going to Bible study, and I made my brother drive me into town. But he'll know, soon enough. Daddy finds out everything." She turned to face him on the sidewalk. "June...Daddy didn't say you was no-good. Well, not just that. He said you was a devil-worshipper, and that all your family was devil-worshippers, and..." Tears spilled from her eyes, hot and unexpected. June took her in his arms, unable to do anything else, not caring if everyone in town saw him holding his beloved. It seemed a silly thing for Old Man Byrne to say, a silly attempt to tarnish the neighbors he just couldn't understand. But they were deep in religious country, and Mary'd lived her whole life under the thumb of a hellfire-and-brimstone Bible thumper. Even if you hate a thing, casting aside a lifetime is no easy feat. It was a truth June would learn about himself someday.

"I ain't, Mary. You know I ain't." Mary closed her eyes for a moment, almost speaking her doubts: how she thought of him constantly, how his hand on hers made her blood run hot, how she thought about his lips, his lean and muscled body beneath his blue jeans and shirt, and how she worried it was the devil himself sending these thoughts to her. But she took a steadying breath and kept those words inside herself. *Hell with it,* she thought. If it was the devil making her feel this way, let the devil take her. She nodded into his chest, pushed him away primly, and began walking smartly along the side-walk. June hustled to catch up and held her hand once more.

When he walked her over to the Kash 'n Karry, Matthew was already waiting outside for her. June held tight to Mary's hand, defiant, and even leaned in to kiss her on the cheek before tipping his hat to her brother and slipping around the back of the store to head back to the farm.

"Old Man Byrne will listen," he said to himself, picking his way up the trail over the ridge. "He has to." June didn't know how lucky he was at that moment; Matthew's car had already carried him and Mary back home, and if their daddy had known where June's path over the ridge was, he'd have flown with the fury of righteousness, pointed his hunting rifle, and shot that young man in the back. As it was, he raged at Mary, Matthew standing with his arms crossed, eyes dark. He'd raced home with his sister, eager to tell tales of her sins to their daddy.

"What kind of harlot is my own daughter? Stepping out to the sody shop for every pair of dad-blamed eyes to see, kissing that devil in the damned parking lot!" The old man slapped her face, hard. Mary's eyes flashed above her cheeks, pale, except for one vivid red hand print. Matthew snickered.

"And you!" Byrne roared. "You're just as bad, whoring your sister out of a Saturday!" His fist was closed for Matthew, knocking him to the floor. Mary hated the hot tears that streamed down her face. She hated this man who'd frightened her all her life. Without a thought for the consequences, she spat at her father's feet and turned to leave, running all out. She heard him coming after her, tripped up by something—his own anger making him clumsy, probably. She ran out of the house as fast as she could, passing through the gap in the old fence out back, running, running, running through the woods to her beloved's home. She hadn't been there since she was a small girl, creeping through the trees to spy on those strange neighbors of whom her father always spoke with such venom. She'd climb to the tall limbs in the woods and watch them, doing all the things normal folks did. And the boy—June—he'd always moved with sure deliberation, kindly tending animals, working on fences, and doting on his mama. Mary had watched him with a little girl's eyes, thinking he was unusual, even then: a kind male. Now, she trusted her legs to get her to safety, to get her down to the Whitts who were her only chance of salvation, for her daddy would surely kill her if he caught her. She'd spat at his feet. Defied him. Run away.

Young June had a lot on his mind when he burst through the kitchen door that afternoon. Most of it was Mary. So it was no wonder that when he saw her right there in front of him, sitting at the dining room table with a bruised cheek and burning eyes, he almost didn't believe she was there.

"Mary?" he said, just about rubbing his eyes. "What are you doing here?"

"She's runnin' from her daddy. That damned fool." June's mama came down the hall toward them, flannel and herbs in hand for a poultice. "And you! You're a damned fool your own self, June Whitt!" The old woman—even more full of piss and vinegar back then—brandished her herbs and things like a weapon. June went to his beloved, crouching down next to her chair.

"He hit you?" June reached up to caress her cheek. Mary turned away, more than a little embarrassed by the closeness of him—the smell of him, so different and yet familiar. Compelling.

"Get out of the way, you besotted buck," Mama (she'd soon be Granny) said, pushing him to the side so she could get to work on Mary.

"Well, I reckon he ain't gonna consent," said June, getting up off the floor.

"No, but I ain't a-going back there," Mary growled, suddenly. Unwelcome tears welled in her eyes. "It wasn't no good place to be before, but now I reckon he'll kill me." She'd made a choice and jumped fully out of the pot. She just hoped she hadn't landed in the fire.

"He won't," said June. "Not if I can help it, he won't." For once, Mama was quiet. She nodded her agreement and gently pressed the poultice to the girl's swollen cheek. Mary's tears slipped down her face. They meant it, these Whitts, with their queer ways and earnest faces. They meant to keep her safe. She'd been running on the wind of her rash decision, but now she collapsed under the weight of it, knowing she'd never go back home again. Never see her own bed, never have her hairbrush or her favorite sweater—the one with the strawberry embroidered on it, something nice her mother had made for her. Mary's daddy'd probably burn it for spite.

Later on, after the sun slipped down over the back ridge, giving its last glow like a sigh, June took Mary's hand in his.

"I love you, Mary," he said. "What's your middle name?"

"It's Litha," she said, caught off guard.

"I love you, Mary Litha." June smiled down at her. "I figure two names sounds mighty official, don't it? I don't want to call you Mary Byrne because you'll soon be Mary Whitt. And you'll be here, with me. Always." His frank way of speaking embarrassed her. His tenderness, too; she was used to men who viewed love as weakness, as women's folly.

"You're so...so open. Wide open, like the sky, and raw." She caressed his cheek shyly. "I never would have thought a fellow so quiet and gruff was really so soft. You're all marshmallow on the inside." June leaned close and kissed her mouth for the first time. She sighed against his lips, and he was completely powerless to stop his arms from pulling her body against him. They might have stayed like that all night, embracing in the dark, fireflies dancing and frogs singing as though it were all just for the two of them. And maybe it was. After all, what was anything worth, if not for love? But Mama discretely cleared her throat from inside the screen door, and June—a young man in the full bloom of love—was still a gentleman.

"Goodnight, darlin'," he whispered in his beloved's ear, and it left a tickle that would keep Mary awake, tossing and turning into the wee hours before dawn.

While Mary thought about June's lips and worried over her daddy's vengeance, June slipped into the night with his hunting rifle in hand. Old Man Byrne had grown up in this valley and knew most of the hollers in it pretty well, but he saw the world through superstitious eyes. That made him fearful, and the two things that'd cloud a man's judgment right down to mud was fear and anger. Old Man Byrne had plenty of both. He might as well be looking at the world through a tin bucket.

On the other hand, June knew these hills and fields, woods and valleys like a child knew his mother's caress. He knew where the sparrows and jays nested, knew where the box turtles crossed from one cow pond to the next. Knew how to listen to the creatures and ask them what he needed. So it was that Old Man Byrne lay on an outcropping of crumbled granite, thinking he was hidden and safe in the trees. Thinking maybe he would fire a warning shot into the yellow square of light, he figured was likely to be a bedroom window. Maybe he'd wing a Whitt or two when they ran from the house in fear. Even in the dark, the Lord would give him sight. He shivered in righteous anger, and the anger gave him pleasure. Vengeance was indeed sweet, it was the only sweetest thing worth living for until the day his angry God took him on home to sit at his right hand, to pass the judgment of the righteous and sentence the unworthy.

Byrne was so taken with his visions he never heard June creeping up behind, never knew there was the barrel of a gun pointed at the back of his head. A chicken startled—a damned fool bird that should have been in the coop hours before—and the sudden explosion of wings in his face and near-deafening squawking made him jerk hard enough to smash his mouth against the rock and piss his pants. His heart gave a lurch, and he was close enough to meeting his maker...something that should have made him rejoice, but only made him roll onto his back and pant, gasping for the good Lord to spare him, scrabbling his hands around for the shotgun that he lost.

"Listen here, old man," June said, gently pressing the cold, round eye of his own rifle against Byrne's head. "You get up, and you get off my property. I was fixin' to ask your permission to marry your daughter. But now I ain't askin'. I ain't askin' nobody but her, and it's her answer that matters. I'm taking her from you, you Old Scratch, Uya, and you ain't never deserved her. Now git." The old man lay shaking with fear and anger, still gasping for breath, willing his hate-decayed heart to beat regular. He hesitated, then nodded. When June stepped back to let the old man up, believing the moral high ground was safe—a stance he'd lose right quick when he left to fight in the war—Byrne flailed his body around like a fish and took June down to the ground. Now they were both wrestling around. Byrne's gun was kicked down the hill, lost and forgotten until days later. June's gun was almost lost, and June himself almost a dead man, but it was too long to bring around and point between two men so close together. Both men grabbed at the barrel of the thing and at each other, and June finally gripped it well enough to crack Byrne over the head with the wooden stock and scramble backwards. As fights went, this one was none too dignified. But it was absolutely, deadly serious.

"I said, git!" June, breathing hard, pointed his gun once more toward Byrne, who knew he was again close to death, even if he could barely see the youngest Whitt boy in the starlight filtering down through the trees.

"Gawddamn you," said Byrne, and he spit on the ground. He struggled to his feet and made his way back up the trail in the woods he thought he knew so well. But now they looked strange. Unfriendly. The trees loomed over, threatening. Even the damned Whitt land was cursed, full of devilry. He imagined he could hear June behind him all the way back up the ridge, all the way to his back door, but when he turned around to curse the young man once again, he realized all was silent. Byrne strained his eyes, sure he'd see Whitts and demons and what-all dancing in the trees, yes, even his Mary, that harlot of a daughter, she'd be there, too…naked, probably, copulating with devils. Or with June Whitt and that was even worse. He sucked in a shaking breath, hair standing wild and glowing in the light of the moon that rose just over the top of the treeline, gazing down and judging silently the world beneath. He started to scream out his curse, scream out that vengeance would come, but he stopped. His anger trickled away like air from a pierced balloon, replaced completely with fear. For it wasn't total silence, not total: Byrne could hear the thrumming, rhythmic beat of June Whitt's feet, could hear his voice rising and falling faintly, and he knew in his heart the boy was dancing out one of them Indian spells.

Byrne took one step, then another toward the fence that measured off his land, separating it from the Whitts'. He reached out a finger to touch it and yelped when a spark of electricity arced from the barbed wire into his hand.

⇒⟫⟫⟩ ⟨⟪⟪⟸

Coming out of his memories, June sighed deeply. He and Lacey weren't far from the spot where June and Mary's daddy had scuffled. June pointed it out to his son.

"Your grandfather was so angry," June said, gazing into the woods. "When I took your mother and married her. I thought he might even hurt her bad. And I couldn't let that happen."

"I know, Dad," said Lacey, patting his father's knee. "I know it." It was why June'd made the boundary on the fence line. Of course, Old Man Byrne could have crossed over with harmful intent to Whitt land anywhere else, so June's wall really went around the whole place, and it kept out all the Byrnes except Mary, June's new wife. But it had to be anchored somewhere, a spell like that; it was a living thing.

Remembering through the wash of years, June saw his mother sitting in the shadows on the porch, rocking quietly. The set of her knees under her skirt and her hands clasped in her lap, all illuminated in the alabaster moon glow, were commentary without words.

He sighed, stopping at the bottom step. "I sealed them out. Old Man Byrne and his close kin—those that live in the house with him."

"Another boundary."

"Yes."

"Set in fear? Set in anger?" Mama's questions were sharp. "You know it matters, son. You know what draws the haints. And jumping all over their bed, getting them all jiggled and riled up...now, one or two might just fall out, mightn't they?"

"Set in love, Mama."

She rocked a while longer, and he stood, waiting for her dismissal. Finally, she said, "Yes. I reckon you set that boundary in love. As good a foundation as any—duty, honor, all wrapped up in there, too. You done stole yourself a wife, young man. Now what will you do with her?" He couldn't see her smile, hidden in the shadow, but he could hear it.

"Reckon I'll do my best by her," he said. He climbed the porch steps and leaned over his mother to kiss her forehead, before going inside to bed. To bed, but not to sleep; his beloved lay not five paces across the hall from him, and their trepidation and longing for each other was thick as cloth laid between them, tangible enough it felt like one could tug on it and pull the other in. But they didn't; June's mother was in the house, and while Ms. Elvola Whitt's views may be different from the cutting chastity Mary's father expected, she was riled up about how it had all gone down, and that kind of feeling made everyone hunker in like birds before a storm.

In the morning, June and Mary practically buzzed with nervous energy at the breakfast table, trying not to look at each other, looking too long when their eyes met, flushing and glancing away.

"Going out to help Granddad with the fencing," June said, finally, getting up to put his dishes in the sink. He went toward Mary as though to hold her, but thought better of it at the last minute and gave a half-wave before disappearing out the screen door. She gave a secret smile to herself, looking both serene and excited despite the ugly bruise on her cheek.

"Come help me with these dishes, girl," said Mama. "You're going to live here, you do your part, too." But she said it with such welcome that Mary could have cried. Her own mother had been dead for years, died of being beat down in her heart, Mary suspected. It was a miracle she'd inherited her father's stubbornness and not his meanness, and she had no idea what she had of her mother's...but she intended to do better by herself than her mother had done. This family, this strange family she'd watched from tree branches when she was little, they had a way about them, as though life itself were thicker in their hands. Everything they did was more...more tangible: not just chores, but a dance of duties, like an agreement between them and all they tended. The land, the animals, and even the soft breezes that blew through the ankle-high hay out in the field yonder: they all seemed to say, "I'll do my best for you if you hold up your end."

She started scrubbing the dishes, rinsing and setting them in the drying rack.

"You absolutely sure, darlin'?" The older woman asked, coming up next to her and taking up a dry dish towel.

"Sure?" Mary had been lost in her thoughts, jumpy as they were.

"Sure this is the life you're after? Whitts ain't exactly well thought of in town. We're respected, at least by some, but we ain't getting asked to lead the Homecoming parade at the Fall Festival, if you know what I mean."

"Oh...yes, I'm sure, Mrs. Whitt." She wanted to tell her everything, wanted to tell this strong, comforting woman about all the hurts and frustrations, the certainty that her father was wrong, completely wrong about the world and God and sin. That she wouldn't put up with a man slapping her face, not ever again. That the small-minded people in town weren't her people, never had been. But she settled for, "I love June, Mrs. Witt. I...I love him." And her beloved's mother nodded, and Mary was certain the woman had heard all she'd wanted to say in that small handful of words.

"I b'lieve you do. Call me Ella, or Mama, since you're going to be my daughter."

Chapter Twelve

WHILE JUNE AND LACEY SAT there in the woods, and the rest of the living Whitt family congregated in the southwestern upstairs bedroom at the family home, Lily Watson sat on the shady back porch, just over the ridge. Dark smudges under her eyes testified to how little sleep she'd gotten the night before. The dreams had come back worse than ever. When her little brother died, Lily had dreamed of him every night, had played with him, and talked with him. Sometimes she woke up with a pillow soaked in tears. But she'd rarely had nightmares about him.

Last night, it was as though he'd found all her secret anger and guilt and used them as weapons, hurting her over and over until she cried out and woke herself up before dawn. She'd been sitting out here ever since, sad and tired and ragged. Maybe she'd go in and have a snack. She didn't really want one, but when she was little, she used to forget to eat. She'd be playing so hard, her mom said, that she'd forget all about coming in for lunch, and her stomach would hurt. A sandwich always helped. Maybe one would help her now.

Lily got up to go into the kitchen, but something stopped her—a peculiar noise, over at the neighbor's house. She walked down the length of the porch and peered through the woods toward the trash-heaped house next door— she could barely see it through all the trees. She imagined that was why her mom had agreed to buy this house; she'd never have wanted a neighbor with junk piled up in the backyard where she could see it.

There it was again. A whimpering noise, almost like...almost like a kitten, stuck in a tree or something. Maybe Lily should go check it out. She rubbed her eyes, hard, and took a shuddering breath. A few years from now, she'd take her first drink of liquor, which would lead to many more, and she'd go to sleep bubbling with all the immortality of youth, but when she woke up she'd feel just like she felt this morning. She didn't know what to call it, but she felt hungover, soaked through with grief and wrung out. Her eyes were gritty. She jumped off the porch and jogged her way through the woods, veering around dense patches of undergrowth and clambering over fallen trees, almost falling down twice, losing her balance. She paused a moment, willing her heart to beat quieter, so she could hear it again...there! Yes, she was certain something was whimpering over *there*. Lily headed closer and closer to the Byrnes' place, sneakers kicking through dried leaves, birds chirping overhead. She absently wondered what Vola was doing at her house down in the valley. Maybe later she'd try to find her way through the forest to see her. Maybe she'd have a kitten to show off.

At that moment, down in the valley, Vola lay in her Granny's bed—and she didn't. In an early summer that happened long before Vola was born, her great-grandmother—young and strong and flushed with life—took her hand and led her through the hayfield to the old, tumble-down house where Whitts had once lived. Except...it wasn't tumble-down. It was whole, with whitewashed clapboard siding and a tall, strong chimney. The porch didn't sag like wet cardboard; it was level and inviting and bright with whitewash. And, yes, there were five ways into the house. Vola exclaimed with delight and ran into the yard, no longer overgrown with blackberry brambles but trim and soft under her feet.

"I want to see!" she yelled, turning back to Granny's younger self. "I want to see the inside and go in all the doors!" Granny laughed and followed the girl into the yard and up the porch steps. Vola ran through one of the five doors, and Granny grinned impishly before she turned and jogged over to the next door. Here, in this world made of threads of the past, Granny could go where she pleased. She could open the door from the porch to the kitchen, and slip her way through cracks in the long boards on the wall, their bright blue paint like new. Vola bounced on her toes in sheer delight when she saw Granny appear before her in the sitting room, making her own door between rooms where there had only been solid wall.

"That's a neat trick!" she giggled. "Is that how it used to work? You made magic doors to go through the house?"

"Aw, no, child!" Granny caught the girl's hand in her own, giving it an affectionate squeeze. "Them rules didn't work back then. Or, rather, they was rules I had to follow, then, and now, here...I don't!"

"Oh!" Vola exclaimed, traipsing to the book shelves, trailing her fingers along the fireplace mantel, now whole and glowing with the beeswax polish Granny's mother had used. Vola turned around and around in the sitting room, delighting in its...its *intactness.* Everything had faded with years and weather and the lack of human care, in Vola's time. It was all so gray. But here and now, in Granny's youth, the past was vibrant and alive! Granny gazed around, smiling softly.

"This is amazing!" Vola cried. She stopped short, looking over at her great-grandmother. "Is your mom here? Your dad? Are they here? Can we see them...?" Granny was already shaking her head.

"No, young 'un," she said. "They're gone."

"I reckon that makes sense," said Vola, turning back to her inspection of books on the shelf. "This ain't real, is it?"

"Well, that's a matter of perspective," Granny said, softly. "Is time real? We're just in another part of it, another rock farther up the stream." She pronounced it *fuh-thur.* "You know, I once read in a magazine that when

136

you close your eyes and imagine practicing piano, the same places light up in your brain that would light up if you were *actually* playing." Vola listened, brow furrowed. Granny smiled as though she had a sad, quiet secret. "Seems like your brain don't know the difference between what's inside it and what's outside it, sometimes." She sounded different to Vola. Her voice, and even some of her words weren't quite what Vola'd tuned her ears to, these last twelve years or so. Soon as she had the thought, she knew why: they weren't really talking, not really. They didn't need to, not in this place. Her mind sort of put the words in.

"Come on, honey," said Granny. "Let's get us a look at my old bedroom." She opened a small, wooden door to the right of the stone fireplace to reveal a staircase that wasn't much more than a narrow, wooden ladder leading to a hole in the ceiling above.

"It's the only place in the whole house you could get to from the inside, back then," she said, winking at Vola, then turning to climb up. Vola followed eagerly.

⇒⟫⟫⟫⟫ ⟪⟪⟪⟪⇐

Clary trailed along behind her daughter and her grandmother like a shade within the dream. They went into the house, and Clary felt a little thrill: she was going to follow them there, too! She was just as excited as Vola to see her grandmother's childhood home whole and sturdy. But, oddly enough, she couldn't follow...at least not through the door Vola used. In fact, she couldn't turn the corner on the porch and follow through the door Granny used either. She was called, ever so softly, like a tickle through the air, and she went along until she reached a door that seemed to welcome her. She pushed through to see the kitchen, with its cast iron stove resting silently against the far wall. She might have been in a one-room cabin, though; there was the door at the other end of the room, where Granny had come in, but there wasn't any other door to the rest of the house. Movement over by the stacked stone fireplace

137

startled her. A woman seemed to look over her shoulder—just a glimpse—before fading away.

"Mama!?" Clary called out, and she ran to the place. Reaching out, she discovered she could simply remove part of the wall, like a panel, light as air. When she looked up, she saw Vola's foot whip up and over the edge of the ceiling—what would be the floor to Granny's old bedroom.

"So cool!" Vola said, when her head popped over the edge of the unfinished wooden floor. Golden summer light streamed in through the window glass, old and rippled. Somebody tall wouldn't have been able to stand all the way up except in the very middle of the room; the ceiling was rough-planed boards, and it sloped steeply like the inside of an upside-down wooden ship. Granny's bed was tucked under one of the eves, with a small table and kerosene lamp next to it. The short walls were tacked up in old newspapers. A huge hooked rug covered the floor. It was simple and cheerful, and Vola could happily have spent hours just sitting here. She tried to imagine how this room had looked when she'd last seen it. The narrow wooden stairs had long since rotted away, so she'd had to climb the crumbling chimney instead, and when she'd gotten to the old attic room, much of the floor had fallen through. She'd had to hop from one joist to another, holding to beams overhead to keep her balance.

"Come, sit with me," said Granny. "We got to talk about some things." Vola sat cross-legged, facing her on the hooked rug.

"Is that Mama?" Vola pointed to a shadow of a woman sitting under the eaves in the corner of the room. Clary waved tentatively back. "Come over here, Mama!"

Granny looked over her shoulder and sighed. "She can't, baby."

"Why not?"

"Because she decided she can't," said Granny, "long ago."

"But...she's here! Can't she just...decide she *can*, instead?"

The young Granny nodded. "She can. Decisions can be changed, sometimes." The way she said "she can," Vola knew Granny meant Clary hadn't yet done it. So her mother stayed over in the corner, there but not there. And Vola put her hands in Granny's, fingers linked in this vision, this version of the past, as they linked in the present, where the two lay together, forehead and knees touching.

"Let me tell you," Granny began, "and let your mind open to receive the story..." Her voice took the rhythm of the old words, the driving ululation that Lily had called Indian sounds. It was the language of their ancestors, the Whitts before they'd taken that European name, when they'd been the tribe of shamans that stayed in this peculiar valley when other tribes—hunters and wanderers—avoided this place, with its malevolent spirits. Vola saw it all: the ancient shapes of their valley and hills and forest, streams, and tiny, trickling waterfalls. All familiar, yet disconcerting because the contours were there, yet not. Centuries of erosion, of subtle and obvious changes, things built, animal paths carved out with hooves and lost again when migrations were disturbed, then halted by the wave of people who pushed through and then stayed—a tidal wave that left houses and great swaths of cleared land for grazing and fences and crops in its wake.

And through all this, Whitts stayed on, each generation tied ever more intricately to the land until there was hardly any difference at all between the two: people and earth, heartbeats and the ebb and flow of water etching through bedrock below. Love and family and the deep, interlocked roots of the forest. An aching desire for freedom: flocks of birds lifting in a cacophony, escaping into the blindingly blue sky beyond the north ridge. Vola saw the blue of the sky as though reflected in her mother's brown eyes, felt her yearning to leave...and her resolve to stay. She saw something else, too: Granny's heart. Clary'd hunkered down inside herself, had pushed her desires down and stayed here like a ghost, but if she'd only known...Granny had felt the same way. The young woman sitting with Vola now; she'd wanted to run free, to escape to Knoxville, Cincinnati, New York City. She'd wanted a life far from here. She knew her granddaughter's longing better than anyone.

But the Whitts stayed because they had to stay. They were tied to the earth, their energy imbuing the rock with living strength. Because if they left, the haints would go free.

"Let me show you," whispered Granny. And her vision filled the room, filled the air, filled the farm all the way to the furthest reaches of their land, and washed over everything like a warm summer breeze through time. Outside the room in the bigger house around the bend, where Clary's solid body sat in the corner, where her grandmother and her daughter lay in a soft bar of summer light, birds hunkered in their nests to watch Granny's vision. Insects, squirrels, turtles, deer...June and Lacey, all caught in the wind.

"Granny's showing Vola," murmured Lacey. On the log next to him, June nodded. They sat and waited, caught in the vision now.

⇒≫≻—≺≪⇐

The little boy ran through the trees, gasping, chubby brown legs pumping, leaves slapping his thighs, his face, his unprotected belly. Eyes wide. Staring. He couldn't stop seeing the thing from the dark.

It took his brother.

The boy, First Star, had not meant to wander so far into the gloom. He had been with his older brother, Bugling Elk, who was tasked with protecting them both. They were playing, following animal tracks, and finding plants and secret nests in the dappled light from the forest canopy, when they came upon the sinkhole. It had opened up under a young tree, its roots dangling and grasping for the earth that had only recently been there. The brothers stood gazing into the maw of the earth, taken by the sight. A breeze sighed from the dark, pushing the scent of moss, of cool, wet clay—and something else, something sharp, like smoke from the special leaves the grandmothers threw down on the solstice night fires—into the boys' faces. Bugling Elk walked hesitantly toward the dark, bending to see under the tree roots. First

Star held his arms out, wishing to grasp him, to pull him back. He knew it was wrong; they should stay in the light! But he couldn't speak. The wet breath of the earth had stolen his voice.

Sobbing aloud, First Star stumbled as he ran toward his village. The wet breath of the earth had stolen his voice, and he hadn't been able to call out to his brother. As though he could make up for that awful silence, the boy wailed aloud now.

First Star had lost sight of his brother, but only for a moment, the time as slow and as quick as the flick of a bird's wing. Bugling Elk crouched down and into the earth, disappearing into the dark. He came back again, crouch-crawling out of the dark toward his younger brother...

The little boy ran into his people's village.

"I have seen the bad dream of the earth," he gasped, chest heaving, tears streaming. He stood, shaking, before his mother and his mother's father, the village healer and venerated elder. They studied his scratched and dirty skin. He stood before them, naked like all the young ones during this warm season, but now with eyes much older than others his age.

The tribe knew of these bad dreams, these spirits from deep in the earth that were drawn to their children. Other tribes, who forsook this otherwise fertile valley, told them of the spirits. They would not camp here, not even in the warm months, for fear of the spirits who came from cracks in the earth. Other tribes' storytellers told of a time when their children had been taken. The dreams from under the earth—they were like the larvae that grew from tiny eggs laid in baby animals, that fed on the living flesh until they could emerge in a new stage of life. The animal—sometimes it lived, left with a puckered scar where the festering wound had been. The children, though—they rarely lived when they were chosen to host a spirit from the dark. Grown men and women had been taken, too, although it happened more to the young ones.

And before the spirits ate up their prey from the inside out, the infected people did terrible things. They killed their brothers, their sisters, and their children. They pulled the skin from their bodies as though they would make jackets and leggings out of it.

"They want to be us," Grandfather had said, listening quietly to the other tribes' stories and smoking his pipe. Considering. "They want our flesh and our hearts, and that is why they infect us and eat us from the inside."

Now, one of them had taken Bugling Elk. First Star had done what he must. Grandfather had long supposed that high emotions were what excited these parasites, that they loved the little ones because they laughed and ran and whooped with the joy of it. They also cried tears untempered by experience or resignation. Life flowed through them in its purest form. So the children were all cautioned against dark places. Deep, rotten stumps, sinkholes, abandoned dens...all were fascinating for curious young ones and all very dangerous.

"And what," asked First Star's mother, "happened to your brother?" She stood tall, her face hard. Other tribespeople gathered around. They already knew the answer to her question; there could really only be one answer.

"I killed it," the boy said, tears streaming—but the weeping was gone. His voice was strong. "It," not "him." First Star had known Bugling Elk was gone as soon as his body shambled out to clutch at him, snarling like a wolf, eyes flat. First Star had never been to the ocean, had never seen the dead stare of a shark. If he had, he would have thought his brother's eyes had been replaced by shark eyes.

He had acted without thought.

He took up a long stick from the forest floor and pushed it into his not-brother's eye. It had taken a moment—one beat of the bird's wing. If the boy had been older, he may have reflected that it had been so easy only because the parasite, the bad dream that took his brother, hadn't yet become used to the unfamiliar body. It was still dizzy behind the stolen face.

At the village, First Star keened, his sadness echoing in the valley, mouth opened wide in anguish, eyes squeezed shut. He honored his brother with his cry, grieving at the last sight of his beloved face when it had no longer been his own. His brother's strong body and friendly face, terribly empty.

The clan gathered around the small family: grandfather, mother, and smallest son. They made a circle and held each other, but they did not touch the three in the middle. It would not have been respectful.

⤜⟫⟫⟫⟪⟪⟪⤛

The wind passed on through the valley ringed by seven hills, Granny's vision ebbing.

"Why did they stay?" Lacey asked, his voice almost a whisper, though it was loud in the still wood. He'd never understood that part. As though echoing her uncle in her great-grandmother's bedroom, Vola asked the same question.

"Why did they stay, Granny?" Her young face was stricken, caressed by muted sun streaming through the memory of Granny's childhood bedroom window.

And together, Granny with Vola and Grandpa June up in the woods answered, "Because they had to." And even though all of them, even stalwart, unbreakable Granny, wished it could have been different, wished they could have laid down the weight of responsibility and gone out into the world beyond the seven hills of the Whitt farm, they knew it was true.

⤜⟫⟫⟫⟪⟪⟪⤛

Up on the southeast ridge, Lily didn't find a kitten. She found Boyd Byrne, filthy, his stench reaching her even from where he squatted on the other side of the fence. He mewled softly as he looked into her eyes, and she felt both repulsed and fascinated.

"Help me," he croaked. She took a step back, stumbling and landing on her butt in the leaves and stubby underbrush. He looked pitiful. He looked sick, and she'd never in her life seen a human being in such a condition—

143

crusted with dirt, skin red and cracked in the creases of his elbows, around his mouth and nose. He needed help, needed her to run and get her mother at least, but his eyes...his eyes terrified her, arrested her. *They're not his eyes,* she thought. It didn't make any sense, but it was true. Those eyes did not belong in that face.

He began to crawl toward her, not like a person or even an animal, but like a miserable, dying thing. He dug his ragged fingernails into the dirt and pulled himself toward her, clutching clumps of grass and crumbling clay as though he didn't trust himself to stand, as though losing a grip on the ground would mean the end of him.

Through the trees, Lily's mom drank coffee at her kitchen table, boxes still stacked around. Jayne Watson hadn't seen her daughter come down this morning. *She must be still in bed, little sleepyhead.* Maybe she hadn't rested well last night either. Jayne felt a vague sense of dread, but she often felt like that—it wasn't anything really unusual for her since her little boy died. She took a sip of lukewarm coffee and rubbed a shaky hand through her hair. The dreams last night—oh, God, the dreams were terrible. Her boy had accused her of the most horrifying things. Had told her she'd killed him and that it had been her fault because she was a terrible mother. And it was all true; it had all come from the center of her, everything he said. She put her head on her arms and cried like a little kid, coffee and Lily both forgotten.

June and Lacey hauled themselves up off the log and walked along, climbing the path toward the southeast boundary. Toward the Byrne fence. They were uneasy but not anxious, not yet. They should have been.

They should have been terrified.

Back at the southwest corner of the big farmhouse, in Granny's bedroom, Clary wiped the tears from her face and crept to the bed where her grandmother and daughter lay, caught in the vision. She climbed onto the bed next to her daughter and curled up with her, putting her nose in Vola's hair and reaching across to lay her strong hand on Granny's frail shoulder. Gitli lifted her head as though in greeting before settling back down.

In the bedroom of Granny's childhood, Vola and Granny opened their small circle to admit a third, and Clary sat with them on the hooked rug. Vola squeezed her mother's hand but even having Clary there with them didn't ease her dismay.

"What do we do, Granny?" Clary asked. "If the threat is back again. If the haints rise."

"We kill the haint," said Granny.

"Kill the haint...but that means we have to kill the person, doesn't it?" Vola asked, anxiously. Thinking of the little boy and the stick he'd used to kill his brother. "To kill the haint inside." Neither woman answered, but Vola saw the truth in their eyes.

Before she could ask any more questions, a piercing scream broke the vision, shattering the memory bedroom and rudely pulling the three Whitt women out of their palaver. Clary and Vola sat up in Granny's bed, wide-eyed.

"What the hell was that?" Clary said.

"Lily!" croaked Granny, still curled on her side. Vola was shocked to see her as she really was, old and frail and sick. "Vola, your friend don't...she doesn't know about any of it. She's up there now."

"What? What do you mean? Do you mean Lily's in trouble?" Vola asked, but Granny's eyes had already slipped close once more.

"Mama, I have to go," Vola said, sliding off the bed and running out of the room. She was already down the stairs and pulling on her old sneakers at the kitchen door before Clary could sputter out any objections. Granny reached out to grip Clary's wrist. *Stay. Your daddy and brother are up on the ridge. They'll be with her. Stay here with me.* Clary sat on the bed, resting her back against the headboard, stroking her grandmother's thin, white hair. She would stay. *Be careful, Vola,* she thought. That scream...

Outside, Vola ran up the cow path, her world reduced to stripes of deep shadow and bright morning light passing over as she ran, her vision narrowed to the next step, navigating rocks and roots and loose scree, all treacherous if she lost her footing. Clouds of insects followed as she went, her retinue of tiny white butterflies and dragonflies, honeybees and even hopping, flying grasshoppers, swirling, roiling around the girl in pajamas and beat-up sneakers in flight through the woods.

Further up the path, June and Lacey had heard the scream, too. They wordlessly picked up their pace, not knowing it was Vola's new friend in trouble, only knowing in their bones that Lacey's worries had come true, that the crack had pulled wide between the Byrne boundary and the wall Granny's father had laid down under the land.

Chapter Thirteen

BOYD'S BODY REACHED THE RUST-ROTTED strands of barbed wire between him and Lily. He reached out tentatively, as though afraid it was electrified. Lily thought it was strange, how he seemed afraid of the fence. But then again, everything about this man, this...sick thing...was all wrong. When the fence lay quiet in his dirty fist, Boyd's lips widened and cracked, the brittle skin bleeding over his meth-rotted teeth. He began to pull on the wire, slowly, steadily, unblinking stare fixed on Lily.

"Please," she whispered, tears spilling onto her cheeks. "Please stop. Please go away." She couldn't move. She was pinned by his eyes, fascinated and horrified by his inexorable pulling on the rotten fence wire. Lily was frozen by the sense that she was still dreaming; all the horror she'd felt in last night's nightmares, the guilt and profound sadness and a kind of deep-down foreboding that she deserved bad things, because her brother was dead. She deserved to be...*got* like the boogeymen of her primal childhood fears would get her.

"Please," she whimpered. Still he pulled until the wire snapped with a twang that reverberated through the woods.

"Was that the fence?" Lacey stepped faster, almost running now, almost to the top of the ridge. That strained plucking like a terrible guitar string breaking had beat through their heads like an earthquake—felt, more than heard.

"Yes," said June, saving his breath. He didn't know how it could be possible; neither Byrne nor haint should have been able to cross the fence, let alone break a strand, even if the crack in the boundary was weak. And if they had breached the fence, there would have been so much more than the eerie twang echoing in the woods. It was pure energy and time and the Whitt family heart and soul that held the haint ceiling under the earth and the boundary protecting the Whitt farm. And June was absolutely certain he'd know when they broke. Knew he'd feel it in his very skin. So the fence had to remain intact. Unless...had it broken on a different boundary? Maybe between the Byrnes and the Watsons on the other side... *Vola's new friend,* June thought, and he suddenly knew who'd screamed. *Ah, shit.*

⇒⟫⟫⟫⟩⟨⟪⟪⟪⟸

Lacey followed right along with his father, knowing in his muddled way that his fear didn't matter. He knew it was there, like a living creature curled in his belly, but it just...didn't matter. It could come along for the ride, could watch everything they did, but Lacey knew it didn't have much of a say in what was to be done. But, curiously, he didn't *want* to go with June. It wasn't so simple as wanting to avoid danger or even wanting to be home, eating a boiled egg and washing it down with orange sugar-juice. It was like the woods themselves, the trees *wanted* him to go somewhere else. Every time he came to a branch in the path, a barely noticeable track in the underbrush, his feet seemed to want to take him back down the ridge toward his trailer house in the valley. He felt the tug at his belly button, and he didn't think it had anything to do with the furry, scared creature crouching inside him now. Branches scratched at him in a way they rarely did; Lacey normally moved through these woods like he was a part of it. Birds and squirrels started a-running alongside, like they were encouraging him, coming along, and

148

then they veered off down the ridge like they were trying to say, "Come on! Come on this way!"

Finally, yelping with pain, Lacey stopped and said, "Gosh-dammit, Dad!" He cupped his bad eye in one hand. A bigger branch had walloped him good.

"What, son?" June was in a hunting mood—all deep thought and strategy.

"I don't think I'm supposed to come with you," said Lacey.

"We don't have time for this. We got to go, now." June turned and took up his marching pace once more. Lacey sighed and followed, completely unsure of what his belly button wanted of him. He couldn't leave Dad up here to deal with Byrnes and haints and what-all by himself.

They just about crested the ridge when the old man raised his hand, fist closed. *Stay. Quiet.* They could just barely see trash heaps beyond the sagging barbed-wire fence. The Byrnes' trash. They were at the boundary. Still and silent, father and son strained to hear something, anything...there. There was a whisper, a whimper. Rustling that might have been rats in the junk piles, but they knew it wasn't—it was coming from the Watsons' place, yonder.

June looked back at his son and pointed, silently, toward the far end of the Byrne property, where it met with the Watsons'. Lacey nodded and began picking his way down the ridge, but not all the way down, the way his belly and the forest seemed to want—only making a loop far enough down to keep their heads below the ridgeline, to keep out of sight of whatever it was on the other side of that fence.

***

Farther behind, on the cow path, Vola's lungs screamed, breath jagged in her throat. She stumbled over a root, panic working against her, and fell hard. Her knees scraped in the loose, flat corners of slate that jutted edge-up from the earth. She rolled and lay on her back a moment, trying to get her breath back, butterflies and insects whirling slowly above her, as Gitli lay next to her, anxiously licking her face. Vola hadn't even noticed the dog loping along the trail behind.

Granny was dying. Vola didn't need anybody to tell her that was why the old woman could bring her into her time, her memories—it was because she now lived in the in-between. The house that was made of old stories, Granny's moments of girlhood, days spent shucking corn on the porch, evenings observing the stars, performing the old rituals. Vola had some of them now, Granny's memories, even though she hadn't told them to her. She hadn't needed to; Vola had come with her to Granny's real childhood home. The one that lived in her, not the one that worked on becoming dust back to dust in this day.

Granny was dying, but it wasn't like real death. Granny was so, so old after all. She had lived so long, the world didn't know how to be itself without her. It didn't really want Granny to go, surely. So maybe if Vola could get rid of the haints, maybe that would bring Granny back. Maybe it was the haints doing it, making Granny sick. Without realizing it, Vola dug her fingers into the shallow dirt to either side of her, still breathing hard, tears streaming along her temples, into her hair and ears. She poured her anguish into the dirt and rock below her. *Go away, go away, go away...* She tried to push the haints back down, to push them away.

Lacey and June looked at each other, both feeling more than hearing the eerie, twanging hum tuning up in the fence just twenty feet away.

"Haints doing that?" June wondered aloud. "How can they...?"

"Vola," said Lacey. He was certain of it. In the same way he'd wandered the deep corridors of his logic, knowing about the cracks between walls, the answer came to him by way of his cedar tree. Vola had done that; she'd pushed its roots down and its branches up, had sung it to grow full of vitality. And Vola was near them now. Singing to the earth. Lacey couldn't hear her, but he could feel it in the air around him, could feel it in the peculiar hum of the fence yonder.

"Yes," June agreed. Vola was calling the haints.

"What do we do? Find her?" Lacey made as though he would go back down the way they'd come.

"No," said June. "We don't rightly know where she is—"

"I can find her!" Lacey pointed to his belly. "I can!"

"No," June repeated, putting his hat more firmly on his head. Shifting his shotgun. He spoke furtively, trying to keep his voice down. "What's done is done, haints is called. Probably been called for months now. Maybe years, for all I know. Now we got to move forward, do what needs doing." He turned to climb back up the ridge, but Lacey gripped his elbow.

"Vola's been calling haints for years? Is that what you're sayin'? Why didn't we know about it?" But even as he asked, Lacey had a flash of intuition: the Whitts always called the haints. Vola and Granny and Clary, Lacey, June. Even Mary. They were the yin and yang, just like Granny always said. Lacey hadn't really understood it before. The Whitts were the other side of the haints, the other half of a set of magnets. The Whitts were here because haints were here. Haints were here because the Whitts were here.

"I'll be damned," Lacey said, softly. "It's why Granny always said *when*. When, not *if* haints come back." Like seasons wheeling, haints would always come back because the Whitts were here. His dad turned to climb back up the ridge, heading to the other side of the Byrne property, thinking he'd come at the problem from another direction. Lacey scrambled to follow, but he lost his footing. He made a garbled cry as he slid...he couldn't seem to get a handhold, couldn't seem to stop the slide downhill! It was the kind of fall that seemed to last forever, leaving no room in Lacey's head for anything but trying to make sense of what was happening—*I'm falling. I'm falling.* Leaves and twigs and little rivulets of dirt cascaded down with him until a turn in the earth shifted him into the edge of a boulder. He cracked the side of his head on the rock and caught a shadowed glimpse of June looking down at him from the top of the ridge—so far up!—before he passed out.

He was only out a moment. The long blink of an eye. But it was enough.

He saw. He saw butterflies, thousands of them, their wings made of shimmering time. He thought Granny was there, too, and Clary. They didn't speak; it was like when they all watched the dying embers of a bonfire in summer, standing in the dark together, only visible as shadow-people in the gloom. But he could feel them nearby. It was like that, here in this place of butterflies.

Wings cleared out like mist in the high morning, and there was a door. White-washed, and familiar...except, last time he'd seen it, that door had been warped and barely hanging by a rusted hinge. It was one of the five doors into Granny's old house, the one where she showed Whitt young 'uns the archived family memories. And the door wanted him to go inside.

He came back to himself and wished he hadn't. His head ached fiercely.

"I know what to do," he said, and sat up. He'd landed in the shallow creek that fed their pond. He was east of his trailer house, and if he cut through the old stand of pines—many of them fallen and others dead where they stood, killed by the pine beetle invasion—he could get there quick.

Up on the ridge, June watched anxiously as his son tumbled down the ridge, clutching at a tree as though he could hold Lacey with sheer will. He didn't dare call out, didn't yet know the threat behind him, the whispering, rustling thing. He did know all hell was breaking loose! First his mama taking sick, now the damned fence, and haints, and his boy falling down the damned mountain! He took a deep breath.

"That's a hell of a thing," he muttered. But he didn't worry—he didn't have room for worry, not right now. He would wait until his boy got up on his feet. He counted slowly to three, breathing in. Pushed his air back out, counting to three. Once more, breath in. Once more, breath out. Sure enough, Lacey only lay at the bottom unmoving for a few seconds before he stirred and struggled up to his feet, moving to cut through the steep, narrow valley...in the wrong direction! June swore softly and shook his head. If his boy's head was addled by the fall, he'd be a liability anyway. June still had a job to do.

⇨⇨⇨⇨ ❬❬❬❬

Vola lay on the ground, her shaking slowly subsiding. Her panic had ebbed, poured into the ground. She didn't know if it had done any good, telling the haints to go away. Couldn't feel them. But she never had felt them, not that she'd known. She'd always known about the haints, but they were distant, like a fairy tale. Like the sun-welcome rituals and putting pie out in the field to honor the ancestors. Important, but not...not imminent. She felt a quick pulse of denial: she didn't want to have to fight haints! She hadn't chosen this!

But Vola was part of the family, wasn't she? And it hadn't done her mother a lick of good to try and push the family away. It was time to go on. Her friend needed her. Gitli, as though sensing her shift in thoughts, licked her hand and whined.

She opened her eyes to see light pulsing and beating in every color imaginable, felt the whisper of soft wings on her cheeks, forehead, arms...the butterflies! The wonder of it—all these gorgeous, ephemeral creatures kissing her with their wings, beating tiny breezes against her skin—it shocked her into the clarity of the here and now.

Grandpa June. Uncle Lacey. Lily. They were at the end of Vola's path, and it was time to take it. She got up, her fluttering entourage bursting into flight around her.

Chapter Fourteen

I'M TRAPPED LIKE A RABBIT, thought Lily, frozen by the sight of the emaciated creature clutching the ground, dragging itself toward her. Too late, she tried to scrabble away, but the *zombie! It looks just like a zombie!* reached out a hand with dirty, broken, bleeding nails and gripped her ankle tight. The spell was broken, and she kicked out with her other foot, twisting to crawl away, to grab a tree trunk, a tangle of blackberry thorns, anything! It was too strong. The thing pulled and pulled her, backing away by inches. Lily called out, turning her face toward her house. Her mother was inside there; if her mother could hear her, she'd come! But doubt flooded her… *She couldn't rescue Conner. She won't come for me.* Her brother's mangled body filled her mind, and Lily opened her mouth to scream, but she couldn't breathe, couldn't get air and when she did, she choked on a mouthful of dead leaves and dirt.

Inside the house, Pauline Byrne flicked her lighter to burn the first cigarette of the morning. She'd woken up from bad dreams in the night and slipped back into an uneasy doze until something woke her for good. She thought it may have been a scream, but she couldn't be sure. There had been screams in her nightmares, too. It was the kind of morning where dreams slipped over life like a sheer curtain, blurring what was real. She took a drag from her Marlboro, closing her eyes for a moment before blinking them wide open once more. She'd heard a commotion from out in the yard. *What in the world is that boy up to?* She shuffled her feet in battered slippers to the kitchen sink and peered out the window into the back yard. She could make out the top of her boy's head; he was crouched down, doing something (but *what?)* and was hidden from her by brush and junk. Was that—was it a scream, all choked up, like? The sound made her uneasy; there was a struggling way about it, not a bright, quick reaction as though a body had been startled with a fright. Pauline stood a moment. She wasn't one for hasty action. She was still alive because she knew how to fade, how to go unnoticed by drug-addled men. There was no need to change her ways now, as far as she could tell.

Her attention was caught by movement in the woods—those dreaded woods beyond, that her husband and father-in-law had warned her against. A battered hat glimpsed through tree branches. There, it was that old, godless bastard! June Whitt, that's what was bothering her boy! And a gun in his hands! Goaded at last, Pauline turned and made her way to the back bedroom, where she'd once shared a bed with her husband, though she hadn't seen that sorry devil in weeks. She rarely slept in there anymore, preferring to drift into oblivion to the flickering late-night television on the couch, overfull ashtray on the floor beside her. But she knew right where her old man kept his guns, yessir.

⫸⫸⫷⫷

The thing that had pulled Lily into the Byrne yard was up to something. It was scrabbling at her hand, tugging at it, but it was hard to…well, hard to care. Fog drifted over her, its dewy drops settling on her face, her clothes, making her heavy. *It's haints.* Why did she know that? Why in the world? The fog told her somehow.

She turned her face to where the battered creature that had been Boyd was pulling at her hand. No, not pulling...he was scratching at it. Scratching at the skin, the blood welling and slipping over her arm, down into the dead leaves. *They want your skin. The haint wants to wear it.* Now who said that? Lily's wondering thought was distant. She was at the bottom of a well, somewhere deep inside, her horror far above like a bright coin of sunshine. The tugging, the pulling on her skin...it was repugnant. There was no pain. She was a little worried about that; it was like waking up at the dentist's office before he was quite finished and feeling him poking around in her mouth: She knew it was going to hurt later. And her blood slipping around like that, it was...it was indecent, she supposed.

A pair of tears trickled from the outsides of her eyes, over her temples, into her hair.

"Help," she whispered. "I don't...I don't want it." The tugging kept on, and she felt more skin rip, felt him using his jagged, broken nails to break her skin and pull it off her in small chunks and strips. *He's not doing a very good job* and the thought brought her horror closer to her, and the world contracted, suddenly crisp and close. She heard him slavering, his labored breathing broken with little grunts of effort. He smelled like pee and sharp sweat and the kind of dirty that borders on rot. And on top of it all, like a thin spread of syrup: the iron, salty tang of fresh blood that coated her mouth and made it flood with spit like she was about to throw up.

She fled. She went under, away, anywhere but here. She went deep enough that she couldn't feel the tugging, couldn't hear him working to take her skin off.

⊱⋙⋘⊰

June should have seen it, should have had his damned eyes open and *seen*, but his head was still full of Lacey falling down the ridge, and the fog was coming on—the haint fog, he knew that—and when he came around to the break in the woods, just enough to see the girl Lily on the ground, enough to see what Boyd was up to, blood everydamnwhere—*it ain't Boyd Byrne, it ain't nothing human*—he was back in Italy once more. Nothing working right, nothing making damn sense, bombs hitting and earth pelting, and when it was too late, he saw Pauline coming out the back door. A wraith in a tattered bathrobe, hair brittle and wild, the barrel of a gun aimed directly at him. He had time to hit the ground before she shot, showered by bits of bark from the tree above. And there was Vola, running up the path toward him, wearing her spirit-shawl of tiny white butterflies and other creatures, the dog running close behind. *No,* he thought. *No, this ain't the time for you. This ain't the time.* It didn't make sense, none of this made sense, but he called out to his granddaughter to get her ass down. She stopped, uncertain.

—»»»»—‹‹‹‹‹—

Vola'd heard the shot, big enough to shiver the woods, and she heard her grandfather's voice, but the words wouldn't come through. Vaguely, she thought somebody had shot at a person. She couldn't quite get to the conclusion that someone had shot at her or at Grandpa June; people didn't do that, did they? People shot at targets, at sheets of plywood leaned up against trees, with crude circles spray-painted on them. Or they shot at deer or turkey. But not other people. Especially not at *her* people. All these thoughts jumbled through her at once before the old woman standing at the back of the house across the fence shot again, this time at her. Vola was still incredulous, but getting shot must have been what happened, because Vola felt punched, and she knew she was bad hurt because her arm went immediately numb. It was like the time she come crashing out of the tall oak and landed funny. Kids know it ain't the amount of pain that tells you whether you're bad hurt; it's the numbness. That's what sets in the panic, 'cause you know that when the pain does come in it will crash over like a wave the size of a house.

She fell against a tree, face a mask of hurt and confusion. Gitli gave a sharp bark, tail tucked and quivering; she never had liked loud noises. Vola's flying nimbus, all the grasshoppers and honey bees, moths and butterflies, they all fell in a heap around her, abruptly still. She got right up and went over to her grandfather. She'd show him what happened. He'd know what to do. That's what she did.

Except...when she blinked and looked around, she hadn't moved. She was still sitting on the ground, propped against a tree, arm numb and useless. She knew she should hurt and worse: she knew she was about to hurt. Bad. Tears of absolute terror streamed down her face.

⇒≫≫≻ ≺≪≪⇐

Pauline shot the girl. She'd seen movement in the trees. It was another of those godless Whitts; they were *godless*, not washed in the blood of the lamb, and she pulled the trigger of her shotgun before she'd meant to. Fueled by fear or the devil or God, she pulled the trigger and a spray of blood flew from the girl's body, and Pauline dropped the gun, hands trembling. She stumbled into the yard, thinking she'd go to the girl. *I shot her*, she thought. *I'll see if she needs help.* She'd shot her, but it didn't feel like she had; it only felt like something she'd witnessed. She would help the girl. That's what she would do. She forgot all about Boyd out here in the backyard.

And that was a mistake.

⇒≫≫≻ ≺≪≪⇐

June ran to Vola and scooped her into his arms, his own shotgun forgotten on the ground. He laid her out on the ground and examined her shoulder, muttering the whole time that she was all right, she'd be okay, he was just going to check her over. The bullet had punched through the top of her thin shoulder, shattering her collar bone, shredding skin and muscle. The old woman had been aiming higher—if she was doing much in the way of aiming. She'd shot at a full-grown man first, then swung over to Vola. That's why she'd hit Vola so high up. His mind was picking out logic, checking off a list of details, trying to make sanity out of pure craziness, trying to see all around the thing and avoid the big truth of it. *If she'd pointed the barrel of the gun further to the left*, he thought, *it would have been my girl's face.* And that's

158

when the shakes set in, deep, wracking. This was worse than the war, worse than Mary dying; this was his granddaughter, and she'd been shot—*oh god, she was shot...*

Screams pierced the air and then more, like two people screaming—curiously harmonious before they cut off abruptly.

"Lily," said Vola. Blood soaked her tattered pajama shirt. "Lily, Grandpa." He nodded and stripped off his flannel shirt, tying it across her body, under her right armpit, looped under the left one and tight up over her ruined left shoulder. When Vola gasped at the pressure, Gitli whined and stretched out her face to lick at the girl. Butterflies were everywhere. Butterflies and dragonflies and honeybees, all lying still. Vola shifted, her face drained of blood. The sun lay on her skin like a caress, and she suddenly glowed. June gasped and fell back.

"Vola?" he reached out a trembling finger and stroked his granddaughter's cheek. It came away dusted with a fine powder. *The butterflies.* They'd covered her in their wing dust.

⇛⇚

In the dirty, trash-strewn yard, Pauline stumbled over her son—except it wasn't her son. It wasn't even human, anybody could see that; it was an abomination. A demon-possessed monster that wore her son's body and...and what was it doing with that young girl on the ground? Pauline stood confused for a moment, trying to see, trying to comprehend. Blood everywhere—was that the girl she'd shot? No, no it was a different one; this one blonde where the other girl was brown-headed. The blonde girl's eyes gazed up, unseeing, and Pauline was afraid she was dead. Boyd was pulling on the girl, ripping her skin off, and he turned his face up to look at Pauline, still tugging the girl's wrist. Almost like a young 'un playing in the dirt, innocently looking up at its mama. Except for the thing's eyes. There wasn't nothing innocent about them. The old woman stuffed her nicotine-stained fist into her mouth, horrified beyond all rational thought. The face that had once been her son's was a death mask, its lips cracked and bleeding, its teeth dirty. Its hooked claws finally stopped scratching at the girl to reach up and pull at Pauline, dragging her down. Down to hell. She didn't know she was screaming, could only hear the roaring of her blood and terror in her ears. The girl on the ground—not dead, not yet—screamed with her. Then they both lay silent, and the haint behind Boyd's ruined face surveyed them both with horrible satisfaction.

The young one was better. They always were. But the old one…a haint tried slipping in, tried pushing in with swirling, foggy fingers through her eyes, her nose, and her mouth. She gave one heave. A buck that arched her old head down into the dirt and about broke her back, and her heart galloped once, twice, and finally quit.

"Oh, well," croaked the swollen, cracked vocal cords inside Boyd's throat. "Might be worth a meal."

⇒⇒⇒⇒⇒ ⇐⇐⇐⇐⇐

Down in the valley, Lacey burst through the little aluminum door to his trailer house. *An old door new again, the wooden chest at the end of the bed, the cocoon jacket inside.* These three marched through his mind, one after the other, like his cards of fortune flipped up by unseen fingers, over and over and over.

"I know what to do!" he called, running unsteadily through the doorway to his bedroom and falling to his knees with a thunk. *Damn*, but his head was pounding. Throwing open the wooden chest at the end of his bed, Lacey pulled out the cocoon jacket—gently, very gently—and bundled it under his arm. Outside, the sun battered his eyes, and he groaned; he'd hit a fair few rocks on his shortcut down the ridge, and frankly, the thought of climbing back up—the short or the long way—made him want to cry.

He leaned against a fence post and bleakly gazed around.

"Got to get back up there," he muttered. He'd thought he heard gunshots earlier, but it was hard to tell. He'd been crashing through the woods like a durned bull stung by a yellowjacket, and his head…damn, his head *ached*.

160

Chickens squawked from inside the henhouse, mad at him for neglecting their breakfast. Morning light twinkled off the rearview mirror of the old farm truck, parked at the barn. He turned his poor, tired eyes away, groaning. Even the bad eye was a-hurting.

The light...that bright light...coming off the farm truck! He snapped his head back to look at the truck again, barely registering the way his brains felt like they sloshed. He was already trotting off down the road, praying his dad had left the keys in the ignition, the way he mostly did in the evening.

Sweating and breathing hard, Lacey rejoiced when his right hand closed around the familiar jumble of metal. He leaned his head against the steering wheel and sent a prayer around to the ancestors, the winds, the hills, hell— the haints too, damn 'em. Vola was probably up at the Byrnes' by now, and nothing was stopping Lacey from getting there. He gave a pat to the pile of cocoons sitting next to him on the bench seat of the truck.

"I heard you," he said. "I heard you, and I got you, and now we're going up there." Resolutely, he started the engine and drove out of the barnyard, down the dip in the gravel driveway and past the big white house. He went past the old, tumble-down house, too. He knew one of the doors was his door (*an old door made new*) but he also knew it wasn't time to seek that door, not yet. And maybe not...*here*. Time made a place just as far as distance, and it wasn't time for the door. He clutched the wheel with both hands, willing his blurred vision to clear up, his muddled head to get him where he was going. And if it couldn't, he willed his strong gut to pull him along that invisible line that wanted him to get where he needed to be.

Chapter Fifteen

CLARY GENTLY STROKED HER GRANDMOTHER'S hair away from her face. There had been shots earlier, two muffled cracks rolling through the valley, sounds jumbling up in the trees and hills so that it was hard to know where they came from. Sounds of gunshot were common enough: hunters or folks just shooting at homemade targets in the backyard. She knew it was too much to hope that's all it was this time, knew that this time guns had been fired up at the Byrne boundary, but she set it aside for now. Her father was up there and her brother, too, and they would do what was necessary. She sent a brief, quiet prayer that Vola hadn't made it up there yet. Clary's hands shook as they brushed Granny's soft, wispy hair—once vibrant and thick. Pale and dry and diminished without the fire behind it, Granny's face was still familiar. Clary loved her so. She buried her sobs in her hands, feeling completely lost. The women who came before her—her mother, her grandmother—knew just who they were and, with that knowledge, anchored Clary right down to the earth. Without them, without either one of them, how would she find her way?

"I know how you feel, honey child," said Granny so softly it was almost a whisper. "I'll miss you, too, my girl." Clary looked up from her hands to see the old woman's eyes open, her gaze sharp. "But your part is coming up.

You can ignore who you are, but that don't mean you can escape it, sweet girl." It was a harsh dig and worse because it was close to her own thoughts. Clary shook her head, annoyed that even on her deathbed, the old woman would sting her. It was one of Granny's special talents, one that had nothing to do with being a Whitt and everything to do with being just who she was: she could unzip Clary's insides and make her feel so painfully exposed, then patch her back up again with love all at once. Fresh tears slipped down the younger woman's cheeks.

"What's my part, Granny? What do I do?"

"Do you hear that?" Granny pointed at the ceiling, eyebrows raised. The old farm truck rumbled by, disappearing around the curve of the driveway and leaving behind the echo of its tires on gravel.

"The truck?" Clary asked, perplexed. "But who's driving it? I thought Dad and Lacey were already up…?" She gestured out the window.

Granny was already nodding. "Up, and Lacey back down, and now going up again. The time is growing nearer and nearer. Not just one slip, this time. Not just one haint, my girl. The seam…it's got to be sealed up."

"I don't know how to do that!"

"I know. Get down to the old house, child. Get down there and wait."

"I don't want to leave you!"

"*I can't, I don't*…Clarinda Whitt, stop whining! I'm an old woman, and this is my dying damned command! Get on down there!" Clary was already out of the house and halfway across the yard before it occurred to her that dying folks got requests, not commands. She turned back, thinking she'd yell at the open upstairs window, but the sight of it, like a sad eye, stopped her short. She shook her head and turned back toward the hay field. She'd stay off the driveway, with its twists and turns, and instead hop the creek and cut across the field to save time.

Up in bed, face turned unseeing to the soft, white curtains wafting in the breeze in her room, a ghost of a smile played on Granny's wrinkled lips. She knew just what Clary had almost turned and shouted…didn't need any kind of spirit sight to know she could get under her granddaughter's skin. That girl had a stubborn streak a mile long. It made Granny proud. But her smile faded just as quickly as it had come. Granny was deeply worried, even if she hadn't shown it to Clary. Poor little Vola, up on that ridge…it was getting bad.

Outside, fireflies drifted up from their daytime beds in the hayfield, wakened by Clary's passing. Their soft glow—so brilliant in the twilight of the day—barely showed in the fierce, late-summer sun. Cicadas and crickets, too: they woke up and gave a few notes of their nighttime song, and it added another cord to the daytime hum of insects. Clary barely noticed, thinking only that her own sense of unrest made the farm around her seem off-harmony.

Granny noticed, of course. They were part of the rhythm of the earth, those night bugs, and the rhythm of the earth was all wrong.

⇢⫸⫸⫸⫷⫷⫷⇠

Lacey pulled up short at the end of the Whitt driveway; June had closed the gate and locked it last evening. Lacey cursed, stopping the truck. He didn't know if he'd be able to get his sorry ass out of the truck and over to that damned gate; everything ached worse, now that he was sitting down. Almost without knowing he'd made a decision, Lacey put the truck in reverse, rolled back a few feet, and put it in third. The old rust bucket wouldn't like taking off in third, but he could make her do it…and, gravel flying, he charged the metal gate.

"Aaaah, damnit!" he yelled. The truck crunched to a screaming stop, metal squealing against metal, hard enough to jump Lacey to the side. He almost crushed the cocoon jacket on the bench seat next to him, making his head throb even worse. The gate wouldn't give!

"This is so much easier on the damned TV," he moaned, putting the truck in park, though it hardly mattered; it was stalled out. He yanked the handle to open the door, just about falling out in the gravel. He made his way over to the gate, now bent all to hell—the fence posts, too—and unlocked it. Opened it. Swung it wide as its twisted hinges protested and shuddered. It mostly flopped down into the weeds to the side of the gravel drive. Wasn't much good as a gate anymore. He knew he'd have to fix it, but he felt somewhat victorious: at least he'd beat that damned gate.

"Now," he muttered. He staggered back to the truck, climbed in, and started it up before he drove by the wreckage.

Clary heard the racket, but she just missed her brother driving away through the farm gate—which looked like hell, now that she saw it. Dad would be mighty angry when he saw the mess. But that was a worry for another time; there in front of her was the old house, looking like it always did. Try as she might, Clary couldn't see the ghost of Granny's childhood home, whole and strong as it had once been. Houses needed people in them, to breathe and eat their supper inside and touch their walls. Human lives have substance, and a house needed that magic, that *vitality,* to keep upright.

Completely unsure of what she should do, Clary clambered up the drunkenly sloped, rotted old porch boards and stepped into the gloom of what had been a sitting room. She didn't even realize she had chosen to go in the door that had called her in Granny's vision. She had, in fact, circled the house and gone past another door to get in here.

"Hello?" she called. But she got no answer, not even a feeling of welcome or of malice. It just felt like so many planks of old wood and chunks of rock all piled up. Soon to be unrecognizable as anything *but* a pile.

You ever lost something?

Clary had grown up on her grandmother's stories about this house, and the five doors that lead from the outside only to one room on the inside, with no way to go between, 'less you went back out on the porch first. Clary could hear Granny's voice in her head, the earthy cadence telling about haints, how they'd get confused when Granny—then, just a girl, just Ella—had run in a

165

different door every twilight, run in a different door and giggled with triumph when the haints wandered around the outside of the house, frustrated, only to fade away again like mist when they couldn't find the girl.

What did Granny do, then? Clary gazed around the decaying house. Now, she could go between rooms from the inside. Time and neglect had made their own doors inside the old house: rusted nails had come loose, letting boards tumble down from the walls. What had Granny done when she was young, after the haints went away? She probably went back out onto the porch, with no small amount of spooky feeling in her spine, now that she'd had a brush with haints in the dark. And then she came back into the door that led to the sitting room. And she'd climbed the narrow stairs to her own attic bedroom. Spent some hours daydreaming or reading. Knitting, perhaps, before the time came to blow out her kerosene lamp in the dark of night.

You ever lost something?

Clary had lost something. *The thing is*, she thought, *I don't know if I ever knew where it was in the first place.* She'd been a stranger in a family of hillbilly outcasts for as long as she could remember. She wandered in the house, stepping through the walls where their boards had fallen away. She didn't need doors between the rooms, not anymore. Something caught her eye—was that paper? She squinted and bent down to pull it out from between exposed studs, where it had been wedged in the wall. Yes, it was paper, faded and nibbled by generations of bugs, but there was spidery writing on it. If she tilted the letter toward the light...*Dearest Clary*, it began. She gasped, skipping to the ending. Who wrote this letter? Was it meant for her or for some ancestor of hers... one who shared her name? It wasn't signed. She went back to the beginning.

Dearest Clary,

You can't make the truth. The world marches forward so fast, and the outside part of it calls us, with its bright lights and motion like so many whirly-gigs in flight, all the time. I know you long to go, just like your own Granny longed to go, just like all of us have longed to go at some time or another.

If you're reading this letter, my girl, you stayed. That was hard. But you're not done yet; the hardest part is coming. I don't know what it will be, your task, but I have seen you. I can see what's to come, at least part of it, and I have seen you. It's my shine.

"Shine," murmured Clary. Her family had used to call their talents "shine." She liked it better.

You got to find what you lost, girl. You got to hold your truth, not make it something that it just ain't. Your own little girl needs you to do that.

She needs you right now.

There was a mark, like the author had started to write something else before being disturbed, and then hastily stuffed the letter in the crack between two boards of the wall. Vola needed her now? Clary looked around, aware that she'd been hearing something for the past few minutes…a fluttering, soft roaring, like the susurration of a wind working itself up to blow through the tall pines. She absently put the letter in her pocket and picked her way over to the glassless window. Something was coming.

➤➤➤➤ ◄◄◄◄◄

Vola struggled to get up, despite June's protests.

"Help me!" she cried. "What are we here for!?" He recoiled as though slapped.

"I…" June shook his head, to clear it or to say "No," or both, and left off trying to stop her and pulled her up, her blood staining his white undershirt. She was right. They had a duty. Even Gitli came along, on alert like she often was when farm duties needed done, though she whined, smelling that things weren't right up here on the ridge. Not right at all.

Somewhere in the back of his mind, June wondered where in hell Lacey was. They shuffled toward the boundary, Vola clutching tight to him with her good arm. She was pale, but he tried not to see it. She'd be all right. He didn't have room for any other possibility.

167

There was the barbed-wire fence, sagging even more, now that it had been broken. June felt the tingle of its deeper boundary, and he closed his eyes, beginning the old chant. He thought he might try to strengthen it—the deep boundary wasn't broken, after all, not when he could still feel its energy. Maybe he could stop the disaster before it started. Vola cried out and broke free from his supporting arm.

"Lily!" Vola stumbled around a fence post, ducking under the highest strand of wire and crying out as her knees hit the dirt, jostling her ruined shoulder. She had eyes only for Lily, even through the sick throb of pain. A few of her winged little creatures fluttered around, listlessly following.

June, coming on behind, saw everything:

The thing that had been Boyd, wasted and sick even before the haint had started to feed.

Pauline Byrne, that unfortunate woman who had pushed down everything she'd ever wanted or hoped for, lying in the dirt, face twisted in horror at the last thing she'd seen in life.

Lily's face, like wax, eyes closed, pale as death. One hand stretched up in the dirt as though she knew the answer in class, blood slicked up and down her wrist where the skin was gouged. Boyd sat nearby watching, watching like a dangerous animal, hands covered in gore, face streaked in blood. Shark eyes set deep in darkened sockets. June shivered when he saw them, recognizing the haint inside the lost man with the blood of generations of shamans. As though he knew, as though the cursed haint recognized June in just the same way, Boyd's face stretched in a sickening parody of a smile. Watching June, relishing his horror, Boyd's fingers plucked at something in the dirt and brought it to his face, laying it on his cheek. It was a tiny strip of skin, bloody and dirt-flecked. *They want to wear our skins.*

"But you got a skin!" June croaked, struck suddenly by the absurd gruesomeness of it. Boyd didn't say anything at all, but June got his answer, delivered up through the very wind rustling leaves at his feet. *Evil is greedy.* It was true, and June knew it in his very bones.

168

Vola hadn't paid more than a glance to the haint. She thought only of saving Lily. Like a small child leaping the last two feet to the bed in the dark of night, believing that if she simply didn't *see* the boogeyman, then he couldn't get her, she put him out of her mind. Shaking with the effort, pale and sweating in the onset of shock, Vola scuttled on her knees and reached one good arm toward her friend. She crossed the line, that boundary that June had sung up years and years ago, thinking maybe he'd reconcile with his wife's family someday, thinking it wouldn't matter at all to those vile spirits bumping along under them like blind sea creatures in their net. Forgetting that all things are connected somewhere, not knowing that by wanting to protect his family from that crazed old man threatening to kill Mary and June and anyone else he could get to, he would weaken their defenses against an even worse threat. Vola crossed over, and that boundary died in a searing light and a high whine that came and went like a freight train.

Vola fell like a puppet with her strings cut, unmindful of her wound, now bleeding afresh.

The haint came at her fast, faster than June would have thought possible, and June's gun was lying too far away. Gitli barked with a fierceness he'd never heard from her, baring her teeth and hunkering low between Vola and this new threat—man-shaped but smelling like death. June picked up the thing closest to hand, a fallen branch, and he swung it. It hit the mark, knocking Boyd over, but it almost didn't matter: pain wasn't a problem for him. Fresh blood seeped from an undoubtedly broken nose, and the white of one eye was sickeningly bloody, but the Boyd-haint only slowed down. Vola lay over Lily, still unmoving. Boyd, and the thing inside him, picked himself back up and came toward Vola once more. June stood ready. He'd swing and swing, no matter how many times the damned thing came on.

And, suddenly, that haint in Boyd was the least of June's worries.

Haints were a-coming by the dozens. By the hundreds. The crack had been ripped open wide—the steadfast wall that had held them down below in the dark since June's grandaddy built it—was crumbling. All over the farm they pulled themselves out of it, two, three, a dozen at once. Like the silver mist in the early morning, like the drifting fog at night. Eyes and gaping mouths, clutching fingers made of fear. Shapes seen only from the corner of the eye in the twilight and moonlight. They sought bodies; they starved for laughter and shrieking hysteria, tears and joy. And fear. Delicious terror. June's vision faded. He fell. As though from miles away, he heard the dog barking, the sound of it drifting, caught in the fog. There was Vola, and there was Lily, neither moving. What would it feel like, to have one of the haints inside him? Would he know it, feel it like a prisoner in his own brain?

Dimly, June saw Boyd shudder to a stop, hanging in the air like a badly used marionette. His face contorted, as though all the emotions a man could feel were running through at once. His skin swelled, bubbling like a sack trying to contain boiling water, and he collapsed to the dirt, oozing and bleeding, mist seeping from his eyes, his nose, and his ears. There had been too many haints, too many trying to feast on the boy's heart and mind. June had never even heard of such a thing happening before.

Chapter Sixteen

LACEY CAME RUNNING. HE'D PARKED the truck in the Byrnes'
front yard, all grown up with weeds. He'd grabbed the cocoon jacket and
ran like the wind—tried to, anyway, busted up as he was, heedless of fences
and boundaries and any hell-born thing. The jacket told him what to do now.
He came around the back of the house and stopped short, head pounding,
good eye pulsing with each heartbeat. There was his daddy, and there was
Vola and piles of trash all around, the fence broken and the little girl Vola
had befriended on the ground, too. There was the dog, lying still. There was
an old lady all crumpled and probably dead. And a dead man next to her,
looking half-skinned. And haints everywhere. Lacey had never seen haints
his own self, but he knew what his belly told him, and that aching, bright
pain in his belly button said it all.

He threw the jacket over his shoulders and shoved his arms through the
sleeves, distantly registering that he ripped them in doing this, but it didn't
matter; the whole thing was exploding in light and wings and the power of a
thousand years of human hope and love all bundled away with each passing of
a Whitt life. Brown, orange, bright yellow, iridescent blue, white…every color
of moth and butterfly imaginable burst free. Lacey fell to his knees, unaware
completely that he was screaming, screaming, letting all his ancestors pass

through him to attack the haints, to beat against the mindless desire to rend, to eat, to thoughtlessly destroy. The ancestral butterflies exploded from him in gorgeous righteousness. It was ethereal insects against the fog: writhing, rippling, fluttering columns and swirls and shapes like stars in the sky. It was sparks exploding from a campfire, and ancient people dancing with the heads of wolf and eagle and buffalo.

In her bed, in that borderland of life and beyond, Ellie Whitt longed to join them. She felt their joy almost like pain. But she wasn't ready yet. Granny still had a thing or two to attend.

$$\rightarrow\!\!>\!\!>\!\!>\!\!>\!-\!\!<\!\!<\!\!<\!\!<\!\!<\!\!<\!\!-$$

Vola lay motionless, Lily pinned beneath her.

She was…somewhere else. Someplace else completely. As soon as she'd touched her friend, as soon as she'd crossed the boundary, Vola disappeared, and she understood. *This is where the haints are.* No wonder haints craved human bodies; people could feel warmth and satisfaction and all kinds of things a hot-blooded body was necessary to feel. This distant cold, this untethered drifting…it was like eating a meal of bitter ash. No nourishment, no pleasure of sensation. No comfort.

Panic hit her, then: she wasn't inside her own body! She couldn't even *see* her own body, couldn't turn her head, couldn't feel the ground beneath her. Was this it? Was this *it*!? Was she in the purgatory of the haints, stuck in the in-between, the darkness, forever? Vola had no voice to cry out. No tears to weep. It was just her, in here, with panic consuming her like fire. Or like drowning. And no way out.

Where her body lay, so still, the faithful winged creatures began to stir. The butterfly dust on her cheeks and hair began to sparkle, as though they'd stored a bit of the now-dim sunlight. The butterflies and damsel flies and mosquito hawks and legions more of insects of the wood were bound to her, this girl Vola, and they rose, ready to serve. Ready to carry.

"Clary!" Granny called from her bed, not bothering with the triviality that her granddaughter wasn't actually within hearing shot. She'd hear anyway. "Clary, you go get her! Vola is drifting! Call her!" She saw them, up on the ridge, like looking through a film of milk left at the bottom of a glass. Her people were all faded, all used up and on the ground...but the haints were stronger, filled with palpable malice, and they were everywhere—still unsure of themselves above the ground, some sticking by the boundary they knew so well. The ancestors beat their wings against the haints on the ridge, but there were so many. So much malice. They'd spent long years like smoke pressed up against glass: looking without eyes, scrabbling, seeking warm bodies and human minds to take. To eat. Now they were free.

Granny was a little girl again, running, running around the house with five ways in, choosing the entrance that would most confuse a chasing haint. Her heart pounded.

And Clary heard it. She heard her Granny, and she heard the soft whispers of thousands of wings like a roar, and she closed her eyes and reached out to find her brightest spark, her treasure, her baby girl. And in the dark, inside the drifting, something touched Vola: words and a lilting, nonsense tune—the lullaby Clary'd sung for her since before she was born. It was a sweet sound, sweet like the soft nubs of her worn baby blanket, sweet like the scent of her mother's skin. And the sweetness made a path for Vola, and she found that she had feet to set down upon it. She took a step, and then another, but it was curious: the more she stepped, the more she felt as though she floated, as though she were borne on a thousand wings in the dark. *I don't have a body*, she thought, and the panic started to rise again. She didn't have a body, and she knew her panic was going to call the haints to her; they wouldn't stay distracted up at the ridge, not for long.

"Mama!" she cried out, and it was a voice made of bees, fireflies, and midges. June bugs, moths, and butterflies, all moving the air with their wings and all taking her along with them to where her mother waited, still singing, still singing. Vola did the hardest thing in the face of blinding panic.

173

She let go of all of it.

That's it, she thought she heard Granny say, her voice a sigh through the trees up on the ridge...and there was her mother's face, framed in the splintered wooden window, looking up at Vola. But it made her dizzy, seeing her mother from so many different eyes, so she closed her eyes and looked at her from inside, instead.

Clary saw the cloud of insects, and she knew her daughter was there.

"Come," she said, opening her arms wide. "Come on to me, my girl."

"I don't have a body," Vola said. She was so dismayed by this, by how lost she felt without it. "Like the haints. They don't have a body either." She didn't have a mouth to say these things, but Clary heard it anyway. She heard it anyway. Something had been let loose—had become unmoored—on the Whitt farm. The ancestors flew outside their cocoons, haints drifted up from their dark prison below, and little restraints, like time and space, they just didn't matter. Up on the ridge or right here in Clary's arms, Vola was with her.

"Yes, you do," said Clary. "You got a body. But you need to leave it behind for a little while." And somehow, she took the cloud of fireflies, of tiny, flitting bees and dragonflies and anything else that flew, into her open arms. She called her daughter to her. That was her talent. It was her shine.

⇒⟩⟩⟩⟩⟨⟨⟨⟨⟨⇐

Up on the ridge, Lacey stretched tall, his arms flung wide. The hot string that had pulled his belly button up to the fence had broken into thousands of strings, each one connecting his body to a flitting ancestor-butterfly or moth, some luxuriously exotic—there was a lunar moth, the size of a saucer, glowing in its own unreal light. Others were more plain, like the tiny yellow butterfly that Vola had spied after they buried Granny's brother up on the ridge.

He marveled at it, the energy burning from his body in pinpricks all over, pulling life's force from him. *What if they drained him*? What if they sucked the life out of him? He wasn't ready for that, wasn't ready to pour his life out in tiny strings, not even for his family, not even to fight the haints; he wasn't ready, wasn't ready, *wasn't ready*!

Lacey began to sob, unable to break the strings, unable to bring his arms down, unable to fall to the ground.

Granny saw him from where she lay. She felt his panic.

"Lacey," she whispered. "Lacey, darlin', you calm down now."

But he couldn't hear.

Granny saw her boy June, lying in the dirt, somewhere deep inside his mind. None of this was going well. Centuries of preparation, centuries of stars wheeling overhead. The earth turning and turning, the seasons rolling through the valley, bringing with it war and peace, discovery and isolation, the rise and fall of human endeavors. Granny saw all of it: the glint of a button from a Civil War soldier, hiding in the cave behind the trickling waterfall. The moonshine still that came later. Two girls playing at catching crawdads.

It had to be something. Had to *mean* something! Granny could see them all—Lacey, June, Clary, Vola. Even the troubled little girl, Lily, and her mother, Jayne, and poor, dead Pauline Byrne and her boy Boyd. All of them, linked with crystalline bridges of light, delicate and breaking and regrowing in fractals by the second, their thoughts...their thoughts making all the bridges, and the haints swirling around, crashing into them, breaking the chains like fragile diamond necklaces. But they kept growing, kept connecting, and Granny could see all of it! But she couldn't make them hear her on the ridge.

One of the haints caught on to Granny's own crystalline thread. It shined and glittered, prettier than anything it had seen in years and years: an eternity or the glint of sun on a ripple of water. Time folded in on itself here in the valley, and the haint remembered. It remembered! Who would have thought a haint could do something so human as remembering?

This pretty crystal chain, this particular one...the haint had followed such a thing before. It had followed along, crashing and bumping blindly, following a girl's joyous giggle, her love of the fields and hills and trees and even the blowing breeze above it weaving a net all around, but she always escaped. Always chose a different door to go in, and this family of people, this clan of shamans, these Whitts, they knew how to send the haints away.

But now...

Now, the haint knew the girl wasn't moving anywhere, and that glittering, glinting chain was both delicate and wide as a highway, and the haint took turns dancing along it and swinging like a child on monkey bars, its grasping, clammy form coming ever closer, and it was going to get to the girl, finally!

⇒≫≫≫—≪≪≪⇐

Ellie Whitt was in trouble. The curtain-softened sunlight set the room aglow, but her face was pinched and dark on the flowered pillowcase, her white hair stringy and plastered to her forehead by sweat. The haint was a-coming—her haint, she knew it now. Recognized it by the smell of late evening dew, the sound of twigs crackling underfoot, and the feel of the heat running out of the day. It was coming for her, coming, and this time Ellie was no young girl, full of life and the complete certainty that bad luck was for other folks, never her. Ellie was old. She'd turned into an old lady, and she no longer could run to a new door each evening, bounding up the porch steps to slip through one of the five entrances to the Whitt family house down in the shady valley. She was stuck, stuck here in this damned sick bed, and she couldn't even send out to help her people, her family, her blood warriors in this fight against evil. She couldn't help in this fight to keep those damned parasitic spirits pressed tight underground, where they could no longer menace those souls caught unawares in the dark places of the woods or the lonely pathways along the bottom of a mountain. She rocked her head left to right, eyes shut tight, thin lips drawn down in a grimace.

⇒≫≫≫—≪≪≪⇐

176

It quieted, the storm of butterflies and moths, the swirling fog of malice, the terrifying pull on Lacey's life. He collapsed, sobbing, grateful for the grit of dirt underneath his cheek. It was over. They must've won; the ancestors had beat away the haints, and Lacey was still alive.

But if they'd won, why did he feel so helpless? If they'd won, if they'd sealed the haints back in the ground, why did Lacey feel ashamed?

The clump of weeds just beyond his nose was pitiful. Yellowed and dry, half-laid over and pounded into the ground, maybe even by Lacey's own feet when he ran from the truck with the ancestors' coat. He lay listlessly, reflecting that he seemed to be ending up on the ground a lot lately—dropping off the ridge, getting knocked down here behind the Byrnes' house...*I'm tired.* His very bones were tired. He had no way of knowing how he mirrored his grandmother in that moment, his face hopeless and drained here in the dirt, hers much the same in her upstairs bed.

A butterfly came down, almost lazily, twitching a wing once or twice to help it aim for its landing. It stood with delicate black legs on the part of the weed that still stuck up out of the dirt, its blue wings shimmering in sunlight. Lacey's eye was drawn to it, that shimmering, iridescent blue, so gorgeous, stark, and singular against the backdrop of misery. Tears tracked through the dirt on his face, tears of exhaustion, of failure, of profound sadness. Of plain old achy pain, too. The butterfly walked along the leaf toward him, delicately placing each of its feet until it reached the tip of Lacey's nose, unfurling its tiny, black proboscis—Lacey *saw* each detail of its actions as though it were magnified, the marvel of it nudging through his exhaustion—to sip at his tears.

And when the ephemeral creature touched him, his clay-lump of a bad eye sparked alive. Lacey saw.

There was the door. Lacey's door, the one that he knew from the tumbledown house down in the valley, though it was whole and strong in front of him. He went through it, and there he saw...

The ancestors, the first of his people, who fought the haints…the first little boy who took up a sharpened stick and pushed in through the flat, predatory eye of a haint in his brother's body…there was more. So much more. The story went on, the murky depths of it calling him to know it, to know the rest…Lacey's body tensed as he saw, his head grinding back into the dirt, his spine bowing upward, scenes of deep, ancient woods, of people singing and dancing under the stars, of fires and smoke.

⇒⟫⟫⟩ ⟨⟨⟨⟨⟸

Lily was in hell. That must be where she was; she felt cold and burning all at the same time. She was sad and alone and completely lost. There was no anger; anger would have meant there was a sliver of a chance that she shouldn't be here in this desolate…what? Place? Not-place? Now that she thought about it, Lily was somewhere she knew. This was her neighborhood back home, robbed of all color. This summer that had seemed like a dream, with its simple delights dappled in the forest light—now it was over. She'd known deep inside it wouldn't last: that kind of happiness, that almost-contentedness. She pushed her body toward the entrance, toward the brick sign that proclaimed "Shady Oaks." Sounded like an old folks' home, her father had always said. *The perfect place for you, then,* her mom used to reply. Back when they had joked together.

No, she wasn't angry. Just sad. And bleak. Like her sadness didn't even really matter. She kept going toward the entrance to the neighborhood, toward the highway beyond, and beside the blacktop: the ditch. Conner's last landing place. She knew what she would find if she kept walking on feet that prickled in pins and needles; all the blood had left her, just like her anger, her happiness. But she kept going forward. Somehow she needed to see. Needed to see, to feel the pain again. Pain was sharper and brighter than bleakness, than bland, gray sadness.

There, in the weeds, there was a dirty white sneaker. And his tiny leg, so much smaller now that the life was gone out of him. Conner had had a kind of force field around him, breaking things and banging into furniture, making Lily outraged and laughing and full of emotion. She missed him so much.

Her legs gave out, and she fell on the ground next to her dead brother, embracing his cold body lying in the ditch. It's where she belonged.

Granny knew the haint was coming for her.

She was afraid.

Nothing was going right.

Chapter Seventeen

"MAMA," VOLA HAD SAID, "WHAT do I do now?"

"Well, I think you have to let go," Clary had replied, and so her daughter had, but Clary kept hold of her and held on tight. She turned, her arms full of her daughter in the form of fireflies and bumblebees, dragonflies and the hundreds of tiny, white butterflies that had marked Vola's path since she'd been born. Clary felt like she'd never felt before; there was a lightness in her, and she knew she was close to something. She was about to open a door inside herself. The shine! The letter in her pocket was proof that she could do what needed to be done, even if it didn't tell her *what* to do. *Let go*. It was the hardest thing to do, even harder when what you clutched in your fists was hurt. Why was it so easy to push away happiness? Clary'd held tight to her misery for so long that she didn't know how to breathe without it, and yet...yet, there was one bit of joy in her life, wasn't there? Vola. Clary had Vola to light her way.

Eyes closed tight, Clary stepped onto a path she'd never seen before, one not followed for hundreds of years, not since the days of buffalo and elk and huge, lumbering bears in the valley. She climbed and climbed, and the steps that started as the splintered wooden ladder up to Granny's girlhood bedroom gave way to rock, carved deep into the mountainside. Even that rock path faded into gray, into the velvety black of sky. Her heart was pounding in her throat, her arms quivering with the effort of holding onto Vola.

"Let go, Mama!" Vola's voice bubbled with laughter. Now it was Clary's turn to open her arms and her heart and release it all. "Open your eyes! Let go!"

"I can't!" Clary sobbed, trying to clutch tighter to her daughter, trying to hold a girl whose body wasn't here. She was ready—she knew she was. She'd come here, hadn't she? But she suddenly felt like a tiny young 'un, climbing too far into the towering pine. She'd gone too far up before she'd even realized it, fueled by excitement and curiosity...now, uncertainty paralyzed her. Clary was terrified of what she would see, terrified of falling, terrified of losing Vola.

"Mama, let me go," Vola said, still laughing. "Just like you said to do! I have wings, Mama. You can't drop me. Open your eyes!" With a shuddering sigh, Clary uncurled her arms, and Vola burst forth like a tiny storm, swirling around her in sheer joy. Clary opened her eyes, and she knew Vola could have burst away at any time, but she'd waited. The knowledge made Clary both sad and proud.

"How beautiful! They feel like cattail fuzz!" Vola called.

"What?" Clary gazed around, arms and legs tensed for a fall that didn't come. "What's beautiful? I can't..." She could see only black and could feel only air beneath her feet. She dropped to a crouch, every muscle tight, holding hard lest she fall into the abyss. But...but there was nothing to hold on to. Nothing at all. Vola's gails of laughter faded. She was leaving...

Clary opened her eyes, then, *really* opened them. She sobbed aloud, tears streaming down her cheeks, releasing her fear and her sadness and opening herself up in a way that was both painful and healing all at once. She was rent by lightning. She was laid low and thrown high, and *she let go*. Stars were all around, swirling in an ancient contra dance, and Vola danced with them, reaching out to trail her fingers in the starshine. Clary's little girl turned and twirled and leapt and sang and embraced the stars.

It was time. Clary took a shaky step onto the lush velvet sky and hummed along with Vola, adrenaline quivering in her voice. She felt her thighs bunch, responding to a desire she didn't dare examine head-on, because she would completely lose her nerve, and she let her desire loose and jumped as high as she could, stripping away the years of being responsible and shouldering burdens that never needed to be picked up at all. She was a kid once more, screaming "Cannonball!!!" and smashing her little body into the pond, causing fish and turtles and tiny water skaters to tumble around her, making a fountain of sparkling water that reached all the way up to the sky. She was one with the cool water, with the caressing breeze and the glowing sun. She was whole.

Vola was right; starshine did feel like the white fuzz inside a velvety brown cattail.

As she danced and sang and swam in the stars with her daughter, Clary's body lay peacefully on the crooked, dusty floorboards of Granny's girlhood bedroom in the old, crumbling house. The note she'd read, the one that helped her grab hold of her shine, peeked out from her jeans pocket. A whisper of a breeze tugged at it, and the bug-eaten paper tumbled down between cracks in the floor, blowing along to wedge between the studs of a wall that wouldn't be there much longer. It was temporary, like the house. Like time. Clary never would find out who wrote it.

⟫⟩⟩⟩⟩⟨⟨⟨⟨⟨⟪

The whole farm was caught in a spirit walk, and folks outside the spirit-gripped valley could feel it. All around the county, folks shivered involuntarily in the sticky, late-summer morning. One or two old-timers, in their battered armchairs in the old folks' home or sitting in their dim living rooms, took up humming a song that was part hymn learned at their own grandparents' knees and part driving, keening, warbling that rose the hairs on the necks of nurses and younger kinfolk nearby.

Back on the ridge, June wasn't surprised to see his old war companions once more. It was inevitable, really, that he would meet his end with these men who had died next to him—some, by his hand. They boiled toward him like a swirling smoke of rage, their howling starting like a distant hum, becoming louder in his ears. They caught among the blackberry brambles and in the lower branches of the sapling oak nearby, reaching, reaching for him. Vola had banished them. It seemed like years and years ago that she'd cut the cord that tethered June to all his demons. But they came back. He welcomed them. After all, why not? Why not?

Nearby and eons away, Lily embraced her dead brother, and Lacey shivered in the ruined cocoon coat, ashamed and grateful that the ancestors hadn't sucked the life from him completely, caught in the grips of a powerful vision. The thing that had been Boyd lay silent, his skin ripped and bleeding, teeth rotten and grimacing up to the sky.

The ancestors—butterflies and moths in a kaleidoscope of wings—listlessly settled over everything, lighting on Vola's pale hands, Lily's blond ponytail, Gitli's black and white fur, and June's weathered brow. His hat had long tumbled away. Gorgeous wings carpeted the trash in the backyard where Pauline's body lay, and the blackberry brambles, coating old barrels and dirt patches in the yard with undulating colors. Haint-fog still seeped and swirled, spreading through the trees, seeking, seeking the neon color of human life.

The butterflies fluttered up and away as June's war-demons came closer. They reached out their hands and clutched at his shoulders, his hands, his legs, and they pulled him...

To the last door in his mother's old home, its wood busted and its doorknob long since fallen out. It wasn't new for him. The old house was just about used up. June reached out and pushed open the door.

And there was his own sweet Mary, smiling without a lick of guile, just like he remembered her.

"About time, June Whitt," she said, and she stepped forward to kiss him. "You got to go down to Florida."

"Oh, Mary," he said. "My Mary. I messed up."

"I know it," she said, her teeth flashing that fierce grin of hers. "But what else could you do?" June stood with his love in his arms, breathing in the smell of her like memories: the soda shop about a million years ago...sun-warmed laundry...their infant children bundled in her arms.

"You're a man, June Whitt." Mary leaned back to look up into his face. Her expression of gentle reproach was so familiar it almost made him cry. "You're a human person, and that's a critter that's bound to make mistakes. Remember what I always used to say?"

"Burn your bridges when you get there?" He tried on a crooked smile through his tears, thinking she'd bristle with his teasing, as she'd done in life. She cocked her head and nodded thoughtfully.

"You're a-learnin' after all," she said, smoothing his hair back. "Sometimes a bridge needs burning, honey. Sometimes, when you think a wall needs built...what it really needs is bustin'." She kissed him once more, and with a sigh she was gone, and June was someplace else.

It was coming. The haint. Granny felt its loathsome fug seeping, reaching, creeping along toward her from way up high on the ridge. She knew it had friends, other haints coming up out of the ground even now, releasing out into the world, going after Lacey and June, Vola and her friend Lily...she was stretched thin, unable to get through to them up on the ridge, unable to get her old bones out of the bed. Panic came in like a foreboding wind before the storm. What could she do? What could she do, lying abed in this house that was wide open on the inside, where anybody could walk from room to room without having to go outside? The old house was abandoned, had been left behind, an old fortress made obsolete by the slow tide of time. What could Ellie do now?

"It's time to go back now," Vola sighed, glowing with starshine.

Clary knew she was right. "I can see it all, from up here," she said.

Vola nodded. "They've all lost their way." Clary sighed and let herself fall like milk dropped into warm tea, down, down toward her body. The velvety rich sky faded from view. They were once more in the old shell of a house with five ways in. But she could still feel it, as though she somehow wore the night sky: Clary felt the rich night against her skin like a sumptuous cloak.

"Not that way!" Vola was butterflies again and thousands of buzzing, vibrating dragonflies and other wings and tiny feet. She swirled around Clary, nudging her with hundreds of minute bodies. "We have to get to the ridge."

"Well, how else am I supposed to get up there?" Clary was starting to feel the itch of anxiety (*Nothing is going right*) that wasn't entirely her own (*They're coming. Coming for me*).

"Go like me, Mama." Vola's cloud of insects swirled, as though she were pirouetting, before she flew out the glassless windows like a storm.

"Vola! I can't do what you do! I can't do that!" Clary was starting to panic now, and she almost dropped back into her own body on the floor below, when an echo came to her through the house itself: *Use your shine, Clary.*

"My shine." Clary took a breath in, watching her own chest rise and fall on the dusty, gapped floor. "Okay."

She called. She called fireflies and June bugs and cicadas—awkward things that they were. She called carpenter bees and monarch butterflies. And they came to her. She rode them, like dandelion fuzz on the breeze, like a soldier on the charge, like a bombardier broken into hundreds of tiny, buzzing bodies, she flew through woods and over the small livestock pond just visible from the upstairs windows of the house, where Granny lay. She followed Vola up to the southeastern ridge. She didn't know what they would do when they arrived. They had no plan, no *protocol*, but she felt the joyous abandon of running for the sake of running, leaping into the air because it was a thing to be done, and for right now it was enough—flying, sweeping through the air like a childhood fantasy.

Chapter Eighteen

WHAT COULD THE OLD WOMAN once known as Ellie do? Only one thing.

She ran.

Stuck in that bed, all her family up on the ridge or in the old, crumbling house around the bend, Ellie turned tail inside herself and ran. She sensed the haint with her, around her, trying to close her in, trying to lay on her like a shroud of wet fog, trying to hold her, to drag her under, to suck on her youthful heart like a morsel of sweet spun-sugar candy. She ran and she ran, her body twitching in the bed upstairs, the soft sunlight through the curtains indifferent, and inside herself…she ran! The haint pushed her on, reaching, grasping, seeping. With a mighty leap that sent her heart plunging into her stomach, Ellie jumped off the edge of a boulder that jutted from the side of a hill in the wide, northern pasture. She was no longer running in the dark trap of despair; she was back home again, running to the house. The house with five doors to the outside but none between rooms. Her legs were young, strong, marred with blackberry bramble scratches, and tanned from hours of running free. Years and years of worries, of cares, of all the constrictions laid upon her by a world of people who let fear reign—all of it fell away like ill-fitting clothes.

She looked back, a glance like a dagger thrown over her shoulder, tangled hair flying like a banner, and the haint took form for her, an image plucked from her own mind, from the pages of fairy tales chanted to children like spells since the dawn of time. It was a wolf, an exaggerated wolf, with huge teeth and menacing eyes, slobber dripping into its neck fur. With massive paws and muscled haunches, it was so big, and so frightening that she stumbled midstride. It would be on her in a moment. The stumble cost her all the momentum she'd built, so she did the only thing left: Ellie turned and planted both feet strong, and she threw her head back, opened her mouth wide, and laughed out loud.

A false laugh, of course, as fake as Ellie's favorite tin pendant, but the act of it, the sheer audacity of it, confused the wolf, and it shuddered mid-leap, like a film with a flaw in the reel.

"Hah!" she crowed. "HahahahaHAHA!" It was absurd, the laugh of a child's-play pirate, but it felt wonderful! In her aged, bedbound body—it couldn't be her *real* body, for who can tell what a real body is, in times like these?—mirth welled up until it spilled out, faint giggles escaping a wrinkled mouth that grinned with a mischief Granny hadn't felt in far too many years.

It was all real, genuine laughter now; it was too funny, pretending to laugh at a fairy tale wolf! Each "ha!" and chortle and chuckle became an arrow, a buckeye aimed with precision, a cow pie (those were the most effective weapons in a battle like this) that hit the mark, pelting the wolf (the big, bad wolf) until it shrunk and whined and cowered back with uncertainty. Ellie grinned, and she turned once more to run to the house, bounding up the porch steps like a deer. She knew now; she understood: the house with five ways in had been built for this. It wasn't a solemn reason, why her ancestors had made this old place without doors between rooms. It was a silly reason. It was why, when kids play, they can't touch the living room rug—because it runs with molten lava! It was why "safe" in tag was unduly complicated, why each and every game where somebody can crow "I win!" has a multitude of rules, of slide-arounds, of bases to touch and ritual dances to shimmy out.

Swapping names for "In the White Daisies," telling tales on Foolish Jack, climbing trees ever higher...the rules of childhood games are baffling and overly complicated, and each new addition adds a thrill, and nobody ever really wins, not really.

But there is a clear loser: haints can't survive those pure, unadulterated expressions of whimsy.

All through the years of Granny's childhood: passing tiny notes to her brother through cracks in the plasterless walls, contriving knock codes, skipping porch boards as she flitted out one door and bounded into another. Treasure hunts, hide-and-seek, all of it: the perfect weapon against sadness and despair, against indifference and rage and meanness. Ellie Whitt was beginning to understand something. Outsmarting the haints was never about logic. It was never about killing people, not until the last possible resort.

Ellie looked back again and saw a skinny, cowering coyote. The kind of varmint that was only ever dangerous if it sensed weakness. She spared it only a glance before she ran around the corner of the house, then ran around another, and then circled back on tip-toes to slip inside. She waited in the gloom of the kitchen, glass chimneys of freshly polished kerosene lanterns glinting on the mantel. Herbs hung in bunches to dry. She heard it out there, the haint, its paws whispering through the grass, as it softly whimpered and growled. And then she didn't hear anything. She opened the door cautiously, seeing only bright sunshine and green, waving fields of hay almost ready to be cut, and the tall, deep woods on the ridge beyond. It was all gorgeous, as though the scenes of her youth had been cut into stained glass. Ellie opened the door a little further and crept out onto the porch. She kept a keen eye on the grass in the yard, on the patch of blackberry brambles just out of reach of the porch, and she saw what she was looking for.

A rabbit, sitting meekly in the shade of the blackberry brambles. Ellie grinned and leapt into the grass. She kept her eyes on the rabbit, pinning it with her stare, and she caught it—but not before it bucked once in her hands, jerking her arms into the brambles. She kept hold of the thing, though, and shook her head ruefully at the long bramble-scratch on her arm. *Haints'll still get you.* Pain...it was a constant possibility, a companion of living. A companion of happiness and joy, really. Back in bed, Granny's wrinkled arm bore the long, red scratch, too. A blood sacrifice, after all.

The fire was easy to make in this place. The work of a thought. Ellie skinned the rabbit and cooked it and ate it. She did it in the yard, not the house, and while she ate and sang and danced, the stars wheeled overhead, and the sun took its place once more. Time was a game, after all, with obscure rules and rivers of hidden lava. Even the "safe base" really wasn't, if time was your playmate.

⇒⇒⇒⇒⟨⟨⟨⟨

Lacey lay in the dirt of the battlefield on the ridge, his eyes wide and staring, but only one of them seeing. The world around him faded into nothing as the spirit world—the world of the blue butterfly—took him under. Swarming sparks from a fire, branches collapsing deep in its heart as they burned to cinder. Fireflies dancing their own swirling tribute to the night. People dancing around the fire—people, yet not-people, with heads of coyote and buffalo and even the moon woman. He was one of them, dancing, and he looked up into the black velvet sky with fiery stars laughing down, and he fell into them. They brushed against him; they felt like (*cattail fluff!*), and he saw the haints.

They chased young ones, followed them along paths wending through the forests, and tried to surprise them at the edge of cliffs, where they climbed for the joy of it. Haints had taken more tribespeople after First Star had pushed the point of his stick through Bugling Elk's eye. Always it was the same; always people were taken, and they grew sick with soul rot. They hurt and they stole and they hungered for skins. Eventually, they were killed to protect the others living in the valley.

But First Star wondered if killing was the right action. He wondered, as he grew tall and sturdy, as his rounded baby belly muscled and his legs became fast and strong. He listened to the trees and the elk—especially the

190

elk because they spoke with the whispers of his dead brother, who was named for them. He listened to turkey and the winds and the fish in the creek. He took their counsel, as he was not convinced his people should kill when one of them was haint-ridden. Bugling Elk was with him, always, with the sadness that came from regret, and because he wished his brother was still alive, he always wondered if there could have been a way. There must be a way, must be *some way* to push the haint out, like a fever, to help people heal, as from a deep heartache.

Of course, not everyone who became infected could survive the haint. For some, it was simply too much. Like childbirth was too much for some young mothers, like poison from a plant could take a child. But for others... might they not survive being haint-ridden? Might someone who was strong enough push the haint out, somehow?

Haints grew bold and feasted on despair; First Star knew that. Haints lusted after human emotion. They craved joy and happiness, but after they sucked those emotions away, like a sweet treat, like the ripe berries of summer, what was left was deep despair. What if a person's joy was stronger than despair? What if the haint could drink and drink until its belly burst and never reach the bottom?

But how to test this strategy?

First Star would have to find a haint to take him. It was the only way. He began to seek the darkest caves, the new sinkholes, and the small valleys that seemed to repel sunshine, even when the sun was highest. The other villagers thought he was crazy. Touched. He'd killed the haint who took his brother, after all. And at such a young age. They respected his craziness.

Eventually, First Star found a haint, a dark, seeping thing lurking in the hollow of a log. He crept toward it, but as he moved past the log's broken stump, a ripple of light caught his gaze. He leaned over the jagged, punky bowl of the rotten stump, filled with water from the last rain and squirming, flicking mosquito larvae. What he saw looking back at him was not his usual reflection: long, black hair and skin brownish-red like clay. He saw a man with one ruined eye: a spirit-world eye, under a shock of yellow hair. First Star froze like a great, startled cat, unsure of the man in the water—was he a malicious god? Another manifestation of haint? He passed a hand over the stump, and the man's hand mirrored his own. He nodded, and the man nodded, too.

As Lacey realized it was his own face reflected in the water, First Star received the knowledge. A descendant, then. Seeing with First Star's eyes, Lacey had come to watch him defeat the haint. Revelations crashed into First Star: if he had descendants, if the man with the spirit-world eye came back to witness, then it meant First Star would be victorious. He grinned the fierce grin of a warrior who could not lose, and Lacey's face grinned back at him. Together, they turned toward the lurking haint.

It was unused to being hunted. Unsuspecting, eagerly, the haint came to First Star/Lacey.

They took it in, breathing deeply, embracing it.

At first, it was suffocating: First Star and Lacey felt their confidence, their assuredness ebbing away as the haint fed upon them. Tears leaked from their eyes; how could they have ever thought they'd be victorious? No human being could fight terrible sadness. Nobody could defeat despair. Happiness was a waning thing, sparking bright in childhood and leaking away as the hardships of life marched on and on.

First Star took a shuddering breath.

He whooped.

It was a sad, pitiful sound at first, and he thought, *Any warrior would be ashamed of such a weak war cry*. He breathed in, deeper, and whooped again. It was better. He stood on trembling legs and began to trot through the trees, singing softly.

The haint quailed.

First Star grinned once more. He ran faster. Sang harder. Leapt over logs and rolled down grassy hills. Filled his lungs with sweet air and yipped like a mad coyote. Sang the dove songs, howled the wolf calls, danced and danced, and ran again. The haint inside tried to get free. This was too much, this joy; it was too strong for it, and it struggled, a cornered animal, all claws and teeth and snarls, and First Star reached inside himself to grip it, this pitiful thing, this sad and cowardly predator, and he ripped it apart.

⟫⟫⟩⟨⟨⟨⟨

Lacey gasped as though he'd been doused in ice water. He was lying in the dirt once more. The blue butterfly launched into the air, fluttering fiercely on glimmering wings.

Joy. That was the answer. Lacey rolled to his side and pushed himself out of the dirt, standing on wobbling legs. He started to shuffle-dance, to sing softly, thinking of joy, calling it to him: a wide-mouthed animal, ready to gobble up the haints that now seeped up from the cracks in things, from the discarded jugs and splintered crates, from the mouth of the cool, dark cave where Lily and Vola had turned over rocks for crawdads, from the dark hollows and downed trees, and from the undersides of boulders cresting from the earth like great whales frozen in time. The ancestral butterflies responded, fluttering wings and taking to the air once more, dancing to Lacey's song.

But pain smeared over his vision, and he couldn't see joy. He stumbled, his bruised head dizzy, his aching body unable to dance. He lay in the dirt once more and keened in frustration. He sank back into himself, feeling unable...just unable. The butterflies drifted down listlessly once more.

⟫⟫⟩⟨⟨⟨⟨

Jayne Watson's face was puffy and pale from crying. She sat quietly in the kitchen, cradling a cooling cup of coffee in her hands. Her thoughts fractured like light on water. Jayne sank into the jumbled, shadowy mess of her mind, into the state she was so used to...into sadness, like a shroud that hid her away from the world.

A jarring noise that may have been a scream pierced the lightening shadows in the kitchen of a house that didn't feel like home, and Jayne startled, knocking cold coffee all over the kitchen table. She swore, looking around her with clear eyes. The house looked like hell. She was certain she looked like hell. In Florida—in her old life, back in time, when her family was still intact—she'd never have let herself go like this. She stood to wet a dishcloth and wipe up her spill but stopped cold when she heard it again: an animal sound of grief so deep she wasn't sure if it was sound or elemental feeling. She understood that grief. It called her. She suddenly wasn't sure if Lily was upstairs in her room, wasn't sure at all, and she hurried through the house to check.

The twisted sheets on the floor left no room for doubt; Lily was nowhere in her room and nowhere in the house. Jayne called out for her daughter, knowing she wouldn't get an answer, and in her mind she saw Lily's face alongside Conner's, dead in a ditch in the Florida sun.

Without thought, without planning, Jayne left the house and ran through the woods in her coffee-stained pajamas, calling out for her children. Thin branches whipped at her and burrs caught in her hair, once perfectly permed and cared for, now wild and frizzy.

"Lily!" she cried, her voice cracking. "Conner!" She was startled to hear sobbing. Even in her hysteria, the deep, wracking cries surprised her into stopping, leaning against a tree, and looking around to see who was crying... it was her. Jayne herself was making those ugly noises, wrung out of her by spasms in her diaphragm, hitting her hard enough to take her breath until she could suck in air to fuel the next round of paralyzing sobs.

She might have collapsed completely then, but she saw June Whitt lying on the ground. He looked familiar, though she didn't really know him. She thought he was her neighbor. And he seemed to be covered in butterflies. The sight—beautiful, yet eerie—shocked her out of herself.

"H...hey!" she croaked, still gasping. "Hey! You...you okay?" She wondered briefly if he was a hallucination. She chucked a small pinecone she hadn't realized she'd been clutching—she'd picked it up while stumbling around these woods. If he was a hallucination, he'd just dissipate when the thing hit him, right? Or was that ghosts? The pinecone didn't go anywhere near June, but the absurdity of Jayne chucking things at old men lying in the woods seemed to bring her back to some kind of logic. She wiped at her face, bringing the neck of her pajama shirt up to do it, like a small child might, and picked her way toward June. She was barefoot, she realized, and her feet were terribly scratched up—would probably be pretty sore tomorrow.

"Hey!" she called again, before the absurdly gruesome scene that was the Byrnes' backyard opened up in front of her and seemed to reenact her very worst nightmares: there was Lily, dead on the ground, with a girl—Lily's friend, Vola—collapsed and bleeding over her. A dog lying nearby. And a dead woman, and a dead…corpse…he was too horrifying to recognize as something that was once human. Jayne forgot all about June and ran the last few feet to her daughter's side, and as she reached out to touch her, she had two thoughts before her world washed away in gray.

This is exactly why they tell you in First Aid not to run in when people are lying passed out…you don't know if there's poison gas or something, and that's what this is, and now I've got the poison gas…

and

…there are butterflies everywhere, all over the people. I hope the poison doesn't kill them…too.

Jayne found herself in a completely colorless version of their old neighborhood in Florida, standing in front of the sign that announced the subdivision to passersby on the highway. *Shady Oaks.* Her husband—soon to be ex, as she thought when he came to mind—had some kind of quip about the name of the place. She shook her head, disoriented. She turned, almost against her will, toward the place she knew she'd see her dead son, lying in the ditch.

Mary had let June go, had turned him around and pushed him back through the doorway into this gray place, and she'd sent knowledge with him.

Mary had always known what was most powerful. She, with a headful of memories that would make strong men quail: her hellfire spitting daddy, beating her and her brother and her mama most of their lives. Feeling like a caged animal with no way out. But never giving up on hope or losing that fire, that fierce hold on the idea that life could be good, that she could figure a way to make it good. Mary knew what a precious thing joy was and how to make it and how to keep it stoked inside like a pilot light.

"That's how we'll beat the haints," June murmured, looking around with some curiosity. He must be in Florida; that's what Mary had said. It was a mighty gray place, this dream. It would be hard going, sparking up joy here. June set off down the road, trusting his feet to take him where he was needed. Mary had set this in motion, and she was his compass—even though she was dead. June saw Jayne Watson ahead, saw the two young 'uns in the ditch.

That's your new neighbor, Mary whispered to him. *That's her boy, lying dead. And that's Vola's little friend. Help her. Help Jayne find her way.* June nodded.

"Let's go," he said.

⇒⟩⟩⟩⟩⟩⟨⟨⟨⟨⟨⟨⟵

Jayne took a few steps, but before she could get much closer to that terrible ditch, a man called out to her, walking along the centerline of the highway, wearing a battered work hat and jeans. But, curiously, no work boots. She'd expect work boots on a man like that. He was barefoot.

"Mrs. Watson!" It came out sounding like "Mizruz Watson." He waved to her, striding purposefully, going right by the scene of her son's death, where he lay now...and what was that in the ditch next to him? Lily? But the man took her attention once more.

"Mrs. Watson." Now he was next to her, holding her elbow and holding her eyes with his.

196

"That's...those are my kids," she said, pointing at the bodies lying in the ditch. He nodded.

"They're dead. Both dead, now," she shuddered, a tear sliding down her cheek.

"No, Mrs. Watson."

"Alive? Conner...?" But the man shook his head again.

"Your boy is still dead, but Lily is alive. She needs you. We all need you." The last part made not a bit of sense to Jayne, but she knew he was right, knew Lily was alive, in the ditch next to Conner's body. Jayne knew it with absolute certainty because this was a dream, right? And you can know things with certainty in dreams. You can also be confused, all at the same time.

"Mrs. Watson," the man said, taking her attention once more. "We need your joy." The wind seemed to sigh through the live oaks all around, disturbing the Spanish moss hanging like beards.

"Who are you?" Jayne asked, wondering who could have the audacity to ask such a ridiculously impossible emotion of her, especially if he knew about her dead boy and her daughter there in the ditch. It was obscene, using a word like "joy" with her now.

"I'm your neighbor, June Whitt." He looked for a moment like he might stick his hand out to shake but gave a rueful quirk of his mouth instead.

"Okay."

"We got ourselves a fight back home," June said, searching her face. "And we need...well, we need joy. That's our best chance against the haints."

"I...," she shook her head. Had he said *haints*? What was that? She shook her head again and took a shuddering breath, reaching up and clutching at her hair with both hands in a way that was unabashedly childlike. "I don't have any left. It's gone. It died with Conner. How can I..." but she didn't know how to finish, didn't know what it was she wanted to ask.

⪥⪥⪥⪤⪤⪤

Away, where Jayne lay in the Tennessee woods, butterflies drifted through the fog to settle on her hair and her hands, where they lay, still reaching toward Lily. The butterflies delicately stepped across Jayne's eyelids. The ancestors did what they always do: they made the space between here and there much different. They hopped along the coils of the spiral of time, each delicate beat of dusted wing starting a wind inside them, inside everyone caught in the haint fog.

Conner.

Conner, his baby-fine hair plastered to his forehead, sun sparkling on the water drops clinging to his face as he crowed with laughter, crouching to spring into the swimming pool. Conner and Lily giggling in the backseat of the car, trying to keep their voices down (and failing miserably), so Jayne wouldn't yell at them for telling fart jokes again. Conner, learning to walk, his stubby legs stomping, chubby face jutting out so he looked like a little Franken-baby.

Jayne was full with him, with her baby boy who would never grow to be a teenager, never get acne and crash their car, never take a girl on a date. He would never grow to be a man. There was no room for anything else, not for Jayne. On the ridge, haint-fog settled over her, and she shivered in the chill in the colorless Florida deep in her mind.

This man, this...Whitt. He stood impassively, watching her in her grief, and she felt suddenly annoyed. It was intimate, this grief, and it belonged to her, and here he was *watching* her.

"Do you mind?" she sniffled. Her words sounded more pathetic than acerbic. He didn't answer, just started humming. Very lightly, almost without melody. Jayne took a step back, affronted. This was weird, even for a... well, a dream. Or whatever.

"I can't do this." She crossed her arms, wanting to wake up, now. "I can't be here. I've got..." but she couldn't remember what she had to leave this place for. There was something...something important Jayne needed to take care of, she was certain of that, but she also wanted to lay down here and stop... everything. The Whitt man kept humming.

"Please stop." Jayne took another step back. He didn't stop.

"Please." She was whispering now. "Please." Still, he kept on humming, now swaying ever so slightly, as though he were made of the Spanish moss above his head in the breeze. It was too much; he was too much, and she made as though to push him, but when she did, she remembered again. There was a girl. Her daughter. Her first-born. Jayne couldn't abandon Lily, even if she couldn't save Conner.

Jayne shuddered, and she said, "I don't have any joy left, Mr. Whitt."

"Then," he said, "I reckon we need your hope." Sobbing again, the kind of wracking, hopeless dream-crying that pierced through to waking, Jayne searched his face. He pulled her to his chest and hugged her, and she let him. When she pulled away, he nodded at what he saw in her eyes. She crossed her arms under her breasts and walked away from him, toward Conner and Lily in the ditch, dreading what she would see. But facing it anyway.

Jayne fell to her knees by her daughter and stroked her hair. When Lily didn't turn, didn't move, Jayne lay down behind her and slipped one arm under her daughter's head, one arm over her chest, and Jayne held her tight there in the ditch, pressing her face into Lily's hair.

Behind her, on the blacktop, the man started to shuffle-dance. He sang softly—some kind of Indian song, sounded like. Jayne really didn't know. But she felt a faint hum in the earth below her, and she breathed deeply, taking in the scent of dried sweat and strawberry shampoo from Lily's hair. She let out her breath and with it, took up a hum that went right along with the man's song. It wasn't the same, not the same murmured sounds or the same rhythm, but it seemed to weave along with it the way cricket song will weave along with cicadas and tree frogs and owls calling dolefully to each other in the night.

Chapter Nineteen

WHEN VOLA AND CLARY ARRIVED at the southeastern border, it seemed too late. The morning sun had risen higher, breaking free of the tops of the tall trees, but the mist was growing thicker. It was creeping to this place, seeping along the ground and through the undergrowth, rolling over people and rubble and plants until the edges of everything were blurry. It should have been bright, this late in the morning, but the heavy, wet fog sucked the light away. The haint-fog. Clary and Vola swirled with tiny wings closer to the ground, finding June and Lacey, the poor lost Byrne souls, their bodies just lumps now that their light had gone out. And there was Lily, Vola, and Jayne Watson, too, and Gitli lying there.

"Vola," Clary said, her voice made of the feel of soft moss, "you're shot." It was hard to feel upset about that; Vola's insect cloud was dancing around her in pure energy, meddling with droplets of fog just to aggravate the haints. It was like Clary *should* feel panic, but she couldn't quite muster it.

"Yes, Mama," Vola said. "The lady there did it." If Clary could have shaken a head, she would have. Instead, she lit with hundreds of tiny feet on leaves and trash strewn in the yard and gazed around at a world that would have been familiar if it hadn't been so gorgeous: green, living things exhaling breath so clean it was intoxicating, light sparkling on dew-heavy wildflowers hidden in the tiny folds between fallen leaves. All these people—her people and the neighbors, slumbering deep inside themselves, their colors muted and murky. And then, like motes of dust sparkling in rays of sunshine...

"There are the ancestors," Clary said. In her hundreds of insect eyes, the ancestors didn't look at all like butterflies; they were light, every one of them was a point of light fallen from the sky full of stars. But why weren't they fighting the haints? And why were there so many? In all of Clary's visits to the archives and all the visions from past Whitt shamans, she hadn't seen anything like this.

"They're coming from everywhere," said Vola. "The whole boundary is broken. Haints are everywhere. But...why are they coming here?"

"To feed. To feed on all of us." Clary felt the chill of haints, the bright sparks of the ancestors. The sleeping, dull glow of people. They were at an uneasy intermission, an impasse up here at the broken boundary. Haints weren't trying to eat the people here. It was like they were sizing up their new freedom, sniffing out the world above their years-long prison in the dark below. In a flash of intuition, Clary knew the haints hadn't eaten the people here—her people—because the ancestors had taken them all down deep, down into a spirit walk, where haints couldn't smell them so sharply. But they would figure it out. Would follow along the threads of the dreams, eventually. What could Clary do? What were they going to *do*?

Vola broke into her thoughts, her voice like the fuzzy points of wooly worm fur. "No, I mean...there are people all over this county. All over the *world*. Why are the haints coming here? I would think...well, shouldn't they all spread out, looking for folks to suck dry?"

"Vola. You're right!" Clary looked again, and she saw the patterns in the fog, the slow swirl with the junk-strewn yard at its center. "We're calling them to us! Grandpa June and Lily and Lacey and all of us. But why?" She cast her mind back to the visions in the archives, the stories...they'd killed the haint-infested. Every time a Whitt had needed to cast the haints away, they'd killed flesh to do it...and in every story Clary had seen, there had only been one haint, maybe two. Once, Granny's brother had had to vanquish four haints inside a passel of moonshiners...but never, not anywhere Clary could find, had there been so many haints at once. This was a...a natural disaster. A tsunami of haints. It was so big it was hard to know where to look!

What were they supposed to do? What *could* they do? Oh, how she wished her grandmother was here with her. But Clary sensed this was beyond even the wise Ellie Whitt, and Clary was on her own. She looked at her poor, battered brother lying in the dirt and tasted the color of his visions... Were they supposed to sacrifice themselves somehow? Clary rebelled against this idea; she was too full of life, especially since she'd seen the stars, touched their delicate fuzz, and danced among them with her daughter.

She recognized something about this—it was a warrior's feeling, this rebellion against defeat, against laying down and allowing the enemy to take her life, her...her *victory*. Clary felt more alive than ever, and she wasn't about to sacrifice herself. Wasn't going to lose her family, her daughter. No. She'd go in and penetrate this repugnant haint-fog, this misery incarnate, and she'd beat it.

"Vola!" she cried. "Go get Lily!" Clary approached the ancestors, called them to her, and they embraced her with sparks of light. She was sucked into the colorless void of the haint-fog.

⁓≫≫≫⋘⋘⋘⁓

Clary saw Lacey right away, lying on his back in the dimness, eyes squeezed shut.

"Hey!" she called, running to him. He opened his eyes to see her, which was a relief—until she caught a glimpse of his bad eye. It was no longer a lump of creek clay, misshapen in the socket. It was...it was made of light. As she drew closer, Clary could see things swirling in the depths, and she was entranced, falling, hypnotized...

Lacey yelped and clapped a hand over the eye. "Don't look at it, sister."

"Okay." Clary pressed her hands to her own eyes, trying to come back to herself. "Lacey, it's a spirit eye."

"Well, yeah. I told you that when we was kids."

"You did," Clary shook her head. She'd never believed him. "Come on, Lacey. We've got work to do." But he just lay there, with a look on his face Clary had never seen before. She was shocked to recognize it. Defeat.

"What's the matter with you?" She punched her brother's shoulder. "Get up, Lacey! We have to figure out how to defeat the haints because I'm not going down."

"Without a fight?" Lacey gave a ghostly quirk of a grin.

"No. Not without a fight. Not at all." Her fierceness surprised him. It was so much like their mother, that determination. He hadn't seen it in years, and it acted like a tonic for him.

"Clary," he said, struggling to sit up. "Clary. We need joy. We need joy to defeat the haints. We need to fill them up with it, give them all the human joy we can pour in, and then give them more."

"Isn't that what they want?"

"Yes. It is."

"Oh!" She saw it, then. She saw how it could work. "Yes!" Clary tugged Lacey's arm. "Let's go!"

But he shook his head, and he buried his face in his arms and started to rock side to side.

"What's the matter with you, brother?"

"I can't get up, Clary. I'm so tired. I fell down the ridge, and I'm all busted up, and my head aches so..."

"You idiot." Clary's voice was fat with affection. "You don't have your body here. Get up." Lacey raised his head, and Clary had to hastily look away from his hypnotizing spirit eye.

"Oh," he said.

"You're right," he said.

And he got up from the ground that wasn't really ground, and he gave a rueful chuckle, scratching his unkempt hair like he always did when he felt foolish. He extended his hand to Clary, and she leapt up to join him.

"You're different," Lacey said, appraising her. "You've got starlight all over you. Like dandelion fuzz, or...or like the insides of cattails!"

She didn't answer, just grinned and started to dance a goofy dance and sing out loud, and Lacey couldn't help but join in. They were kids again, barefooted young 'uns running through the trees, feet always landing safely, just shy of sharp rocks and jagged, broken hickory nuts, safe as though the land itself wanted them there. They whooped together, daring each other to leap further, to run faster, to climb and to fly higher.

"C'mon!" Clary called. "Sing Aerosmith with me!"

In the haint-fog on the southeastern ridge, in the dirty backyard of the Byrne property, Lacey's tired body splayed wide, a smile on his dirty, bruised face. And fireflies, dragonflies, June bugs, mosquito hawks, midges, and honeybees and, of course, butterflies all danced around him in a reel as ancient and bright as the sunlight that made its way through the fog droplets to dance along with Lacey and Clary.

"It's working! It's working!" Clary cried out, giggling and breathless. The fog came in, closing over them like the pond over their heads, but Lacey and Clary knew better than to despair. They called it. They called the haints, pulled them in, and fed them on sweet-rich giggles and reckless daring, on the invincible feeling of childhood. And the haints came and gorged. Brother and sister continued to dance, to leap, to sing and call out laughter as musical as a song...but then, Lacey stumbled. Clary paused and turned back to help him up again.

"Something's wrong," he said, smile slipping and breathing hard. "They're getting stronger, Clary. But the joy...it should bust them. Something's wrong." Clary gazed around, her own breath ragged in her chest. Lacey was right. Something was wrong.

"Vola," Clary said.

━⟫⟫⟫━⟪⟪⟪━

Vola couldn't find Lily. She searched the memories of all the places they'd been: the woods, where Vola had shown Lily how to call the wild violets to open up, the sunny, dusty loft where kittens mewed, and the mother cat answered back in musical purrs. The creek, where they caught crawdads. She tried everywhere. Each time she thought of a new place to look, she'd pounce like a kid playing hide-and-seek, feeling that jittery excitement that came with routing a playmate from their hiding place...but Lily wasn't there. She wasn't anywhere. Vola tried to focus, tried to call out to that bubbling friendship that bound them, but Lily was simply...absent.

And then, she thought about Grandpa June's demons. About how he went, shaking and resisting, into that dark place—that place deep inside himself where he nurtured the ghosts of his past, where he gave them all the guilt and sadness and regret they needed to thrive, before Vola had shown him how to stop it. How had she done that? It was like breathing; when she started to pay attention to it, it seemed strange and unknowable. But, here: when Vola held her grandfather's darkness in her mind, along with Lily, right there next to it...yes, there was a kind of path.

"Oh, no," she said. She thought she knew where Lily had gone. Vola turned down a corridor that smelled of afternoon thunderstorms and heat so thick it felt like a creature curled up around you. There was long, curly moss hanging from big, spread-out trees and a sparkling, waving geometry of light (*it was the way their pool water reflected against the roof over their patio in the afternoon*). The rush of knowledge of these things made Vola hopeful: Lily's memories, at least some of them, were open to her. She could still be found. Still be reached.

Moving faster now, Vola called out to Lily: "Where are you! Lily, come here!" But there was no answer. Vola turned around and around and saw that she was in Lily's old neighborhood, back in Florida, and even though it wasn't her physical body in this place, she felt a chill. She knew where Lily was.

Once she thought it, Vola couldn't help it: she made her way to the entrance to the neighborhood, where the blacktop highway and its fast cars ran by like a river, unmindful of the houses and the people inside. There was the ditch; there were two bodies lying in it, impossibly small under the colorless sky. Vola crouched next to Lily and shook her shoulder. Pushed her friend's hair—come loose from her ponytail—out of her face. She tried to pull Lily's arms away from Conner's body...but she couldn't. Through it all, Lily never moved. Never looked at Vola, never did anything but sigh and shift closer to her dead brother, as though she were settling down into a long sleep. Vola tried harder to pull Lily's arms, to get her to see *her,* but she just... couldn't. It wasn't that Lily fought, or that she was heavy. Vola couldn't get a grip. Couldn't make a difference.

"But I helped Grandpa," she said, sitting back in the gray grass, looking around. The world was utterly silent, all grays and dirty khaki. Neither light nor dark. "How could I do that? I helped him set his demons free."

A breeze started to blow. The Spanish moss drifted in the trees, and Vola heard something...a shuffling on the blacktop and soft humming. A shadow drifted over her, and she shivered. A soft warning sounded somewhere in the back of her mind. *Something's creeping after me.* She thought about Granny's old house, the five doors...and she shook her head. *I need to focus.* Of course, something was after her. Something was after all of them. Absently, Vola rubbed at her shoulder: whole here, in this pale dream, but shattered and throbbing back in her flesh. The shadow passed, and Vola put it out of her mind. It wasn't the time to get distracted.

She looked down again, and there was a dim shape there with Lily, holding her just as Lily held Conner. Vola hadn't noticed before. *Mrs. Watson! Lily's Mom!* Like a picture book Vola's mama used to show her when she was little, with paper layers that laid down, each over the last, to add more critters to the scene: Vola saw more of this shared dream. There was Grandpa

June, dancing and singing on the highway. He caught her eye and smiled. She recognized the look: optimism and grim determination. It was how he looked when he faced something difficult, but he'd already decided he would win. He wore it when he was pulling calves, when the mother cow was too exhausted to help, and the baby might otherwise be lost. But he always saved the calves, and he always saved the mother cow.

"I wanted to let them go, Vola," Grandpa said, still dancing, dipping his shoulders down one after the other. He sang, and he spoke to her at the same time because in this place he could do that. "My own ghosts. You helped me because deep down, I really wanted you to."

Lily lay deathly still, her limp acceptance more maddening than her struggling against Vola could have ever been.

"And she doesn't want me to help her?" Vola asked.

"She's been touched by haints, honey. More deeply than the rest of us because she was all alone when it happened. Without the ancestors. Without you." He grinned, as though showing Vola there was a trick to all this. A twist to the puzzle that revealed how the curved metal nails came apart, like at the Cracker Barrel. How the game could be won, if you just quit trying so hard. She blew out a noise in frustration.

"Then, what? We just let her go because she doesn't want help? Grandpa, she's...she's my only friend."

"Well, now," Grandpa danced a little harder. He turned and he stepped, flung his arms wide, and the asphalt beneath his bare feet darkened each time he stomped. The little bit of Spanish moss over his head flushed a deeper shade of gray, and there...there was an acid-green lizard, darting along the live oak branch.

"Well, now!" He shouted aloud, chortling blue into the sky and white into the billowing clouds. "What are friends for?" It was cryptic, and it was darned irritating...and suddenly, like color creeping into this dream world, the knowledge came. Vola thought she knew what he was getting at.

⇢⟫⟫⟩ ⟨⟨⟪⟪⇠

The haint circled around Vola. Vola...such a sweet prize, so full of life. There had been a path, a kind of hole in the boundaries between places, and the haint had slipped into it after the sweet perfume of sunshine and sweat, of youth and happiness that trailed after the girl. It recognized her

The giggle

The root

Follow the giggle-the root-the wisp

from the cedar roots Vola'd sung into the deep earth. She was so sweet, this child, and she was worried. Hurting. Yes, hurting deeply, somewhere, but hopeful in spite of that...it was intoxicating. Irresistible. The haint circled and circled, followed, reaching itself, its unshaped fog of malice, almost—almost touching the girl, but not quite. It wasn't time yet. But she wasn't running. She didn't know the danger.

Not yet.

There would be time soon, to take the girl, to eat her heart, to suck out her giggles and whispers like juicy marrow. The haint had waited for years and years. It could wait more. Then it would wear her skin.

⇢⟫⟫⟩ ⟨⟨⟪⟪⇠

All summer, the two girls had laughed and played together in that peculiar borderland between little girlhood and adolescence, and they held each other's secrets close. They giggled and they sighed over hopes and dreams. But Vola thought of every time Lily flipped her ponytail away from her shoulder and crossed her arms, feigning anger when she didn't get her way. She thought of Lily stomping off up the trail, away from the quiet place they'd made together, their own special place in the woods. Shattering their peace for the sake of a tantrum. Dadburn-it, that girl could irritate the fire out of Vola!

Vola got herself worked up, thinking about it. If Lily wouldn't see that Vola was trying to be her *friend*, trying to *help*, then by gum, Vola would get to her another way. She leaned over her friend's face and blew in it. When Lily didn't move, Vola blew in her face again, imagining her friend pretending to sleep in the dewy predawn, out in the yard. She reached out and took a strand of Lily's blond ponytail and tickled her under the nose. *Was that...?* Vola thought it was: the slightest twitch, a ghost of irritation passing over Lily's brow. Vola grinned triumphantly and kept tickling Lily with her own hair.

⋙⋙⋙ ⋘⋘⋘

Somewhere deep inside, Lily was chafing. She'd been drifting, holding tight with Conner, ready to sink down, down with him. She didn't know where she was, didn't care enough to wonder. It had been blissful in its way: feeling nothing at all, after wave upon wave of crushing sadness had pushed her under, pushed her here, where she could simply drift with her dead brother. It didn't bother her, to remember he was dead; she'd join him soon enough. And that was fine. It wasn't good or bad; it just...it just was.

But something was poking at her. Something tickled her and made her aware, and she didn't want that. Awareness brought pain, and Lily most definitely didn't want it.

But it wouldn't stop, the annoyance, and Lily tried hard to go deeper, to escape the tickle, that giggle that seemed to get to her even in this floating, blissful nothing. It was like a dream just before waking: you tried and tried to grasp it, but it ran through the fingers like sand in the receding tide and waking happened anyway. That was it: the harder she tried to stay here, stay drifting in this place darker than sleep, the more she came awake. And there was something else...something that had followed this fresh irritation, and it was dark. It was clammy and unwelcome and vaguely terrifying in the way something squishy felt on your feet in a murky pond. Lily tried to turn away from all of it.

209

"Come on…," Vola whispered, "come on, you city slicker. You darned prissy girl! You, you…" She tried to think of insults for her friend, but all she had were country bumpkin at best. They sounded silly in her own ears. But that was all right, she reckoned; silly was fine. Sometimes silly insults rubbed even worse because they were funny even while they were hurtful. "You little preppy!" It was something she'd gotten from Lily herself, describing the social hierarchy in the schools back home. A prep was uptight, clean-cut, and snobby. Even someone who probably really was preppy didn't like to be called one.

Sure enough, Lily grimaced, and her eyes opened—just a slit, but enough to make Vola crow in victory.

Mrs. Watson watched all of this with a bemused expression, arms still wrapped around her daughter, slightly appalled at how callously this little hill-child reached over Conner's dead body to tease at her obviously damaged, obviously grieving daughter. But since none of this made sense—the old man who looked like a farmer and danced like an Indian scraping and tapping out a rhythm on the highway, Jayne lying in a ditch with her two children, this dream world that was devoid of color—she supposed she'd let Vola do what she would. Jayne kept on humming, nonsensically, and it wove along with June's call, and it worked into Vola's teasing, and she felt the vibration of the thing deep inside her, inside her very cells. Idly, she thought about something she'd read years and years ago, maybe in an old *National Geographic* or something, about soldiers marching across bridges…in Roman times, maybe? And when they did, they had to march out of step because if they marched all together, it would set up a vibration, and the bridge would start to ripple, and the whole thing would…

"Collapse. Just fall apart," Jayne whispered into Lily's hair. Jayne raised her eyes to meet Vola's, and when she did, Lily pushed her friend's hand away.

"Stop it!" Lily said, and when she spoke, she opened her eyes. Jayne kept singing along with June's life-song, and suddenly their whole world flamed into color so vibrant it hurt. It kept getting brighter and brighter until the dream-world built by sadness, with its pitiful simulacrum of Conner's dead body as the crux, burst apart in a flurry of sparkling blue and white and yellow and fiery orange-and-black stripes and iridescence.

And they were back on the ridge.

A cloud of winged bugs lifted and made its way off through the trees. There were still plenty more here, mostly butterflies, from what Jayne could see, and she was vaguely glad those beautiful creatures had survived this... whatever had happened here. People stirred and sat up. There was a one-eyed man over on the other side of a stained mattress propped up against some old barrels. His hair stood up in curls and spikes, and he held his head as though it ached fiercely. There was June Whitt, over in the trees, rolling onto his hands and knees before pushing himself up. There was Lily, stirring under Vola's body, feebly wiggling.

"Get off!" she screeched, and she pushed Vola into the dirt next to her. She expected Vola to fight back, to tease, to go on letting Lily be mad that she'd been so rudely pulled back into the sharpness of reality. But something was wrong. Vola lay in the dirt, unmoving, her face slack. Lily sucked in a breath at the sight of all the blood—on her friend, on her own shirt.

"Mom!" she cried, "Mom! Is Vola dead? She's dead!" Lily trembled, trying to turn her friend over onto her back. Jayne, still disoriented, crawled the few feet over to where her daughter struggled. The black-and-white dog came, too, on unsteady legs. Jayne reached out to touch the girl, and she knew, somehow. Knew that Vola wasn't dead, but something else was going on. The dog—Gitli, Jayne was sure Lily had told her that was its name—licked at Vola's face, whining.

"Hey!" Jayne called. "Mr. Whitt! The girl, she...come over here, Mr. Whitt!" The man staggered over, looking older than he had in the dream, much less lively in the foggy midmorning light. From several yards away, Lacey groaned as he came back to himself, all his bodily aches speaking up again. He huffed as he pushed out of the dirt, all his parts refusing to coordinate.

"'She's okay," he said, voice croaking. "Vola's in the bugs. She'll be back soon." He made his way over to them, shaking his head sadly at what was left of the Byrne family.

The border between things was still very thin, and Lacey's spirit eye still saw.

"Haints," he said. "This ain't good, Dad." June looked over at his son, uncomprehending at first. There were still wisps of fog, but even they were dissipating rapidly as the sun continued to rise. They'd won the battle. Haints had run off, been spread thin, been filled up and burst with all the strong emotions their unimaginative, hopeless spirits couldn't hold. But...

"One's in her, Dad." Lacey crouched down, his hurting knees screaming. "Vola's gone from out of her body, and one of 'em got in there." June's shock was painful to see. Jayne looked away, wrapping her arms around her own girl, here and safe.

"Oh, no," June murmured. "My Vola." He sank to his knees and tenderly gathered her up in his arms. She opened her eyes, and what looked out at him wasn't his granddaughter.

What looked out of Vola's eyes wasn't anything human.

When the dream world burst apart, Vola should have come back to herself. She should have opened her eyes on the ridge, all her spirit dropping down from the cloud of winged insects into her body (at least, that's how she visualized it). But she was somewhere dark. Somewhere...unknowable. It felt like when she'd first left her body up on the ridge and drifted...but there was something more. Something...predatory.

Vola had never despaired in her life. Sure, there was the fear she'd felt when she was thrust into the dark with no body and no senses, but...but she'd held tight to her hope.

She always met a challenge with determination, with the deep, sure knowledge of youth: that she was bulletproof, that she was unbeatable. Immortal. Sure, she'd been lost plenty. Bewildered in the dark of the cave, turned around in the shadowy forest of unfamiliar trees. But all she'd had to do was turn around and see the familiar trees once more, their trunks like the faces of old friends. All she'd had to do was take a deep breath, and let her body remember the way out, no matter what fix she was in.

But that wasn't completely true, was it? Bulletproof? Why, her own shoulder was in a bloody ruin, her blood leaking out even now. Vola looked down at the shadowy form of her body and saw it was true, as though the thought of the ragged hole in her body reknit her back into being, as though she were reborn—not as she had been, but as a new creature, made out of pain.

And before she'd found the way out, before she'd found light and the sweet air of escape and continued on her way with a renewed sense of security in her own inability to be laid low...there had always been that moment, even the barest touch of time, when she'd felt the panic bubble in her throat, cutting off her very breath.

Stuck underneath Uncle Lacey's froggin' boat. Unable to find the end of the thing, unable to come out from under it, unable to draw breath, or to see sunlight dappling through the murky water to bring her back to the surface... as she remembered, she felt it, and this time, there was no escape from it. She suspended in that barest second of terror, and it became her world.

The haint curled around her like a cat, and if it had been able, it would have purred with the deepest of pleasure.

⟫⟫⟫ ⟪⟪⟪

"What's wrong with Vola?" Lily asked. "Hey! What's wrong with her? Is she dead?" June looked up, still cradling his granddaughter. She was so pale, so bloody, wrapped up in his flannel shirt. Lily felt faintly sick at the sight of her.

"No," he said. "She ain't dead. Haints..." his voice broke. "Haints got her."

213

Lily searched his face for a hint of humor, even though it would have been sick. None of this made sense. No sense at all.

"What does that mean? Like…?" She didn't want to say it, the thing that came to mind. Didn't want to think about the living corpse that had pulled her out of the woods, that had tried to take her skin off. Her wrist throbbed at the thought. It was ugly and swollen, but the blood was already starting to clot. She barely gave it another thought; if one of those nightmares had Vola…Lily pushed away from her mother, crawling over to Vola on knees, and her one good hand touching her friend's face. But she recoiled when Vola's eyes looked her way. They weren't her friend's eyes, not anymore. They were shark's eyes. And suddenly, Lily knew all she needed to know. With the strength of sudden resolve, she grabbed her friend and dragged her halfway from June's lap, and she clutched Vola's body with her skinny arms and squeezed her eyes shut.

"I'm coming after you, you… you *hillbilly*!" Lily whispered, and her body went limp.

"Lily!" Jayne shrieked. "We just got her back! You—you—Whitt, do what you did. What you did, before, when you broke that dream."

"I can't." June shook his head, his face haggard with exhaustion. "That much energy, that joy… it's in a well, in us. I used it all up, and I got to let it fill again. I don't have any left." He stroked Vola's hair, two tears tracking down his weathered cheeks. Lacey buried his face in filthy hands. Jayne looked around the gruesome scene, as though trying to find something, someone who could fix this horror. She growled in frustration, clutching her hair in both hands.

"I just got her back," she said again.

Chapter Twenty

LILY HAD ONCE WATCHED A television show about hypnotism. They'd said that once you were hypnotized, even just one time, it was easy to make you do it again, and you'd never even know about it. This was like that. Lily just slipped right into the dream world, like pulling a sheet up over her. She looked around her, at the dim gray that pervaded. No walls, no ground, nothing at all, just the colorless, floating place she'd just been. It had been easy to go back, almost without trying.

"Vola!" she called, straining her eyes. She was going to find her. Lily was shaky; she was stretched thin and exhausted, but she had a friend who had just made her realize that being mad was better than being...nothing. And that was important. And Lily was going to go back to the dream world, back to the sad and colorless Florida and get her. Even if she didn't really understand it.

Stumbling forward, hands outstretched, Lily strained her ears to hear something, anything. Where was the highway? The old neighborhood? The tall oaks with spreading branches laden with Spanish moss?

"Vola!" Lily was already up to her knees before the shock of water hit her. "What...?" There shouldn't have been a pond here. Disoriented, she scrambled backward, splashing onto a weedy bank. *Gators!* They'd been the boogeymen of her childhood, and she looked around wildly for them now. If she was in a pond, she must be in the cow pasture next to the old neighborhood. Maybe that's why Vola couldn't get out of here; maybe a gator got her, like they used to get small children and pets and sometimes even old people out on docks. Lily used to hear about it, on the morning news her mother liked to watch… but hills loomed around her from the fog, tall hills, and Lily realized she wasn't in Florida, not this time.

Once she realized this wasn't her dream Florida, Lily knew: this was the pond on the Whitt property. Vola had brought her here, leading her through a grove of pines that had all succumbed to the pine-beetle invasion. Some had been left standing, branchless, dead sentries, but the girls had to scramble over others that had fallen, their bark like patches of peeling scales leaving sap on the legs of their jeans. The memory of the dead grove bloomed the rest of the narrow, deep valley around Lily.

"At least there aren't any gators here," she muttered. But there was something in the water, a vaguely rectangular shape just out of reach. It bumped against a submerged branch with a dull *clunk*.

"Okay," Lily said and blew air from her pursed lips. "I'm at the pond. So what the heck do I do now? Where's Vola?"

A crashing in the woods set her nerves jangling, fingertips and legs tingling with adrenaline. Whatever it had been was big; a tree went over, or something, causing an echo that reverberated like distant thunder. What makes trees fall over in a dream? Lily's heart beat fast, her breath jagged.

When the woman walked out of the woods, Lily bit down a scream that had already half-escaped, in a kind of choking whimper.

"Hey there, honey pie," the woman said, strolling through the tall grass that grew between the woods and the pond. That grassy strip was just wide enough for the old farm truck to drive on. "Sounds like you swallered a frog." The woman looked vaguely familiar, with permed hair that had been fashionable before Lily was born, and a smile that made her look adventurous.

It was a smile full of broad, white teeth. She caught Lily's eye and tilted her head in friendly contrition.

"I'm sorry, young 'un," she said. "I ought to not make fun. Ruckus in the woods like that, it's mighty frightening."

"What...what is it?"

The woman shrugged. "Might be a bear, I reckon. Lots of things out here." The overturned boat—Lily now recognized it as Uncle Lacey's old froggin' boat—bumped against the branch in the water. *Clunk.*

"Who are you?" Lily was half-certain the woman wouldn't answer. She thought this was kind of like the hillbilly version of tumbling into *Alice's Wonderland*, with cryptic creatures and quietly terrifying...*things*...lurking out of sight. That cartoon had never been Lily's favorite; it had given her nightmares for a time.

But the woman surprised her. "I'm Mary Whitt," she said, holding out her hand to shake.

"You're Vola's grandmother?" Lily grasped the woman's hand. "But... you're dead. I thought." Mary gave her hand one firm squeeze and let go, her toothy grin dimmer, this time.

"That's true."

"Why are you here?"

"I got to give you something, honey pie." And Mary Whitt took Lily's face in her warm, work-roughened hands, and she pressed her lips to hers and blew into her mouth. She put her breath in Lily, a hay-scented wind laden with the promise of fat summer rain drops, a gale that tore down the late-summer leaves that were already turning for fall—though that was still two months away. Mary let go and smiled down at the girl, and the crashing came again, closer, and Lily could hear more this time: claws gripping the trunk of a tree, scratching into it powerfully enough to gouge to the heart of it. Massive paws pushing the tree over for sport... Mary and Lily looked to the woods marching up the steep rise of land, and the trees going over were close, close, and the creature—*Bear! It's a bear!*—was close, too...

"Is that a haint? Is that what they're like here?" Lily's fear was in her throat, but there wasn't any panic. There wasn't room for panic in her alongside Mary's breath.

"No, child. It's not just haints that stay in the places between. Places... beyond."

Mary took Lily's shoulders and turned her toward the pond.

"Wait!" Lily cried. "Where's Vola!?"

"In the water," Mary said. "Go on, now," and she pushed the girl into the pond. As Lily fell, she saw the bear coming toward Mary, the ends of its tarry brown fur sparking, lightning crackling all over it, and then the water closed over Lily's head.

It was curious, being underwater in a dream. Lily felt buoyant; she felt the water swirling against her, felt her hair spreading out into it, but she didn't feel like she was drowning. Still, she didn't dare open her mouth to call out to Vola. When they'd had a swimming pool in Florida, Lily had taken deep breaths, ducked under and screamed as loud as she could. She and Conner had taken turns doing it, trying to see if they could hear each other. They'd emerged sputtering and laughing, and though they could hear each other, muffled under the water, they'd never been able to hear the underwater scream from outside it. The memory made Lily shiver.

Where's Vola?

Lily swam until she saw a shape loom in the murk. The boat. Uncle Lacey's overturned froggin' boat.

Vola.

Now it was so obvious! Vola was under the boat, *had* to be, and Lily swam like mad to it.

Ellie crouched on the boulder jutting out from the hill, hay swaying and rippling all around like water. She looked more like one of Peter Pan's Lost Boys than the venerable Whitt family elder. And that was right. Mary came to her and sat in the tall hay.

"Hi, Mama Whitt," she said. It gave Ellie a start; everyone had called her Granny since Vola was born. But Mary, her boy's Mary, had called her Mama Whitt or just Mama, when she was alive. Mary might have been the one called Granny, if she'd lived. It was a little sad to think of, even in this place. Life that might have been.

"Hi there, baby," said Ellie. "I saw what you did." Mary broke off a stem of green hay and stuck it in her mouth to chew, gazing out over the farm. From up here, they could see almost the whole thing. Even the deep cleft of valley where the pond was, though that place was out of the sun.

"You did good," Ellie said, softly. Mary's shoulders drooped down, and she sighed, as though waiting to hear those words.

"I didn't get to see her," she said. "Vola. My granddaughter. I was hoping."

"I know." Tears flowed freely down Ellie's cheeks now, but they were good. "She's a good 'un."

Mary grinned her broad-toothed grin, and her face was wet, too.

"She don't take after my side," she said.

Ellie reached over and took her daughter-in-law's hand. "Maybe she does."

⟫⟩⟩⟩⟩⟩─⟨⟨⟨⟨⟨⟪

On the ridge, butterflies walked and stood still and flew lethargically. Jayne sat with both girls' heads in her lap, rocking slightly and humming, stroking their foreheads. Lacey and June held the vigil with her, heads bowed. Gitli lay with her head on Vola's foot.

Clary sat in the old house battered by time. She waited in the raw patience of the utterly powerless.

It was all up to the girls now.

>>>>—<<<<

Lily hesitated before ducking under the lip of the overturned boat—more of a plywood, floating coffin. The idea set her trembling. *It doesn't matter,* she told herself. *It's scary, and it doesn't matter. You have to go under there anyway.* It spun into a mantra, and Lily kept the words in her mind, *doesn't-matter-doesn't-matter-doesn't-matter,* and she put her hands under the lip of the ungainly boat (*coffin*), and she was under.

And there, floating like she was (*dead*) unconscious, was Vola. Lily grabbed her shoulders and shook her, and Vola's head drifted back, her eyes closed. Lily took her friend's arm, hoping she was alive, knowing that she *had* to be because people weren't dead in shared spirit visions, right? Except Vola's grandmother was dead, and she had been here. And Conner had been there, in Lily's dream. *Doesn't-matter-doesn't-matter.* Lily had to get her anyway. And she had Mary Whitt's breath in her lungs, and that gave her strength.

But Vola wouldn't come. She drifted in place, but she wouldn't go with Lily when she tugged her arm. Why?

As though waiting to be noticed, the haint drifted into view. It was different, seeing one out from behind the eyes of a person. It was formless, yet... yet it was all forms. Like the color black. Not a color, but all the colors in one inky shade. It had Vola; it had her trapped in here, and that was its real power, Lily knew. It grabbed you by your fear. The haint was gator and bear and big bad wolf. It was a dead person. It was the misshapen Frankenstein's assistant, Igor...that character in the old black-and-white movie had always scared Lily more than the monster itself. It was Conner.

"No," she said. It wasn't Conner. Not her sweet brother. He was dead, but he wasn't scary, not anymore. A single bubble of Mary's breath escaped Lily's lips, and she could see colors through it: the slightly sunburned skin of Vola's cheek, her rich, brown hair, a vibrant strand of pond weed, green as could be.

Without thought, without plan, Lily blew all her pent-up breath: Mary's breath, the looming summer storm, the hay-scent, the deep-blue sky, and icy-white clouds above! Lily blew it all into Vola's face, and she clutched her friend to her as brilliant bubbles of summer rioted around them, and just before the gray dream broke, she felt Vola's arms holding her, too...

⟫⟫⟩ ⟨⟨⟪

"*Preppy*!?" Lily said, coughing as though coming up from underwater. "That's what you called me!" Vola laughed against her shoulder, even as she squawked in pain.

"I got shot! Stop it! You're hurting me, you city slicker!" Lily gasped and let go, helping to prop her friend on her good side.

"Dadburn, you're a mess, too," Vola said, looking at Lily's ruined wrist. June, Lacey, and Jayne all sobbed, every one of them, in relief at seeing the girls come back. Away at the old, tumble-down house, Clary fell to the floor, sobbing her relief into its dusty boards, which accepted the tears as an offering of thanks. Gitli wagged her tail so hard her body quivered, and she licked every part of Vola she could reach. And she licked Lily, too, for good measure. The mist faded away, quicker than they would have thought possible, and butterflies lifted off into the sky. It was heart-breakingly beautiful. They left behind a battered mess of people, two of them dead. The corpse that had once been Boyd gave a last, gasping spasm.

"Be at peace," said June. "Boyd, go on now." He reached out one hand, crusted with Vola's blood and dirt, and he gently pressed the boy's eyelids with two fingers. Boyd gave one long, shuddering sigh, before he dropped back into the dirt for good. Light flowed through June's hand, and dozens of butterflies swirled around the two of them. When June took his hand away, Boyd was still and...yes, he looked more human now. Whatever had been in him was gone, truly. Jayne looked to Pauline Byrne's dead body.

"What now?" she said. "Are you...going to eat their hearts or something?"

221

"What? What kind of nonsense is that?" June looked baffled. "I'm going to call the law, woman. There's two people dead up here. And we need an ambulance. Got one girl shot, the other girl roughed up pretty bad..." He walked stiffly toward the back door to the Byrnes' house, to find the phone and call the police, muttering something that sounded suspiciously like, "What in the hell do they do down in Florida anyway?"

Chapter Twenty-one

After

＂**W**ELL, SUGAR BUG, I RECKON this is it. Number three.＂ Granny reached out her hand, neither young nor old, and stroked Vola's cheek. They sat together in Granny's childhood bedroom, on the rag rug. Golden sunshine spilled over the floor from the window.

"What do you mean, number three? What's that supposed to mean?" Vola caught her great-grandmother's hand in her own and held it against her face for a moment before letting go.

"Things come in threes, don't they?" Granny held up one finger. "You cut the demons from your granddaddy's heart." She held up her second finger. "Haints come out of the ground." Now, the third finger. "I'm a-going away."

Vola frowned. "But...it's bad things that come in threes. Helping Grandpa June wasn't bad."

"Well, it's things, honey child. Sometimes bad things ain't all bad, sometimes good things got some sad to 'em. It's...things."

"And there's been way more than three! Lily came, and Boyd Byrne got kilt, and his mama, too, and Lacey fell down the mountain, and...and Lily got hurt, and I got shot, and..." Vola flung her arms out in exasperation.

"Oh, for goodness' sakes, young 'un, don't take all those old sayings so seriously." Granny cracked a grin and started to chuckle at her great-granddaughter's expression. "Being superstitious ain't like being religious. Or... maybe it is. Sometimes folks just choose what they see."

"Then what's the damned point!?" Vola was almost in tears, though not because Granny had riled her up. Or, rather, not entirely because of that; she knew this was the old woman's goodbye.

Granny nodded. "That's a good question, young 'un. Come over here." She wrapped her arms around the girl, tight, and even though she wasn't really there with Vola, the girl could smell lavender and earth and a bit of the breeze from over the ridge and beyond.

"I love you, Granny," said Vola. "Don't go."

"Well, now," said Granny. "I love you, too. And we all got to go, sometime. You will, someday. Maybe I'll see you then." Her eyes lit up with such pleasure at the thought that Vola smiled through her tears. It was like...like there was going to be a party, and Granny was so looking forward to it. It was hard to feel sad about someone going to a party, even if it meant she was getting left behind.

⟫⟫⟩⟨⟨⟨

Vola woke in her own bed, down the gravel driveway from Granny's childhood home. Tears streaked her face, and her shoulder ached deeply. She tried to hold onto Granny's happiness, like a shawl, but it was fading. Tears were what was left. And pain in her body.

"Pssst," said Lily, from the doorway. "Check it out." She held out her cupped hands, and a tiny, rusted *mew* came from them.

Vola sat up, barely wincing at her shoulder, and hastily wiped her face.

"You're here early!" she said. Her friend shrugged.

"I snuck it in!" Lily waggled her eyebrows, holding her cupped hands up again.

"Well, bring it over!" Vola scootched in the bed so Lily could sit next to her. She set the barn kitten down, and they both laughed when it gamboled unsteadily on the rumpled blankets.

⸻⟫⟫⟫ ⟪⟪⟪⸻

The morning mist was lifting on the ridge. June had carried his mother up the hill in last evening's twilight and kept the vigil all night. His eyes were clear and solemn under the old, battered hat. Something was over, something big, and June felt washed clean. Ready to receive the years ahead.

Lacey dug steadily, tears dripping from his nose into the good, rich earth. He wore a wool sweater, and it was too warm for the late summer morning, but June thought he knew why. Clary and Vola touched Granny's hands, folded outside the shroud that wrapped her, head to foot. They all four lowered Ellie Whitt's body into her grave, Gitli standing sentry. Granny felt light, in the absence of life. Like a doll.

"She was wrong, you know," said Clary. "Granny. She said we needed to seal the haints back in."

"We was both wrong," said June, turning his hat in his hands. "The wall needed to be busted open, not sealed back up." In the absence of Granny's retort, trees waved overhead in a gentle breeze. A few leaves were turning yellow already, though it would be hot for a while.

"I miss her," said Vola, finally.

After, as they wended their way down the ridge, through the dense woods, a single, brilliantly violet butterfly came flitting. It flew with joy, wings pumping the air as if each motion was a leap of sheer happiness. Lacey stopped and lifted his elbows away from his sides, a crooked, hopeful grin on his face. But the butterfly didn't light, only flew around and around his head, touching his forehead under the shock of unkempt hair with the merest brush before weaving among them all one last time. Without warning, the violet butterfly flapped its wings mightily and flew up into the sky, achingly blue between the tops of trees just starting to turn their hint of fall colors.

And, like that, Granny was gone, following the distance like the flock of birds Vola had seen in her mind. Free.

They all breathed deeply, realizing they'd held their breath until that moment, and they all wiped the tears from their wet faces. They would be sad because it was right to be sad, but they would go on, and they would find joy again. And, until then, maybe they'd have some contentment.

⇒≫≫> ⇐≪≪⇐

Later on, all the survivors sat together at the dining room table—even Jayne and Lily.

"So," said Clary, spooning mashed potatoes onto Jayne's plate, "Y 'uns sticking around here, or moving up by your parents in Maryland? You decide yet?" Jayne gazed down at her plate for a moment before meeting her eyes.

"We're staying," she said. "We figure…we figure we've been through…a lot. And now we'll be okay, I think." She gave a fond smile to Lily, who nodded. Jayne's ex—Lily's dad—he would be moving, though. He'd transferred again, to Arizona. And Jayne was all right with it. She hoped Lily would be, too.

"I took a job at the bank in town," Jayne said.

Grandpa June's gaze lit on the girls, who were whispering to themselves and giggling while the adults talked. Gitli begged for scraps at their knees. Lacey made funny faces at them, setting them to giggling again. Lily still looked peaked: wrist bandaged, too pale, and with dark circles under her eyes. But she'd be all right. And Vola's shoulder was on the mend. Clary had been pleased and surprised that June had been so gracious about the clinic after they'd fixed up Vola. They'd sent her on to the hospital in Knoxville, which had made June mighty nervous, but he settled down now that she was back home. He'd insisted on putting one of Granny's poultices on the bullet wound anyway. Even though it was all stitched up and on the mend. It was a way to keep Granny's memory alive and there with them, even if her body wasn't.

June took another bite of greens, considering. Tonight would do as good as any, he reckoned. There was something else needed done. One last

226

thing, up at the Byrne-Whitt line. June'd asked around, after the police had showed up and took away the bodies—Boyd had gone crazy on meth, killed his mother, went after Lily, and shot Vola, before he killed hisself, that was the official story—and there weren't any Byrnes left, not of this line. All dead: Mary's brother, Boyd's two brothers, all dead on account of bad decisions and drugs. June felt relief, in a way. The old blood animosity was gone.

But, he still needed to...to finish it all the way. For Mary.

June waited until the half-moon had risen up in the clear night sky, and he made his way back up the ridge. He'd sent Gitli back to the house when she'd tried to follow.

"Go on, stay with Vola," he'd murmured, and the dog had turned to trot back. His hips ached a bit—"Old Uncle Arthur" coming to visit. That's what his mama had said when her arthritis flared. He brought Old Man Byrne's rifle with him, the same gun he'd dropped that night decades ago. The gun he'd pointed at the Whitt house, with hate in his heart. With a faint curiosity, June looked around him at the black woods, a few late fireflies flaring a slow beat. He didn't think he'd see any haints there. There were a few faint wisps of mist, rising up from the ground, but that's all they was: just mist. They'd blown open the prison, let all the haints out and gorged 'em on human emotion. There would be more, of course. Haints went right along with people, like love and worry, hate and contentment. Jealousy. Fear. Strength and bravery. But folks wasn't as afraid of the natural world around them; most took for granted that it had been all discovered and conquered, and after all: wasn't fear just something unknown? June understood the dangers of that thinking. He also knew the Whitts would be around when they was needed.

His musing brought him to the broken barbed-wire fence, its strands like thick, tangled cobwebs in the faint moonlight. Slowly, June brought the gun up over his head. He shuffled a little dance, and he started to hum. It wasn't a driving dance, not one full of life's joy. Nor was it one full of hatred or anger. His throat opened, and his wordless song of peace drifted into the night. The song of bygones-as-bygones, of laying dusty bones into the ground for a last, long sleep drifted through the patch of woods over to the Watson house, where packing boxes no longer cluttered the kitchen. Where Jayne had picked a new paint color for the walls, and she and Lily had finally started to settle in, together. June's song filtered into their dreams, and they sighed and smiled, and felt…not that they would forget the horror and badness they'd seen, but that it wouldn't be the most important part of them. In short, they felt that it would be all right.

After, June hunted in the Byrnes' yard for a shovel. He found what he needed buried in a tangle of old weeds, off to the side of the house. Next to a rusted-out lawnmower. He dug a long, thin grave for Old Man Byrne's shotgun, and he laid it to its final rest. When it was all done, he stood and stretched his back, took off his hat and gazed for a moment at the icy-cold light of the half-moon, now high above the trees. A caress came, in the form of a soft, warm breeze and lifted the sweat-damp hair from his forehead.

"I miss you, Mary," he murmured. The wind picked up a small flurry of leaves and danced them around June. He smelled fresh summer hay and a storm on the horizon. And then it was gone, and the night was all that was left.

June went back down the ridge, and he went to bed.

END

About the Author

MEGHAN PALMER LIVES IN KNOXVILLE, Tennessee with her family. Visit meghanpalmer.net to learn more.